FIERCE

A SCI-FI ALIEN ROMANCE

HATTIE JACKS

VIV

I land on a hard, cold metal floor in a tangle of weak, wet limbs. The initial contact makes me gasp for breath, but I can't breathe. Something is stuck in my windpipe. Panic sweeps over me as I raise my hands to my mouth. I'm scrabbling at my lips, feeling for the obstruction. I touch a hard, warm circular pipe and almost recoil that it's sticking out of my mouth until self-preservation kicks in, and I pull at the thing. It slips out easily, but keeps on coming as I retch and writhe on the ground, tugging and tugging at the never-ending tube that stops me from breathing.

It comes free with a soggy pop, and I cough-breathe-shudder and cough again, spluttering up liquid until my breathing is ragged and my heart rate falls. As I recover, I wipe at my eyes, trying to work out what has happened to me.

I'd left the quiet solitude of my flat for ten minutes for god's sake! If I hadn't been fighting for my life a few seconds ago, I'd swear this was a nightmare brought on by the last dregs of cheese I'd eaten with some slightly soggy crackers before bed. The thing is, I can remember putting the key in the lock of my front door, and then as metal clicked against metal, there was another sound, a sharper metallic sound. And pain against my neck.

I've become so desensitized to pain, I guess I hardly noticed. When I put my hand up to touch the skin, it's sore. I jerk back from my exploring fingers. Wherever I am, it's not a hospital. I'd recognize a hospital anywhere.

Plus, they don't usually leave you naked in a pool of goo when you're supposed to be in need of urgent medical care.

The floor beneath me is some sort of metal grating and icy cold. I slowly uncurl from my foetal position to look around. The place is dimly lit and, as I look up, I see four large bags swaying as they hang from the ceiling on hooks. Each bag has a tube running into it. The whole room shudders and the bags bounce. I stare up, horrified as a human foot appears, pressed against the milky plastic. I scramble back, barely registering the broken sheeting that surrounds me. Fear musters the energy I need to scuttle away from the bulbous bags, shimmering and shuddering, as the room continues to vibrate.

Where the hell am I? Why are there human beings in bags hanging like meat carcasses? I only went out for milk and instead of being tucked up in my warm bed, trying to forget the world, I'm somewhere horrible. I hug my knees to my chest, attempting to fire my brain into life, to work out the impossible made possible. There is a whining, grinding sound and the room shakes violently. The bodies in the bags slosh against the sides and I can clearly see that each one holds a woman, all with tubes down their throats like I had. None of them are moving, but I wasn't dead when my bag burst, so it's a rational assumption that they're alive, too.

The bags swing again. The need to release the people

inside overwhelms me. I've never been an action woman, even before the accident, even less so after, but I can't leave these women hanging like sides of beef in a butcher's shop. Because for all I know, that's what we're destined for; some sort of meat or slave market, whatever filthy inventive things humans do to each other. My legs are weak but I struggle to my feet and stumble over to the bags. I claw at them, but the weird, rubbery plastic is tough and thick. Too thick for me to break into. As the room continues to vibrate with the grinding sound slowly increasing in pitch, I look around wildly for something, anything that I can use as a way of opening the fluid filled bags.

My eyes alight on a glint of gold near where I'd been sitting. I race back in an almost straight line to find it's a three-pronged grappling hook, sticking up at an angle from the floor of the room, poking through the grating. It's oddly out of place for this strange room. That doesn't stop me reaching for it and tugging, but it's held fast.

"No! Come on!" I yell, hoarsely. I have to get the other women to safety, or at least out of the bags. Nothing has ever mattered more at this moment.

With a shrieking groan, the gold hook tensions against the metal. I watch, helpless as the rear of the room is ripped away and as it does, an incredible suction takes me, too. Wind howls, whipping around my naked form, chilly fingers of ice exactly where I don't want them. Not that I have much time to complain, not when I see that I'm falling from the most enormous...spaceship?

It's not saucer shaped, more like a flying house brick. Slab sided, matte black and lit with the strangest glow, lights undulating over its surface, pinpricks of blue, green and red. It distracts me for all of a second. Until the falling and the wind reminds me of my dire situation. I know I'm going to hit the ground. I know screaming won't help me, but I scream anyway, screwing my eyes closed as if that's going to cushion my brain hitting the rear of my skull. Out of nowhere, I'm hit hard in my side, knocking the limited breath I have out of me. Something has me, something dark and something with claws that dig into my exposed skin. Regardless of the falling situation, I struggle against it, wriggling my goo covered body out of its grasp and I hit the ground with a thud, rolling over and over until I skid to a stop on my front.

I don't have time to catch my breath. Sounds of beating wings surround me and I flip myself over, frantically wiping evil smelling mud out of my eyes to see if there are any escape routes. I'm in a ruined building. Three walls are all that remain, the rest is open to the elements. The darkening sky above me roils with thunderous clouds. A lightning bolt illuminates the crumbling structure and I can see I'm covered from head to toe in black dirt. A further flash reveals a man, standing above me on one wall, his huge wings outstretched. His eyes glow red. I shove myself backwards, away from him, just as another lands with a thump in front of me. He reaches out his black clawed hands as he's joined by the first bad angel, their laughter echoing terrifyingly around the destroyed building. My body can't cope any more. My eyes can't stay open. I'm not sure I even want to keep breathing, not when I'm about to be ripped limb from limb because I've fallen into a pit of hell.

When the real darkness arrives, it's a blessing I embrace.

JYR

I hear the fight long before I enter the lair. The roars of my younger warriors, the mercs, egging on whatever stupid dispute has resulted in two idiot males knocking the gak out of each other. It doesn't matter the mercs are the bottom of the pile in lair hierarchy; they have to adhere to the rules of the legion, no matter what. One of those rules is no unsanctioned fighting. That's confined to the training pits. It's the only way to keep a hundred vicious males in line.

"What the vrex is going on?" I growl at Kaloz. The warrior leans against the wall outside, swigging from a long drinking vessel. He shrugs, shaking out his wings at me insolently.

For my second in command, he's doing an outstanding job of not caring. I stride past him without a glance and enter the main hall.

The long tables are pulled back, and the benches tossed into a corner as the crowd of mercs surround the fighters. An older warrior with an enforcer band around his upper left bicep is taking bets on the winners from the newer mercs that don't know any better.

A loud crunch and a roar galvanizes me. I leap into the air, my great wings beating down hard, the downdraft hitting the crowd below me like something solid. I land in the center and slam the 'winner' to the ground hard enough that he'll stay down if he knows what's good for him.

"Get him to the healer." I shout at the three mercs nearest to the loser, who's bleeding heavily from various cuts to his head and torso. Fortunately for him, his feathers are intact. If they weren't he'd be no use to me, and he knows it. The crowd reacts swiftly, grabbing hold of the unfortunate merc and dragging him out of my sight.

"What are my vrexing standing orders?" I bellow at the remaining mercs.

Breaking up the fight was Kaloz's job, and, on cue, he ambles in after all the fuss has died down.

"Kaloz?" I say through gritted teeth.

"Fighting is for the training pits only." He says, and the disdainful inflection in his voice cuts through me. I should react, but I need Kaloz. Instead, I glare around at the remaining crowd, who suddenly remember they have other places to be.

"Command, call the seniors to szent." I don't raise my voice to Kaloz. I don't have to, and the entire lair knows my displeasure.

Prime's word is law, and I am the prime of the Gryn Legion, the only Gryn Legion now left on Ustokos after the great reckoning. I walk over to the downed merc and place my booted foot on his chest. I recognize him as one of my recent intakes.

"Fyn, I expected more of you." I remove my foot and hold out my arm. He hesitates for a second, then reaches up as I pull him to his feet. "No fighting here, we're your family now. The only fight is with Proto."

"Some family." He mutters, averting his eyes from mine. "I thought families were supposed to protect each other, not divide to conquer."

"The Gryn is unity, Fyn, and don't forget it." I repeat our mantra, the one that is ingrained into every new merc when they arrive. "So I don't care what it was about." I pull him against me, staring into his face. "Don't let it happen again. If you fight under my roof, it reflects on me. If I catch you fighting outside the pit, I will dispose of you myself." I growl low as I release him, noticing his head is running with blood. "Get yourself checked by the healer." I push him towards the door, and he makes good his escape.

"One of these days someone will accuse the Prime of the Gryn of having a heart."

"Proto cut it out cycles ago." I turn to see my head of security, Ryak emerging from the shadows, secretive bastid that he is. "As you know well." I grin at him.

"Someone called a meeting of the seniors, so here I am." He half inclines his head. I've known Ryak for more cycles than I care to admit, and he still doesn't trust me. Good thing I trust him, given how he prefers to hide in the shadows.

"Szent." I say, and he falls in step beside me.

"About Kaloz—" he says and I hold up a hand to stop him.

"He is my command. Do you challenge me for Prime?" I square up to him. Ryak's been dying to have this conversation, and I'm in no mood. "No? Then he is my chosen second, and that's the end of the matter."

"As you wish." Ryak says quietly as we enter the szent.

The other seniors are assembled and wait until I take my

place at the head of the large round table, fashioned from the twisted metal we have wrenched from every joykill bot we've ever destroyed. Once I sit, the rest take their places. Kyt, our quartermaster in his long and rather impractical coat, sits next to Ryak. Myk, our slayer, slides into his place beside me. The strong and silent swordsmith a reassuring presence as always.

"We're not due to have szent for another turn, Prime, what's the problem?" Kyt asks.

"Other than me coming back to the lair to find the mercs tearing the place apart?" I glare at my assembled seniors. "The mercs should know their place. Next time I find a fight outside the pit, it will be your wings to pay. Understand?"

Silence fills the room.

"Understand?" I roar.

A chorus of 'yes, Prime' replaces the lack of response as I drum my claws on the shiny surface of the table, making small dints to match the many others I've put there.

"I ran into a phalanx of joykill bots earlier when I was - out." The less the seniors know about my recent trip the better. I swallow down the squirm that fills my guts. "Proto has upped the patrols, and we need to work on our strategy to counter the increase, to continue to protect the supplies and markets."

"We can run with extra mercs." Ryak suggests. "We've added a decent number from your recent raids on Proto's control camps."

"Probably why patrols have increased." Kaloz snorts, and I shoot him a sharp glance. "Proto's got to have noticed. It's going to run the numbers. That's what it does."

I sit back in my chair; the metal worked smooth by Myk, each strut that extends to the sky, in a mirror image of a set of miniature Gryn wings, is made out of parts of Proto's bots.

Each one represents a minor victory against the sentient artificial intelligence that made Ustakos almost uninhabitable. The long war that had waged between organics and machines only ended in the entire population being decimated. Members of those species who weren't captured are forced to hide in the ruins of what was once a number of great civilizations.

It's too late to dwell on the past. The Gryn is about the here and now. We survive and we thrive. Our lair is only half full and we need more wings and bodies.

"So you think we should stop trying to save our brothers?" I fire at him. "Like I saved you?"

Kaloz opens his mouth to speak, but his reply is cut off by a merc bursting through the door to the szent. I roar my disapproval of his unauthorized entry.

"Prime!" He skids to a stop at my chair. "You have to come, one of the patrols has found something."

I shoot out an arm and grab the unfortunate intruder by his throat, lifting him easily from the floor as he chokes.

"Patrols always find 'something'. It is not a reason to interrupt a szent, not ever." I murmur before dropping him back to the ground.

"This is different, Prime." He whines, clutching his bruised skin. "You have to see." His eyes are wide, pleading.

"Vrex it!" I swear. "Szent will continue once the Prime has looked over the findings of a merc patrol." I clutch the messenger in a headlock. "Lead the way, merc." I grin at him as he attempts to swallow. "But this better be good, or you're on garbage duty for the next ten turns."

VIV

I spent my childhood wanting to fly. Running around the garden at the back of my parent's house, flapping my arms. Staring up at the birds that soared over me with undisguised jealousy.

Today is the day that my thirty-six-year-old self found out flying using wings isn't all it's cracked up to be. My relief at being back on solid ground after my two bad angels strung me between them is short-lived. The terrain they flew me over appeared like the aftermath of a war. There was hardly a building standing in the acres of scorched-looking black ground. No sign of any life or greenery. Briefly, the clouds parted, and I see not one, but two enormous moons in the sky.

Confirming with a slamming finality to my addled mind I wasn't on Earth anymore. Which means the two creatures carrying me aren't demons from a hell I don't believe in. They're aliens, which I do believe in.

I just never expected to meet one.

The building they've brought me to is marginally less damaged than anywhere else we flew over, although that's not saying much. It's far too dark to see where they carried me. All I can tell is the place is in some disrepair, given that they brought me in via what appeared to be a hole in an ancient concrete wall. With little ceremony, I'm dragged into a windowless room, a heavy metal door slamming shut behind us.

One of the bad angels pulls me in front of him. His huge, round eyes glow red as he stares at me. I recoil from him. He's wearing a mask that makes his eyes look that way, the rest of his face a black blank.

"What are you?" He shakes me, his voice sounding hollow.

"Fuck off!" I retort. "Let me go!" I attempt to bite his arm.

I've been in a bag, dropped out of a spaceship and subjected to the worst flight of my life. To add insult to injury, I'm naked, covered in goo and dirt. I don't have to take this sort of shit from a masked feathery wanker who thinks it's fun to shake something considerably smaller than him around.

He hesitates and shoves me away from him.

"Female." He says with some awe in his voice and retreats from me, bumping into his colleague. "We'd better get Prime."

The pair of them reach up and pull off their masks. I hold my breath, expecting sharp beaks and beady eyes, but they reveal very human faces. Young faces. It fits with their treatment of me so far. Just my luck to end up with a tribe of flying alien kids. I wrap my arms around myself, suddenly acutely aware of my nakedness, covered by a thin layer of mud.

They race out of the room, dark feathers streaking in their wake, the door sliding shut behind them with a metal clang and a further scraping noise that denotes a bolt being slid across.

I'm a prisoner of lord of the fucking flies. Only these are actual flying beings. A wave of cold washes through me. There's no way this should be happening. Oh, sure, I believed in aliens. I mean, how could humans be so arrogant to believe that they are alone in the universe? But I didn't believe in alien abduction. I wasn't arrogant enough to think aliens would have an interest in little old, damaged me. After all, it wasn't as if humans paid much attention to me, either. Why on Earth, or anywhere else would anyone want to take responsibility for the mess I have become? A creature of the night that never leaves her flat. A woman who has been forgotten by everyone she used to know, her work colleagues, her family, and the few friends she had. A woman who wanted to be forgotten.

I crouch in the darkest corner of the room and wrap my arms around myself, trying to look as small as possible. Whoever the kids have gone to get, it can't possibly put me in any worse position than I'm already in.

After a wait that seems to stretch forever, but takes no time at all, I hear the scraping back of the bolt and the door rolls away into the wall. My old friends are back, entering at a similar speed to the one they left, only there's an eagerness in their stride that makes me tremble.

The biggest male creature I've ever seen in my entire life follows them. He must be seven feet tall if he's an inch. His huge dark wings seem to dwarf the other bad angels. He holds himself proudly, his chest bare, displaying the most impressive set of abs. His handsome face sports high cheekbones under a pronounced brow and his dark eyes take in every little detail. Eyes that have a depth to them that goes down fathoms. A slight breeze ruffles the feathers along the edges of his wings, and I get a slight hint of spice. His presence dominates the room, almost as if it's sucking out the air. I'm struggling to breathe again once those incredible eyes fix on me.

It's as if I'm the only thing he sees.

"*EREGRI!*" He roars, so loud in the small space, I clap my hands to my ears.

He's across the room before I can blink, wrapping huge arms around me and lifting as if I weigh nothing. In seconds, we're outside and in the air. His powerful wings carry us higher and higher. I cling to him as if my life depends on it. It does. If he drops me, I will die. Although given I don't know what he wants with me, perhaps that's an alternative I should be considering.

Except I want to live. Doesn't matter what happens to me, how broken I am, life persists. All those weeks spent in a hospital bed; life clung to me. I survive, that's what I do. I bury my head in his muscular chest and think about the other women hanging in the bags. Who has them and are they going to suffer the same fate as me? The spicy scent I smelled earlier is much stronger in my nostrils.

It's my big scary alien. He smells like cinnamon.

His muscles bunch as he moves effortlessly through the air. I risk opening one eye and see that we are descending towards a small platform. Dust swirls as he alights, still clasping me, he strides forward. I see rough-hewn rock walls and feel warmth on my naked skin. My alien lets my legs go, allowing me to slither down his hardened form.

The abs are not the only hard muscle he has. I distinctly feel the long, thick and very erect cock that he's sporting under his trousers. That answers another question I didn't even think to ask. These aliens are more like humans than birds. Although from what I felt, not like ninety-nine percent of human men.

Once hawk-man is sure I stand on my own two feet, he grasps my shoulders and presses himself against me, putting me in absolutely no doubt as to what he wants.

"My *eregri*." His voice is like a quarry full of gravel being rubbed together. "I never thought this was possible. We shall mate over and over until our pleasure produces many young." He lifts his hand and traces a single, black clawed finger down the side of my mud caked face.

"Nope. I don't think so." I raise my knee swiftly and as hard as I can to ensure it impacts his crotch with maximum force.

Big though he is, he doubles over with a high-pitched groan, releasing me to grab at his family jewels.

"I'll give that a hard pass, if you don't mind."

I step back, scanning the cave he has brought me to. I can see that there's a pool of water that steams slightly in the middle. Off to one side is a pile of what looks like furs, surrounded by things that dangle and twinkle. Then I spot what I need and I'm sprinting away towards the rear, towards the tunnel and hopefully freedom from the gorgeous bad angel that wants to give me his babies, whether I like it or not.

I can't even look after myself, so I'm not having anyone's babies. Not now, not ever.

JYR

I had her. My *eregri*. My fated mate. She was in my arms and almost in my bed. Now I'm curled up on the floor nursing my injured cock. If anything is going to cool my ardor, it's going to be a kick like the one she just delivered.

By the time I'm able to look up, she's gone. A delicate creature that smelled like our lands used to after the rain, all sweetness and full of promise. I can find her by scent alone, and I know she cannot leave my nest, given that she is decidedly wingless.

The pain that replaced the throbbing erection brings me to my senses. I grabbed the female and left the lair without explanation, in front of my seniors and several mercs. If they add that behavior to my other recent disappearances, especially the way Kaloz has been acting, it doesn't look good.

I trust all my brother warriors with my life, except Kaloz. If he knew about my nest, he'd try to use it against me. He never believed in the old ways, and he had an absolute certainty *eregri* didn't exist. He would make my discovery into a weakness. He would make my mate my weakness.

And I am not weak. She makes me strong. Stronger than I have ever been. My poor cock chooses this moment to remind me how strong and fierce my sweet female is, aching with her blow and my need. I get to my feet slowly, brushing the dust from my knees.

"You cannot hide from me, my *eregri*," I call out, my voice echoing around the cave walls.

I walk over to inspect my handiwork in my nest. I have chosen only the best furs that the Mochi could provide me. The furred feline bastid's charged me a vrexing fortune for them. I run my hand through the soft pelts, imagining pleasuring the female who stared at me with her beautiful blue and defiant eyes. They were the color of a saphi flower, although I don't remember the last time I saw one blooming. She would wriggle beneath me as I implanted my seed. I nod at the nest I have built for her. I have done well.

"I will return, my sweet. In the meantime, make yourself at home." I say, allowing the natural acoustics of the place to carry my voice to where I know she will be hiding as I head outside.

I reach the ledge to my concealed entrance and hesitate. I've only just found her, and I'm letting lair business drag me away from the only compatible female we have seen in cycles. Proto made vrexing sure that they were all taken from us. Some of the Gryn we free say it forced them to mate whilst in captivity, but Proto kept them so tranqed they couldn't remember what species the females were.

I know she will be safe here. I spent a long time finding the right place for my nest, almost as much time as I spent furnishing it. Reluctantly, I spread my wings and drop from the ledge, allowing the wind to take me up, high enough to avoid the constant bot patrols.

There are females on this planet. Something deep inside

me knew. I knew my *eregri* was coming and I built my nest, but I remain uneasy. If there are females that are not Gryn but close enough to us to trigger the fate mate bond, this has to be something to do with Proto. Anything that involves the sentient AI that rules Ustakos only bodes ill for the organic life forms attempting to scratch a living on this cursed planet.

The lair appears below me, and I circle for a while to clear my head and consider my excuses. But that isn't what bothers me. I'm more concerned as to my reaction to the female. I need to speak to someone about it, but it can't be my seniors, not yet. Not until I've worked out what it means for me and for all the Gryn. They are my responsibility. They require a leader who can protect them. I have to be that leader, and it means I can't let any other challenge me for my leadership.

Because there can only ever be one Prime. To lose my position means death and there's no way any Gryn is ever taking my life from me. I die in battle or not at all.

As Prime I am afforded my own quarters and my own entrance, which means I don't have to answer questions for a while. Even so, I keep my landing as quiet as possible, letting out a sigh of relief as I enter. Heading to my desk, I pull out a flask of lynk and take a long pull. The strong liquor burns down my throat and settles in my stomach like liquid fire.

"You going to share that?" Ryak asks, his voice low and even. He looms out of a corner at me, arm outstretched.

"Vrex it, Ryak! You can't do that to a Gryn!" I laugh, tossing the flask over to my head of security as my heart rate returns to normal.

He's the Gryn I've known the longest. He broke out of Proto's first capture facility with me. Ryak is something else.

He had no designs on being Prime. He performs his duties with a quiet menace that means most others avoid him. I know exactly what happened to him because it was done to me too. The torture we were subjected to might not have left scars on our hides, but Proto made us to be something else, like Kyt and Myk. I know I can trust them all with my life. Shame I can't say the same about my Command, Kaloz.

I sit down heavily on my bed as I gesture at Ryak to do the same, holding out my hand for the flask. If I can't be with my mate tonight, I'm going to get as drunk as I can, hoping it dulls the ache in my heart.

"The female?"

"My *eregri*."

"That complicates things."

"Don't I know it." I tip the flask at him but the alcohol sours in my mouth. "Kaloz doesn't believe."

"I told you he was trouble." Ryak sits back.

He's not one of us.

His voice echoes in my head.

"Don't do that." I admonish him, even though my heart isn't in it. Ryak has a way of using the thoughtbond that is truly disturbing.

"You can't deny our abilities, any more than you can deny your mate."

"Vrex!" I throw the flask across the room. "You know I have no choice. Keep him close or lose half the Legion."

"I don't believe that any more than you do." Ryak inclines his head. "Have you mated already? Is that why you're back here?"

The ache in my heart moves to my balls, and I shift uncomfortably.

"Mating is going to take more time with my *eregri*. She is

not of the Gryn and not of Ustakos." Ryak's eyes widen slightly.

"Then I suggest you get back to her. The seniors and I can take care of things here." The corner of his mouth quirks into an unaccustomed smile, revealing a sharp tooth. The effect is unnerving. I'm tempted to go just so I can get away from that smile.

"I can't, not after I left with her in that way. I have to show my face. To make sure the mercs know who's in charge"

"Go to the main hall, deal with today's fighters, make an example of them. That should give you enough grace to spend time with your mate."

I draw out a sigh that seems to have come from the depths of Hyddar and I rise.

"Let's get it over with."

VIV

I heard him leave. The sound of his enormous wings fades away in the distance. I still waited a while in my hiding place, a rather damp alcove I had determined he probably wouldn't fit into, before I emerged.

What did he call me? His *eregri*? Why are aliens speaking English anyway? I'm suddenly incredibly tired. Too tired to give in to the geek in me that wants out. All of these things were fun to think about when I was sat, on my sofa, in my little flat, eating chocolate ice cream and binging on Doctor Who.

Another childhood dream shattered. The man in the blue box who holds out his hand and whisks you off into time and space. Alien adventures were never supposed to involve flying monsters who threaten to impregnate you within seconds of meeting. It was not supposed to involve being covered in mud and gunk either.

Which reminds me, the mud is setting, and it's itchy. First things first, I need to get this stuff off me. I remember a brief glimpse of what looked like a pool in the main cavern. Providing my aliens don't bathe in acid, that's probably the best place to start. The cave is as large as I remember from my escape. The pool is definitely larger than I thought. Big enough for a swim. I peer in. The water is clear, and I see several ledges, like steps that drop into a dark center. It steams slightly and smells like the sea. I look around for something I can drop in to test if anything melts.

Figuring out problems is part of what I used to do as an insurance investigator. It meant I never knew what would come my way, and I always had to think outside of the box. My fellow humans were endlessly inventive in ways to defraud the system. I like to think I was good at my job. A job I'd give anything to go back to, even though I'd given it up as lost a year ago, whilst I wallowed in my home, hardly daring to set foot outside the door. It goes to show, you really don't know what you've got, until it's gone.

Across the other side of the pool is an enormous pile of fur, surrounded by, well, just about anything and the kitchen sink. Twinkling things hang from the overhanging rock ledge, they spin and flash in the lights that I can't quite see set high in the cave roof, and which flood the place with a white glow. Long pieces of fabric join the twinkles along with items that look like cooking utensils. Basically, if it's shiny or pretty, it's hanging up over the furs.

It's probably the weirdest thing I've ever seen. Given that I've seen women in bags, spaceships and bad angels in the last few hours, that's saying something.

My foot nudges a pebble and I drop it into the water. It doesn't fizz or dissolve, so I risk touching the surface with my finger. That doesn't fizz or dissolve either, and it's with undisguised delight that I hop into the pool, finding the water deliciously warm, and sink down. Although it smells like the sea, the water is fresh, and I take a couple of gulps before wondering if that was a good idea.

I scrub at my body, trying to get off the thick black stuff coating me. It slowly shifts, revealing my normal skin color and the burns down my left side that normally remain covered by clothing. The mottled, scarred skin, sensitive in places, and with no feeling at all in others. Rivulets of white run like a web over the whole mess, giving it texture all of its own. My scars. The things that define me.

The water is silky smooth, and the warmth permeates my bones. I'm not sure I've felt this relaxed in a long time. With everything that has happened, that is a rather odd emotion. I guess it has to be a reaction to the adrenaline draining away. Before I fall asleep in the water, I drag myself out. Other than a few scrapes to my knees and elbows, which have also been soothed by my bath, I'm remarkably intact.

Out of the pool I give myself a shake, like a dog, and squeeze as much water as I can out of my hair, which has returned to its usual dark blond. I used to have sun streaks in the front, but they are long gone. Beach holidays stopped being my thing after the accident.

I scuttle across to the pile of furs to see if there's anything I can use as a coverup. I've no idea when hawk-man is going to return, and he's already seen enough of me, even if I was covered in mud. He might give most Hollywood movie stars a run for their money in the handsomeness stakes, but he's made his intentions quite clear and, hopefully, so have I.

I don't have time to fend off his advances or even make him think I'm interested. Instead, I need to get to the other women and get the fuck off this planet. If that's even possible.

I'm damn sure I will not spend the rest of my life making hawky babies for Mr. Alpha Alien. Anyway, he'll probably change his mind once he sees my scars. I haven't bothered with men since my body was broiled, and that was three years ago. I didn't need anyone else's opinion on how hideous I was. I didn't need my heart broken. I was perfectly capable of doing all that on my own.

I yank on a length of red fabric that's hanging above the pile of furs, pulling it down and winding it around me. It makes a passable, if short, toga and just about covers my damaged skin. It's then that I hear the tell-tale sound of great feathered wings and a thump as my alien returns. In a flash, I'm running across the cavern, back towards my hiding place. I throw a glance over my shoulder and see a whirl of muscles and feathers heading in my direction. I increase my pace and reach my alcove just as I feel a set of claws nipping at my bare heels.

"*Eregri!*" He calls plaintively.

"Fuck off!" I curl up, tucking myself as far out of his reach as I can.

A pair of black clad knees appear in the entrance, followed by a set of tremendously muscular arms that are blotted out by a tsunami of slate gray feathers, and finally a pair of deep, dark eyes peer at me.

"Come out." He demands.

"No." I can't remember the last time I was this bold, but why the hell not? It's not as if things could get any worse.

There's a long sigh, one I find I relate to. It's the sigh of someone with the cares of the world, or this planet, whatever it's called, on his shoulders.

"Please?"

"I'll come out if you promise not to touch me."

There's a long silence. "Please accept my apologies, my *eregri*. I misspoke when we were last together. I will not make you do anything you don't want to do."

He fills the entrance to my alcove and his scent, warm baking with a hint of spice, hits me. Is he just being nice to get me to come out? Can someone who smells that good actually be a bad angel? My mind is scrambled. I'm so tired I can hardly think straight.

"I have brought you food." There is a slight hesitancy in his strong voice that makes my stomach do a funny squirm. It's followed by a low growl from the same organ which reverberates around my hiding place. "I promise I only want to talk, nothing more."

Looks like I traveled a million billion miles to find a male that actually knows the way to a woman's heart.

"Back off, then." I call out. The feathers swish upwards, and I watch as his booted feet retreat from my hiding place. I squirm around, wriggling my way free and get to my feet, straightening my makeshift clothing to make sure I'm fully covered before I look up at my hawk-man in the white light of the cavern.

He is an incredible specimen. He holds himself like a god, wings set close to his back. Feathers shining with life from the deep slate gray on the back to the black and white streaked underside. His hair close cropped and black. His alien skin on his shoulders is dark and leathery, but the rest is pure human. As long as they built all human men like Greek gods. His six-pack is one most athletes would die for. But it's his eyes to which I'm drawn. They are such a deep, dark brown, they're almost black. And they are fixed on me.

They are the eyes of a predator. One I know wants every part of me.

JYR

The female is tiny. She has cleansed herself of the mud from the wastelands, presumably in the healing pool. If I thought she smelled good before, her scent now is reminiscent of a time when Ustokos had grass plains, and rain that didn't burn as it fell. It's sweet, pure and perfect. All I want to do is bury myself in her. It's driving me wild.

But I promised, and a Gryn doesn't break a promise, especially a Prime.

With the mud removed, I'm able to take in her delicate features. Her hair shines gold, like the fur of the Mochi, but she is not a Mochi. Far from it. She has no fur, no ears, no tail and no claws. Instead, she has soft creamy pink skin. Her face is simply the most beautiful I have ever seen on a female of any species. Dazzling blue eyes and a mouth that pouts deliciously as she looks me over. I'm unable to help myself. I puff up my chest and raise my wings higher to prove I am a worthy male. She's wrapped her body in a piece of red fabric that I knew would be perfect for my nest when I found it, and now I know why. The color is stunning on her, and the way she has wound it around herself emphasizes the swell of her breasts and the curve of her behind.

I feel my cock rising, like it did when I first saw her. A further ache indicates that my secondary cock is stirring, and it's both a pleasant and painful experience, given it's never swelled before. I see her eyes dipping towards my crotch and remember my promise, turning swiftly away so that she can follow me into the main cavern.

"Who are you?" She asks as we walk through. "Where am I?"

She's curious, and I like that. Not that I would ever dislike anything my *eregri* did. Although I'm sure my cocks would prefer not to meet her knee again anytime soon.

"My name is Jyr. I am the Prime of the Legion of the Gryn." I glow with pride and feel somewhat deflated when she frowns, although her little brows knitting together makes her look adorable. "You are on Ustokos." I add.

"I really am on an alien planet." She whispers, staring around as if she's seeing the cavern for the first time. "I can't believe it." Her eyes shine with wetness. "How did I get here?"

"My mercs say they were raiding one of Proto's transporters for supplies when you appeared. It's a reasonable guess that Proto had something to do with you being here." I reply and try to draw her attention to the food I have brought and set out on a raised area of rock next to our bed. She's little and could do with feeding up. I want her to eat. "Are you from the lower continent?"

"Am I from this planet?" She barks out a laugh that holds no humor as water slips down her cheeks. "Do I look like I'm from this planet?" She stares at my wings, folding her arms across her chest, which I notice heaves with her breathing, causing heat to pool in my stomach.

"Most of the records were destroyed in the great reckoning. Before my time. There's no knowing how many organic species are left or where they are." I explain, again indicating the food, in the hope she will stop the water flowing from her eyes, which makes me feel all kinds of uncomfortable. My feathers itch. I want her to eat and be happy. I want her to consent to take my cocks.

"I'm from Earth, you idiot!" She spits out, a ball of rage even as her tears flow. "I'm not from here! What sort of aliens don't know who they've abducted and how?" Her arms wave helplessly.

"Please, my *eregri*. Come. Eat." Her distress slices through me worse than a joykill bot's laser whip.

She seems to notice the food for the first time and her eyes fix on it, scrubbing at her wet face with the back of one of her pink, clawless hands. She sniffs loudly, then sits next to the food. Picking up a sizeable chunk of maraha, she turns the deep blue flesh over in her hands before taking a tentative bite with her blunt teeth.

I internalize a groan. All I want to do is tear off morsels to feed to her, imagining her sweet lips taking pieces tenderly from my fingers as she lies in my lap. She shoots me a sharp look.

"Are you okay?"

I suspect my groan might not have been as quiet as I had hoped.

"I am, now you are feeding."

She swallows and slowly puts the maraha down. "What's in it? Drugs? Are you trying to drug me into submission?" She gets to her feet.

"No, no!" I cry out. "There's nothing in the food, see?" I

pick up the chunk of meat she was eating and take a big bite, rapidly chewing it and swallowing to demonstrate that it's unadulterated.

To my horror, further water glitters in her eyes. They overflow, and it runs down her cheeks again. I reach out and gently cup her face, which fits easily into my hand as I swipe my thumb over her soft skin.

"What is your name, sweet female?"

She shudders, but doesn't immediately move away from my touch. It feels like an electrical current is running down my arm. I've not experienced electricity for a very long time, not since I was last at Proto's mercy. This is good electricity. It warms me as it flows through my veins. Her eyes close briefly and for a second, I see a flash of another planet, one that is green and lush.

"My name is Vivian Owen. Most people call me Viv. I'm a human, and I'm not from your planet. I was abducted, I think. There are other humans here, too. I saw them before I fell out of the spaceship. You have to help me rescue them and we have to go home." Her words flow out of her as if she's been holding them in for a long time.

"My sweet Vivian," I try out her name and it rolls on my tongue like the richest ambrosia gathered by the Kijg in their petrified treetops. "There's no escaping Ustokos. As for your fellow humans, Proto will have them deep in its clutches by now. It will take many turns and many mercs to locate them, and we do not have those resources to spare."

Her eyes narrow and she moves away from my hand, the warmth of her skin lost to me and the spark gone.

"Then what's the point in me even speaking to you? I thought you said you were a Prime or something? Take me to someone who can help." She demands.

When I built my nest for my female, this was not how I

imagined it working out. I should be deep inside her, plea-suring her and filling her with my seed. Not staring into a pair of bright blue, red-rimmed eyes that defy me. I feel the anger that simmers under the surface rising. Anger at my legion for not being what I want, anger at having to prove myself at every turn. Anger that even something as simple as taking a mate is turning into another battle.

"I am all you have. You'd better get used to it." I no longer struggle to tear myself away from this frustrating problem and, in a few quick strides, I'm out of my cavern and in the air again.

VIV

Yep. He flew off.

That's how he deals with conflict.

Oh, and well done, Viv. You were just getting some answers and your only point of contact on this planet just flew away. Way to go.

Turns out that not only am I shit with human beings, I'm also pretty appalling in social interactions with other sentient species, too. A wave of self-pity flows through me and in seconds I'm sobbing snot into my hands. Big, shuddering, silent, screaming sobs that are as pathetic as I am. I thought I'd cried enough for a lifetime after my accident, but apparently not.

Being marooned on an alien planet with a growly hawk-man is the catalyst for more tears. I've been on my own for a long time, but as soon as he left, I feel the emptiness. It slams me in my chest as if I've never been alone before.

And when he touched me, it was as if I was made for his touch. That can't possibly be right. I must be having some sort of breakdown to be thinking this way. Just because he has deep, dark brown eyes that are flecked with green doesn't mean he gets into my knickers. If I were wearing any.

I made it through all those months in the hospital without falling apart, and I'm damned if I'm going to now. First things first. My stomach growls at me, and I look at the food that Jyr brought.

It's set out in a simple, but appealing, pattern. The meat that is blue but tastes like beef is closest to where I'm sitting, followed by something that is orangey pink and could be more meat, then a basket of what looks like breadsticks, and finally a pot of golden liquid. I don't think I've had a boyfriend who has cooked for me, let alone taken such care at setting out a simple meal. I dip my finger into the liquid and bring it to my nose, it smells sweet, and I test it with the tip of my tongue. It tastes like honey.

Alien honey.

And it's very, very moreish.

The cave light is dim when I open my eyes. I'm on the bed of furs and next to me is a very large, very warm body. I feel smooth feathers under my hands. For an instant, I let my fingers slip over the silky softness of the feathers and marvel in the thick, rigid feather shafts. These are working instruments. Lifting Jyr, and me into the sky with little or no effort. If I hadn't experienced it, I wouldn't have thought that flying with these wings was possible.

But then, not that long ago, the idea that aliens on other planets were possible seemed like a dream. I wonder if I'm dreaming now. The last thing I remember was eating alien honey. The thought has me jerking upright.

He said the food wasn't drugged! Yet here I am, next to him, on this pile of furs, with no knowledge of how I got here.

"*Eregri?*" Jyr murmurs, his big, clawed hands reaching for me. Even in the low light, I can see he is still asleep.

"Not on your nelly!" I scramble away from him. His eyes spring open and I'm captured by the look of terror that appears there. My mind fills with the sounds of screaming and the smell of scorched flesh. "What the—" I fall back, rolling onto the hard floor of the cave.

Jyr is instantly beside me, his enormous wings brushing the walls as he lands. They encircle us, and I'm enclosed in a wall of silence. There is only me and him.

"I do not wish to harm you."

"You drugged me. You said the food wasn't drugged."

"It wasn't, my sweet female," he puts his fingers to his lips. "I promised, and my word is my honor. I found you asleep when I came back. I only wanted you to be comfortable, which is why you were in my nest."

"Then why—"I ask, until the truth dawns on me. I'm on an alien planet. How the hell do I know what will and won't agree with me. That honey did go down very easily. Maybe it has soporific properties. "The honey." I stutter out, by way of explanation.

"Kijg ambrosia is delicious." He smiles. "It's one of my favorites."

A predator with a sweet tooth?

"We have something similar on Earth. It's called honey, and it's made by bees." Hark at me, the teacher of aliens.

"Beez?" He queries, making the word buzz and revealing an impressive set of sharp canines. His eyes twinkle.

"They are insects. Without them, our planet dies. Honey doesn't make us sleep though."

Jyr inclines his head and folds back his wings and I hadn't realized how warm and safe they made me feel. He straightens up and holds out his hand.

"Tell me more about your planet, and I can tell you about mine," he says. I stare at his hand for a beat and then shrug. It looks like I'm not going anywhere for a while and, if this is first contact with humans, then maybe I should try to be an ambassador.

Because when an alien holds out his hand to you, even if he's not telling you to run, it has to be an adventure. And I've missed the part of me that craved adventure so very much.

Jyr helps me to my feet and, with one hand in the small of my back, he guides me back to the food. I notice it has been replaced with fresh. There's a new pot of honey, and I hold myself back from diving straight in. I'm not entirely sure having any more of that stuff is a good idea. It might be okay for a creature of Jyr's build, but perhaps not so much for me.

"Sit, my *eregri*. Eat." He does his toothy grin at me, and his eyes glitter with uncertainty.

How can a predator as large as him be hesitant? He could easily take what he wanted from me. With his muscles and claws, I'd be powerless to resist. Yet, other than when he flew me to this cave and just now, he hasn't laid a hand on me. A thought occurs that he might have seen my scars when I was sleeping. A feeling of cold settles in the pit of my stomach. Tears fill my eyes and, because I know I have to be strong, I dip my head, my hair falling over my face as I try to get my emotions under control.

Even on an alien planet, I'm ugly. I know I am. I reach for a piece of the blue meat, just as Jyr does. Our fingers touch and that strange tingle is there again. He immediately withdraws. Of course. Whatever he wanted to do to me, that's been destroyed once he saw what I really looked like. My scars destroyed everything. My life, the job I loved. The medal in my bedside drawer was no comfort. Cold metal is no replacement for a life lost.

"How come I can understand you?" I ask him to distract me and to return to the more pressing here and now.

"What do you mean?" He cocks his head on one side as he chews on the orangey pink meat, his sharp teeth making swift work of it.

"You're speaking English."

"I don't think I am. I'm speaking Gryn."

I snort in frustration. "Then how can I understand you?" Is he deliberately playing dumb, or is his brain the only under-used muscle in his body?

"Proto probably did something so you could understand." He says dismissively as he makes his way through a large chunk of the blue meat. "My seniors and I can understand all Ustokos languages after Proto experimented on us. It probably did the same to you."

"What is Proto?"

JYR

"What is Proto?" Viv asks as she nibbles delicately on the maraha.

When I returned to my nest, having wrestled my anger at her under control, she was asleep, having eaten most of the ambrosia. I watched her for a while, trying to understand how something as tiny as her turned my world upside down.

"Proto is the entity that controls this planet, more's the pity." I say, hating to admit it to my *eregri*. "It controls the machines, the bots and anything else non-sentient. It won the great reckoning and considers organics a blight on Ustokos. It wants to wipe us out. It is an unmovable force that is beyond cruel."

"So why did it take me from my planet?" My mate queries, her eyes full of intelligence. "If it doesn't like people- Gryn- whatever?"

I rub at my chin. "I don't know." I can't imagine it's for anything good. "I'm sorry, my *eregri,* but Proto controls all on and off world transport. Even if I wanted to take you home, I couldn't."

She sighs and picks up a piir stick, biting on the end, her lips wrapping around it as it crumbles in her mouth. My cocks perk at the sight, and I shift, trying to make sure she doesn't see. If there's one thing I've learned from having my mate dropped at my feet, it's that mating doesn't come naturally. She can only be mated when she's ready. My balls give a slight throb as a reminder of what happened last time I mentioned mating.

"Why do you keep calling me that?" She says through distracting mouthfuls of piir. "Ere-gi." She tries the pronunciation.

"*Eregri*," I correct her with a smile. It's the first time I've really paid any attention to the fact she isn't Gryn. "It means that you are my fate, my boundless flight, my mate and my heart." I place my hand over my chest.

Her face darkens.

"I'm not your anything. I was brought here against my will, and I want to go home." She's full of fire, flaming like the gold of her hair. Her eyes blaze. My stomach sinks. I don't want to lose her. "After I rescue the other humans."

And we're back to this again. The other humans.

"I have no interest in any other human. Only you."

"There's no such thing as fate. There's action and reaction. That's all. If I believed in fate maybe—" She stops before finishing the sentence. Her eyes are guarded, and she folds her arms across her chest.

"I stopped believing in Nisis, our mother goddess, many cycles ago. Until I saw you." I want to reach for her, to pull her onto my lap, to be close. With an effort, I stop myself. "The Gryn has no females left. Proto took them. In all my efforts to free my kind, I have not seen a female, not since the day my mother was torn from me."

Vivian takes in a quick breath.

"I never expected to find a mate, fated or not."

I get to my feet and pace away from her. Losing my family is not a part of my past I wish to revisit. Shortly after Proto took me from my mother, I felt her life force dim and wink out. After that, it was only pain and torture as they performed experiment after experiment on my growing body. Until the day my seniors and I finally escaped.

"Proto will pay for what it has done to the Gryn and the other legions. Until then, we survive, and we take whatever comes our way. You are mine, Vivian. I will have you."

Viv stares at me, her mouth open. With a few short strides, I am across to her, catching her up in my arms and burying my head against her skin. Her body is delicious against mine, soft and pliable. Her scent intoxicating. I close my eyes, pushing at her down the bond, the fledgling bond that I only know about from stories told to me as a child. A bond she has to have with me for our mating to be true.

She brings her hands up onto my shoulders. Instantly I get a flash of pain and suffering that is so great I can't do anything else but pull away.

Someone hurt my *Eregri*.

She stumbles back, wetness on her cheeks.

"You don't want me, Jyr. No one does." She goes to run, back to the tiny cave I found her in. I grab at her arm.

"It is fated."

"Then fate is wrong." She looks up at me, her little body vibrating with her truth.

She's so close to me. I want to touch her, take her, and make her mine. But I'm needed back at the lair, my absence will be noted, and I have to show my face. The Gryn is the unity, and it is a call I ignore at my peril.

"I have to go, my *eregri*. But fate is not wrong. Nisis is never wrong, and I will prove it to you when I return."

It takes everything I have to leave her this time. I'm almost tripping over my wings, like I did when I was a youngling, with the effort it takes to make it to the outside of the cave.

"Where are you going?" I hear her voice calling after me. I risk a look back to see her standing on the ledge outside the cave, the wind whipping at the fabric she has wrapped around herself, her long golden hair flowing behind her.

"I'll be back." I call out, hoping my words are not lost on the breeze. I see her look around briefly before she ducks back into the safety of the cavern.

I can't remember the last time I offered a prayer to Nisis, but now I do. I hadn't understood my need to nest. Until now, the last few weeks of secrecy, of hoarding and of planning all make sense when I see my female, my *eregri* wrapped in my furs.

When I return, I will show her what it is to be mated to a Gryn, and she won't ever deny the fates again.

VIV

Okay, so the flying away thing is starting to get old. Yet again, I'm left on my own with no explanation. If anything, I'm more confused. He is absolutely sure that I'm his 'mate'. Which, from the sounds of it, means that he has to accept me, scars and all.

He's stuck with me as I'm stuck in this cave. From my brief look outside as I watched him leave, we're way up high in a cliff face. Below, a long, long way below, are the moldering ruins of what looked to be a great alien city. Twisted wreckage of tall towers that look melted. The wind cuts through me like ice, and I hurry back inside to the warmth of the cave.

I'm on the losing side in a war that devastated this planet. Just when I thought my luck couldn't get any worse. At least I'm used to being a loser.

I return to the bed of furs and curl up. Jyr's scent drifts into my nostrils. Spice and a hint of warm laundry. I try not to think that it's comforting, like it was when he wrapped us both in his huge wings. A long time ago, when I had friends, my best friend, Liz, used to joke with me. She said I had to overthink everything, and I should be less uptight. Some-times running with something takes as much guts as standing still.

"How's this for overthinking, Liz? I've got a massive alien who wants to get into my pants and give me babies, and I can't even undress in front of a mirror." I laugh/sob to myself, burrowing deeper into the furs as I don't know how to turn out the lights in the cave. I miss Liz and wish beyond words that I had made it up with her, with everyone, before all this happened, and I disappeared from Earth. Regrets circle and worry at the edges of my mind, but fortunately, in time, sleep claims me.

A weird noise wakes me, the sound of something being dragged. I stick my head out of the furs as slowly as I dare. So far, Jyr has only brought me prepared food, but I'm worried he's brought me something larger, like a cat present, only something a massive flying alien predator might bring.

Jyr stands in the entrance to the cave, clutching at the wall. His side and one wing are covered in bright red blood. As I stare, initially paralyzed at the sight of the huge alien and his horrific injury, his eyes flicker closed and he slips against the rock, leaving a red streak.

"Shit!" I'm off the bed and close the gap between us in seconds, grabbing hold of him and wrapping an arm around my shoulder. "What happened?"

"Ambush. Need to get to the pool." He takes a step forward and collapses against me. He weighs less than he looks, but even so, seven feet of alien is difficult to prop up.

"You need to get that wound seen too." At this stage, I'm presuming it's one wound. "You can't go in the pool."

"Pool." He growls, and I feel a set of claws gripping my shoulder. What I thought was just on his fingertips turn out to be long, black and vicious, retractable like a cat. His face is a mask. Trying to contain the pain. "Get me to the pool, please."

"Let me check you over first, you really shouldn't go in the water." I try to steer him towards the pile of furs.

"No!" He snarls with a strength and ferocity that I didn't think he had. "Don't defy me, female. Pool."

As much as I want to run from this monster, if I left him, he would fall. Yet again, I'm doing something that puts me in danger for someone else.

"Pool it is." I mutter and carefully help him over to the steaming water. "Sit." I risk giving him an order as I deposit him on the edge, moving to his feet to pull off his heavy boots.

He sits hunched over, head hanging and barely conscious as I remove his footwear. My concerns were correct. He has one deep slash running over his abdomen and several smaller, but equally surgical cuts on his chest, arms and back. There's so much blood on his wing, I can't even see if it's damaged.

"Pool." He murmurs. Any fight left in him is long gone.

I shuffle him so that his lower legs drop into the water, and he weakly pushes himself so that he slides into the pool. Dropping under the water. He doesn't come back up.

I wait.

He doesn't resurface. The clear water of the pool is turning red around his increasingly pale form.

I wait.

"Fuck it!" I jump in beside him, ducking under until I get his arm around my shoulders and, with a push against the side, I kick up to lift his head clear of the water.

Jyr coughs shakily, his breathing shallow as I prop him against the side and brush my hands over his face to clear away the liquid. I can feel his strength under my fingers. It's almost as if I can see his will to live, imprinted in my brain like a branding. I go to take my hands away.

"Stay with me, my *eregri*." His voice is incredibly low. "The mountain waters will help me heal. Your presence will help me heal."

"You need a hospital, Jyr. You've been badly injured." I put my hand on the side of his face and turn his head so he's looking at me. "You're losing too much blood. Even for a seven-foot flying alien."

I didn't mean for the last part to come out and I clap my hand over my mouth. In a movement I don't even see, Jyr's huge hand covers mine, pulling it away from my mouth as he chuckle groans.

"I'm fine. I heal fast. See." He pulls my hand down towards the biggest wound, the one on his abdomen. I resist. I don't want to touch it, but I can't escape his grip. The water is dark with his blood, and as he puts my hand on his skin, I can feel that it's much smaller than before. "Takes more than a few flesh wounds to stop a Prime of the Gryn." He laughs, his head dropping back onto the ledge that runs around the pool.

He rolls it over to look at me. "Thank you." His eyes close. "For a tiny little creature, you're very brave."

"Hardly." I reply. "Foolish, yes. Brave, no."

"You underestimate yourself, *eregri*." He coughs again and winces. "I should get back to my warriors. Proto was looking for us, and I only just got away." He attempts to get out of the pool but slides back.

I grab at one wing just before he disappears beneath the dark water and pull him back.

"You've lost too much blood, Jyr. You're not going anywhere."

JYR

I don't understand how the capture/contain patrol had located the small band of mercs, but they were in trouble when I'd reached them on my way back to the lair. One merc was already down, and the load of weapons they'd been transporting was scattered on the ground. It looked as if the matter was under control until a joykill bot appeared out of nowhere. I fought it off while the others made good their escape.

It's what a Prime is supposed to do.

But I wasn't supposed to let the vrexing thing get a couple of shots in, let alone injure me this badly. But it had a new weapon that, in our usual close quarters fighting delivered several serious wounds before I could disable it. Given the precarious state of play back at the lair, knowing Kaloz waits for me to show weakness, the only way I'm going to go back is fully healed and with my mate by my side.

The last thing I want is to share her with anyone, but she makes me strong. And I have to be a strong Prime. My Gryn warriors deserve nothing less. Which left me with no option. If it was a choice between the lair and my nest, I had to return to my nest. I would have preferred that Viv hadn't seen me in this state, either. It's for me to care for her, not the other way around.

Despite my rapid healing, Viv is correct. I've lost far too much blood to be of much use to anyone. I certainly can't fly. Even if I could, I doubt I would be able to fight off Proto again today. With some effort, I pull myself out of the pool. The water has done its job. My wounds are cleansed and closing. After a short breather, I get to my feet. Viv is by my side, holding my torso and staring wildly at my chest and abdomen.

"Wow," she says, tracing a finger over the closed gashes. "I wish humans healed like this."

"You'll never even know I've been injured in a turn." I say, trying to hold myself up but enjoying her proximity.

She says nothing, but a brief image of flames fills my head, along with the smell of burning. I feel my feathers prick and brace myself as each one lifts as I twirl my wings over my head, shedding the water that has covered them.

"What the fuck?" Viv cries out in alarm as I spray water halfway across the cave.

"How did you think I dry my feathers?" I grin at her.

My mood is weirdly euphoric. Perhaps it's being in close proximity to her, perhaps it's the blood loss. Either way, I'm probably going to sit down before I fall down.

"Yeah, well, are you going to dry your trousers in the same way?" She puts her hands on her hips, raising her eyebrows. For the first time, the hint of a smile quirks the corners of her mouth.

"Not at all." I release the mag catch at my waist and shove at the soaking fabric, stamping on each trouser leg until I'm free of the wet cloth. It'll dry quickly, whether or not it's on me, but I want to see her reaction.

"Oh god!" She whirls away from me, running across to the bed and throwing a fur at me. "You're naked!"

She still isn't looking. I leave the fur at my feet. I am a good-looking male, and my primary cock is impressive, or so I've been told by Mochi females who have entertained me.

"I am naked, my *eregri*. Do you not like what you see?"

She turns back to me, one hand over her eyes. Peeping through her fingers, she lets out a little snort of breath.

"Just cover yourself up, okay?" She hesitates for a moment before whirling away.

She wants me.

I grin to myself, but pick up the fur and wrap it around my waist. My gait is unsteady, and I just make it to the bed before I have to sit. My feathers itch for a preen. Viv risks another peep and drops her hand away when she sees I've covered myself. I rake my claws through my damp wings. It feels good, better than good, to be working over each shaft with my mate in close proximity.

"Hey." She puts her hand on my arm, stilling my movement. "You need to rest."

Her brilliant blue eyes search my face. I want nothing more than to taste her lips, which is weird. Lip touching seems like an odd thing to do. Cleansing and preening can involve the lips, but lips on lips? I don't know where the idea has come from, unless it's down our bond.

"I'll rest if you'll stay with me." Well, it worked before, didn't it? "But you'll also need to let your–clothing - dry."

Viv looks down at the fabric she has wound around her luscious body.

"Yeah? You'd like that, wouldn't you?" She backs away.

"I only want you to be comfortable, my *eregri*." I attempt to placate her as I see the fire in her eyes. "I made a promise not to touch you. A Gryn's word is sacred." I place my hand across my chest and bow to her.

She shivers as my imagination goes to a place where I am touching her, all over her body, concentrating on her pleasure. The scent of her arousal fills the air, and my cocks react.

Fortunately, the heavy fur keeps my reaction under wraps.

"Don't look." She hops onto the bed behind me.

"Believe me, Viv. All I want to do is sleep. You have nothing to fear from me." It's not strictly true. I could certainly muster up the energy to mate if she desires me.

She stops moving, and I roll onto the bed, coming up short as I find she has buried herself under the furs. All I can see is her face and her golden hair.

"You are so beautiful." The words escape me without even a thought. Because she is. Viv is the most perfect being I have encountered.

"I don't think so." She replies. "There's probably something wrong with your mate radar if you think I'm beautiful."

"Mate radar?" I query.

"Yeah, you know. Radar, the radio waves that mean you can see objects coming without actually seeing them."

I shake my head. "Since the great reckoning, we cannot use any technology. Proto's algos are in it all. Using anything that has any form of electronics would risk being found and captured."

"No tech?" Viv raises herself up on her elbows to look at me, the fur draped over her chest falling to reveal a creamy expanse of skin. "What about the lights in here?"

"Organic bioluminescent plants. We cultivate them."

"So no phones, no computers, no spaceships?"

"Not the Gryn, not for a hundred turns."

Viv flops back onto the bed, staring up at the ribbons of light and sparkle I put there for her. I knew my mate would be dazzling and they suit her perfectly. She flips onto her side, propping her head up on a fist, and stares at me.

"No hospitals?"

"Probably not. I'm not sure what a 'hospital' is." I get a flash of white rooms and a strange sharp smell. It reminds me of Proto's labs.

And it has come directly at me from my mate. Our thoughtbond has already formed, something I had never expected, not so soon and not with another species.

She truly is my boundless flight.

VIV

O bviously, Jyr will never need a hospital, so he doesn't need to worry about what one is, or how bad it is to spend months in one.

"They are supposed to help you if you're sick."

"Have you been sick?" He asks me. His dark eyes are half lidded and his voice slightly muzzy. "Like I am now."

"I was, once."

"I prefer to be here with you, in our nest. Not in a 'hospital'."

"Our nest?"

"Mmmhmm." He hums. "Made it, for you." His hand waves vaguely at the things hanging up. "You like?"

My chest squeezes. I can't quite grab the air when I try to take a breath. All that time on my own and all I wanted was for someone to care. Jyr built this place before he even knew me. The creature beside me might be supremely strong, arrogant and, well, very proud of his naked body. But he's still hurt, and he needs someone to care for him right at this moment. My stomach warms at the thought of being that person. I reach out and brush the back of my hand against his face. He leans into my touch like a cat.

"I like."

"My *eregri*." His gorgeous eyes close in pleasure, and he shuffles further onto the bed so he can press his head against my chest, one wing covering me. The scent of his still damp feathers defines him. A spicy musk that is both delicate and strong. "I'm pleased you're here, finally." His words tail away as his breathing deepens.

How did I go from hiding from this huge alien to having him in my arms? The thing is, he's soft and warm, like the bed I'm tucked into. His weight alone is oddly comforting, and so is his ability to heal himself. It means that I won't be alone, not if I have him.

Wait? What? Seriously, am I even considering this? Am I considering believing this whole thing about mating?

I look at the slumbering bad angel next to me. He has kept his promise. Other than flaunting himself at me earlier, confirming what I already knew, that he was just as alien big down below as he appears elsewhere, he hasn't touched me. Not since he brought me here. To his nest. The one he made for a woman he had never met.

No one has ever done anything like this for me. Not that I was prepared to let anyone in. When you're alone in the world, it's hard to not stay alone. Besides, I liked my own company for a bit. Okay, I admit it had got boring, but I'd pushed everyone away. I didn't know how to get them back. If they'd even want me after the way I behaved. My family thought I hated them. My sister stopped speaking to me years ago after the argument with my parents. Things were said. Things that couldn't be unsaid.

No one would even know I was missing from Earth until the bills piled up.

This alien, he wants me. He wanted me before he met me. I should find that strange except I'm on a freaking alien planet, with an alien sleeping in my arms! An actual alien! A laugh bubbles up from within me, and I have to clench my teeth to stop the hysteria from bursting out. I have no idea if what he told me is true, about the machines and the tech. I'm supposed to trust an alien I've known for next to no time when I have trusted no one for years.

Outside of the cave, I hear a low buzzing sound. Jyr stirs, but he doesn't wake. He lost so much blood, I'm amazed he's still alive. He'll probably sleep for hours. I carefully slide out from underneath his warm body and soft, feathery wing. Clutching a large fur pelt around me, I pad carefully across the cave towards the entrance. It's dark here, and I press myself against the rock wall as I slowly edge forwards. The buzzing is louder as I stare out into the dim light. This planet's default setting it appears.

I look around for the source of the noise and immediately step back when I see it. About the size of a trashcan, the robot hovers just above the ledge. Three balls covered in spikes make up the body of the thing, although these continually rotate as it hovers, the red glow from beneath indicating its power source. A grating whine is followed by a bright white light that scans the cliff. It makes a metallic chittering sound, almost like laughter as the scan continues. Laughter that is manic in tone.

"Joykill bot." Jyr whispers in my ear, his arms wrapping around me and a hand over my mouth as I nearly leap off the ledge in surprise. "If we don't move, it's sensors shouldn't detect us."

He doesn't need to tell me twice. I'm not moving, no way. The thing might buzz like a bee, but it's radiating evil. I'm not sure how long we stand there, frozen, but I become more aware of Jyr's warm body and his wings gently curving around me, the feathers brushing my bare legs. My heart thunders in my chest. His is a steady beat against my back. His powerful form is reassuring and somewhere in the back of my mind I know he would destroy the thing that hovers over us in an instant if I asked him to. Heat pools between my legs. This terrifying spectacle shouldn't be turning me on. Being this close to Jyr shouldn't be turning me on.

The robot swivels around, each spiky oval turning independently. I feel as if it's looking straight at me, and my breath comes out in short bursts into Jyr's massive hand.

"Don't worry, *eregri*. It'll leave soon." His voice seems to be in my head rather than a whisper in my ear.

It emits a loud, insistent tone that grates in my eardrums. Just when I think I can't take anymore, it stops and shoots straight up, away from us. Jyr keeps hold of me for a beat and then releases me. I stare up at the sky, mesmerized by the pure evil that was contained in that one robot.

"Was it looking for us?" I say, hoarsely. My legs are trembling until I feel Jyr sag against me and I turn to take hold of him.

"It was looking for me." He says, yawning. "It's the same type of bot that did this to me." He runs his hand over the nearly healed wound on his abdomen. "I'm already in the database, so it's no big deal."

"If something tries to kill you, it's a big deal." I pull one of his big arms around my shoulders. He looks all in. "It won't come back though, will it?"

"It might. I guess we're going to have to go to the lair." I deposit Jyr on the bed and he immediately wraps his arms around me, pulling me on top of him and rolling over until I'm underneath him. The action takes me by surprise, and I should struggle.

I should struggle, but I don't.

"What's the lair?" His breath is hot on my face. His lips very close to mine.

"It's where we live, with the rest of my Gryn warriors."

"But this place, your nest-"

"It's only for us," Jyr murmurs, closing his eyes and inhaling deeply. "Your scent, it drives me wild, *eregri*."

His eyes open again, this close up, they are flecked with gold and green. He is the most handsome man-alien-creature I've ever met. My hands on his chest can feel his strength, his taut muscles as he holds himself over me.

"I can't- I can't do this, Jyr. You don't want me. I'm not perfect." I stammer out, as Jyr unwraps the fur from around my body.

"I won't make you do anything you don't want to do." His hands stop and I find myself wanting him to continue. "You are perfect. You are my mate, and the fates wouldn't give me anything less than perfect."

His mouth is tantalizingly close. He shifts his touch to my face, fingers as soft as his feathers brush over my cheek. I press my lips to his. Warmth spreads through me, a warmth I haven't felt in a very long time. With infinite care, I probe with my tongue, and Jyr opens his mouth for me as I reach around the back of his head to run my fingers, first through the feathers that cover his back and upper shoulders and then onto the hard leathery skin that has intrigued me all this time. It's like armor but living and as hot as the rest of him. Jyr seemed hesitant about my kiss at first, but now he reciprocates. His strong mouth on mine, entwining our tongues with delicious fury. He is as dominant in our kiss as he is in everything else. When he releases me, his eyes are still closed.

"What was that?" He breathes.

"I don't know." My nether regions are throbbing with need. "That kiss was something else." I want more. I definitely want more of his mouth.

"Kiss?" He hisses. "Is that what that was?"

"You've never kissed before?" I stare up at Jyr and he breaks into the naughtiest grin.

"Nope. Gryn don't 'kiss', although I don't know why, it's extremely enjoyable."

"What do Gryn do, if they don't kiss?" I'm playing with fire, I know I am, but I can't help myself anymore. I'm stuck on an alien planet with a bad, bad angel, who's never kissed before and has just blown my mind.

Jyr's grin widens, his sharp teeth bared, and he drops his head into the crook of my neck, his tongue swirling over my skin, down and down, over my chest until he reaches my breast. He lifts his head up, his dark eyes searching my face for permission, and I pull at his neck for him to continue. How could I not? His hot mouth fastens over my raised nipple, and he sucks. My back arches and I grab at his head, unable to help myself. He works hard, lapping at my tight peak, and then switches to the other nipple.

The simple pleasure of being touched again overwhelms me, and I let out a high-pitched whine.

"Does my *eregri* require more?" He says, half incoherent through a mouth full of nipple.

In an instant, the remaining fur covering has been stripped away, and I am laid out, entirely naked, for this alpha predator to consume.

Naked with all my imperfections on display. With a sharp intake of breath, I try to cover over the mottled, damaged flesh all down my left side.

"Jyr, I-" But it's too late, he's already staring and staring at the scars that are the only thing that defines me.

JYR

iv's eyes are wide as I take her in. Her creamy skin, lush full breasts that have only ever haunted my dreams, are tipped with rosy nipples that I have teased to bright red peaks. She squirmed under me, her back arching as she pushed them into my mouth. I could have shed my seed from both cocks without even thinking. Between her legs is the sweetest little wisp of hair, and the scent of her arousal is heady in the air. I have to taste her tonight. My primal being will accept nothing less.

She trembles under me, mumbling something about an apology. And then she pulls at the furs, trying to cover her glorious body from my sight. I push her hands away.

"This is mine now. You need not cover yourself from me. I always want to see you like this, spread for me, eager and wanting."

"But," she protests and I run a hand over her hips and onto her waist. She whimpers and scoots away from me, wetness on her cheeks and a stutter in her throat. Finally, she drags a fur over herself and sits, hunched, her back to me.

"Eregri?" I reach for her shoulder.

Confusion mixes with my lust, and I feel slightly woozy. I made my nest for her and she came. I brought her here, fed her, and kept her safe. She taught me her 'kiss' which must mean something to her. And yet, when I pleasured her, she withdrew. All I can see is flashing blue lights as my sense tries to fight over my desires.

"Now you know." She sniffs, rubbing at her cheeks with the back of her hand before turning to face me, her eyes red rimmed. "Now you know just how ugly the creature you've chosen as your mate really is." She spits out the words like a challenge. "I'll understand if you want to give me back to the machine things." Her voice is low, and my heart aches.

I shuffle over on the furs until I'm sat next to her. One wing curls itself around her bare shoulders.

"What makes you think you are ugly? All I see is the most delicious morsel I will ever taste." I desperately want to draw her into my arms, to hold her and to soothe the rawness of her emotions I feel coursing through me.

Like I feel my Gryn warriors.

For an instant, I freeze. I did not know that it was possible to communicate without words with any other than the most senior Gryn.

But I can feel my mate, like I did with my brothers, until it became something more. The mate thoughtbond resonates through us both. Stronger than anything I've felt before. More than just a brief flash of her past or emotion. I fill my mind with softness, like the down at the base of my wings, and give it to her. Beside me, her shudderings slowly cease.

"My scars." She says. "My scars make me ugly." She slowly pulls away the furs to reveal her skin.

It's a similar pink to the rest of her. Thicker, like the skin on my shoulders, the impenetrable hide that ensures the Gryn can fly through anything. I see nothing but perfection.

"Scars tell a tale, my *eregri*. They do not make you ugly. You are the most beautiful creature I have ever set eyes on, and you will always be that way to me."

I brush the knuckles of my hand down her side, which she claims is scarred and she shivers but does not move away.

"Tell me the tale of you."

Viv's eyes are on her hands in her lap. She twists her long, slim, clawless fingers together.

"There was an accident. A car accident." She looks sideways at me under her long eyelashes, making me want to perform another kiss on her gorgeous lips. "A car is a form of human transport, a box on wheels that is propelled mechanically. Our machines haven't become sentient and taken over our world." She adds with a slight hint of a smile. Her face becomes serious again, her bottom lip pouting a little.

"I got out, but there was a woman and a little girl trapped in one of the other cars. I don't know how I did it, but I got the door open and the woman out. Some other people dragged her away just as the car caught fire. The little girl was screaming for her mother and I had no choice." Her breath hitches, her eyes fixed on the other side of the cave. "As I got her out, my clothes hooked on a piece of metal. The fuel tank exploded, and I was thrown clear. But not before I got burned."

She wraps the fur back around herself.

"Humans don't heal like you. I was in hospital for a long time, and when I came out..." She shakes her head.

I feel her loneliness as an empty void of thoughts and nothing. It's how I feel when I'm alone in my quarters at the end of every turn, only she is lonely for the lack of company, whereas I am never alone. Her sadness slams into me hard.

My wing pushes her to me, and she doesn't resist. The fight has left her. I put a finger under her chin and lift her head so I can see her glorious eyes.

"Your story is one of bravery and your scars are nothing to be ashamed of. Your beauty is as exquisite as is fitting for a mate of a Prime."

"You're not bothered?" She says, placing a hand on my chest.

"No." I cover her tiny hand with mine. "Now, I wish to pleasure you, if you'll let me."

Her face flushes a deeper pink, and it is utterly gorgeous.

"I've not been touched that way for a long time." She dips her head.

I let out a low growl at the thought of any male, human or Gryn touching my female, and she sits back in alarm.

"What was that?"

"No one but me is to touch you again. Understand?"

"Depends how well you touch me." She stares up at me, defiant.

"Oh, *eregri*, once you have been touched by Jyr, you'll not want any other male again."

VIV

Jyr seems pretty full of himself. If he hadn't just told me I'm the most beautiful thing he's ever seen, I would most definitely be kicking him in the balls again.

But my horny has been awoken. It's been dormant for so long, I presumed it was MIA forever. This big alien has done something to my insides. I didn't want to show myself to anyone after being rejected, but his reaction was at the complete opposite end of the scale to what had gone before. And as much as I've never been into the whole caveman vibe, his growly alpha behavior makes me want to test him and see what happens.

I don't think I was this bold before the accident. At thirty-three, my distinct lack of love life was hardly anything new, always too much of a perfectionist, wanting it all and ending up with nothing. At thirty-six, it's too late for love.

Unless you're a seven-foot alien male with a wingspan the size of a jumbo jet. Jyr isn't going to waste any more time, and he isn't going to let me tease him any longer. He plucks the fur covering my body away in a single tug. I think

I may have let the predator loose when I goaded him. He hooks an arm around my waist and instantly I'm spread out for him. His head drops onto a nipple, and he does that thing with his tongue again that leaves me panting.

"Let me show you just how beautiful you are." He laps down the underside of my breast. His huge hand spans my waist as his mouth moves over to the scars that flow like water down my side.

I try to pull away, but he holds me in place, his tongue sweeping over my sensitive skin as he caresses my scarred body. The body I've been hiding from everyone, including myself. I'm frozen as he works his way down my side and over onto my abdomen, where the scar meets skin. His touch is so incredibly gentle as he lavishes attention on the part of me I haven't been able to acknowledge, other than to use it as a way to excuse who I have become. Jyr's interest, or lack of it, in what makes me ugly allows a coil of pleasure to unwind inside me.

He doesn't stop at my stomach. His lips move lower. His hands part my thighs, and his massive form burrows between my legs. He sits back, wings looming over us both as he grins at me, licking his lips, one finger trailing over my mound, hovering just above my clit. It slides over the bundle of nerves and down through my folds, slick with desire. He toys with me, his face a mask of delight, like a cat that wants to devour its prey, but wants to make the moment last. A moan of lust escapes me and his eyes blaze. He dips his thick digit inside me, his other hand spanning my waist. I arch my back to allow him to go deeper.

"Delicious, but I have to taste." His voice is deep gravel, and I shudder over his finger.

I can see his cock, thick and swollen. It's even larger than I thought. It tapers from a thick base to a point. A ridge studded with engorged nodes runs down its length. The underneath reminds me of the belly of a crocodile, ridged and segmented. But it's what sits just below his cock that stops my breath.

A second cock, slightly shorter than the first, and slimmer. It too has a long ridge running down it. My alien has two cocks!

Two!

Jyr removes his finger, licking my juices with a smile that melts me even further. He drops between my legs and nudges his way up my thighs before I have time to take in the concept of a doubly endowed male. He latches onto my clit with a force that has me seeing stars. All I can think about is what he's doing with his mouth and those two cocks, ridged and rigid. He devours me, inch by inch, his incredibly talented tongue, just the right side of rough brings me to the brink. He slips in a digit and pumps my tight, wet channel, adding a further finger as he redoubles his efforts over my clit and the stars I saw earlier pale into insignificance with the climax he wrings from my body. I seize up, unable to move or speak as my limbs spark with the fire he has found within me. Pulsing and releasing, gushing into his mouth as I get control of my arms and grasp at his dark hair.

Jyr chuckles, swiping his rough tongue up my inner thigh.

"Beautiful."

I can't yet speak, my chest heaving from the unaccustomed effort of pleasure. I twitch underneath him. He raises himself above me, two cocks ready to spear my willing and soaking holes.

"Delicious." He collapses beside me, pulling me into his side and covering me with furs.

He wanted me, wanted to make babies with me. He has literally wrung my body to its very limit, but doesn't want anything more?

"Don't you want to- you know?" My voice is weak, almost pathetic.

"You have had more than enough of Jyr for tonight. I only take what is freely given, my *eregri*." He pulls me onto his expansive chest. "Tomorrow we travel to the lair. You will meet my warriors." He settles himself further into the furs, like a hen on eggs. "Then we will see about mating."

Oh god, I hope it's not some sort of public thing...

Deep down, the Vivian I used to be smiles to herself. Filthy girl...

JYR

I absolutely would have mated my Vivian as she lay beneath me, boneless and weeping her nectar. It was like the best ambrosia. I would have feasted on her again and again. But her fear hovers near the surface. Fear of rejection, fear of me, and of her surroundings.

Honor means I cannot take a female in that way. She did not feel the immediacy of the bond like I did, and that means I have to coax my gorgeous female around to my way of thinking.

And it's filled with licentious thoughts about her soaking channel and soft breasts. When she came undone for me, I thought I would spill my seed wastefully, as I have many times with the thought of a mate. I have been with a Mochi female, the ones that frequent the trading posts, looking for a barter. They have their own way of mating, no pleasure, only the act. No wonder my secondary cock never rose for those encounters.

My Vivian needs coaxing, and she must want me, completely, before I will take her.

For a male that is used to getting his own way, instantly,

without hesitation, this is going to be a challenge. One I have hardly lived up to. Beside me, her breathing becomes deeper, and her sweet face is relaxed as she sleeps in the crook of my arm. I brush a lock of her golden hair to one side. She is alien and familiar at the same time with her creamy skin and lack of feathers. Only a little bit of fluff between her legs. From what I've been told, Gryn females were covered in feathers. I'll never know and now I have my *eregri,* I don't care. She might not think she's perfect, but she is.

My heart aches deep down inside. We have a mountain to climb together. From what I've seen so far of my fierce little mate, she's more than up to the task and it gladdens me more than I thought possible to have her by my side. I tuck her closer so that I can inhale the scent of her hair and my body drops into repair mode. My sleep deep enough to allow the healing process and light enough to be aware if Proto comes calling again.

———

THE SMELL of dawn filters into the cave. From the red light outside, it would seem that the ion storms that have persisted for the last half a cycle are breaking up. This will mean the Legion will need to make the most of the better weather. It means that even if I wanted to, I cannot stay in my nest any longer.

I have to return to the lair, present my mate to my warriors, and face the consequences. My stomach hardens. They will accept her. I will make sure they do. And I will deal with the Kaloz problem before I risk my name as Prime.

Viv squirms under the furs, and her brilliant blue eyes

open. She blinks a few times at me, and her cheeks darken. The scent of her arousal reaches me, my cocks react. They are going to have to wait, even if taking my sleepy mate long and slow would be the ideal start to my day.

"Good morning, my *eregri*." I wrap a fur around my waist and pad over to the remains of the meal from last night, picking out a few choice morsels to tempt her. I return to our bed and present them.

"I'm not really a morning person, Jyr." She says, clasping the furs to her chest. "I don't do breakfast."

"Today you do. We have to return to the lair. It may be some time before you eat again."

She looks at the food and her stomach gives a low growl, as defiant as she is. I grab a chunk of maraha and chew on it whilst I gather up my clothing. The trousers are, thankfully, dry. Vivian's piece of fabric is dry too, but not the outfit she will be wearing to meet the Legion. Only I get to see that much of my *eregri*. I pull on my clothes and boots before returning to her, noting with satisfaction that she is eating heartily.

"Must be the alien air." She says, her mouth rising at one corner.

"The only alien here is you." I say as I start to dig under my pile of furs.

I need to get to know my mate better, once things are more settled and she knows more of Ustokos. There's so much for her to learn if she is to be the Lady Prime.

"What are you doing?" She asks as I dislodge her, pulling out a pair of trousers triumphantly. I dig deeper to finally pull out a shirt. Both are far too large for her, and the shirt is made to fit over a pair of wings, but they will have to do until I can find a Mochi trading post.

"Here. You can wear these." I hand her the clothes.

"These were here all this time?" She stares at the garments and grumbles a curse. She looks up at me under her eyelashes. I know she doesn't want me looking at her. The thing is, I always want to look at her.

"Eregri," I say, gently. "I will get you the best clothing as soon as I can. I did not know who you would be until you arrived."

"And that's it, is it? You're stuck with me? I'm not even the same species as you. How do you even know we're compatible?" Her words come out in a rush, impossible to unpick.

"You are my *eregri*, my fated one. There is no stuck, and I think last night proved that we are compatible."

She snorts, grabbing at the garments. She stands, clutching them to her, then turns her back on me. Pulling on the trousers gives me a superb view of her ass, and I have to fight with my arousal. She shrugs on the shirt, closing up the slits for the wings easily by wrapping it around herself.

Dressed in my clothing, she looks even smaller and more delicate. Far too fine for a rough Gryn like me. The fates certainly have an odd way of behaving. I reach for her hand and draw her to me.

"Before we go, I have to tell you that my legion is split. I am Prime and my word is law." I take a deep breath. "My second in command was the Prime of another legion. He lost his position when Proto raided his lair and came to me for help. As a former Prime, I had to give him Command. He resents my generosity and conspires against me whilst showing a fair face. Bringing back a mate to our lair will cement my position, but there is still danger." She takes in a breath. "Not as dangerous as Proto. No Gryn would challenge their Prime without good cause. You are safe with me, my Vivian."

"Okay," she doesn't sound convinced and my anger flares. "Thanks for the warning. But-" She hesitates at the look on my face. I don't want to scare her and I attempt to moderate my features. "Why keep him around if he's so much trouble."

I sigh. She's put her tiny, pink finger right on the nub of the problem. Mate thoughtbond or no.

VIV

I suppose flying with Jyr makes a change from him flying away. I'd like to enjoy it more, but the memory of those first two flights is still clinging to me, and I'm terrified that he's going to drop me or something. So instead of doing the whole 'Lois Lane and Superman' thing, I'm clasped around Jyr like a spider monkey.

Hardly a good look, although he doesn't seem to be bothered. He lifts me as if I'm nothing. I can feel his muscles bunching and releasing under my death grip as he soars in the sky, one powerful arm around my waist.

Maybe he won't drop me after all. Maybe I'll be alright. Maybe I'll find the other women and find a way off this planet. Ha. Ha. Ha.

"We're here, Vivian." He says in my ear, and we go into a sharp descent that only makes me cling tighter to him.

The rushing of wind and the hard beats of his wings denote we have landed, and I try to let go. Turns out that's harder than I expected. My limbs seem to have frozen, and I pry myself loose awkwardly. We stand on a ledge of a building that looks like they made it out of concrete. Then bombed it. Then burned it and bombed it again. The blackened structure crumbles and twists. I don't move away from Jyr, I don't want to risk the very, very long drop that I can see just behind us.

Jyr is looking over my shoulder, his dark gaze hard. He takes my wrist as I turn.

Arranged in formation on the ledge are the biggest, baddest looking set of warrior angels I've ever seen. Each one has similar wings to Jyr, slate gray on the back and mottled underneath. They are all huge, muscular with dark hair and eyes, except the one standing a little way back. His eyes are a pale blue, like a husky. All of them slowly flex their wings as we enter into a staring contest that I'm pretty sure I'm not going to win.

"This is my mate, my *eregri*, my female." He snarls the last word as he pulls me against his hard chest, one arm possessively slung over my shoulder and down my abdomen. "She is mine and you will afford her the utmost respect."

One by one, the other warriors take a step back and bow. "Prime." They chorus. Their wings are dipped along with their heads in clear deference to my powerful alien angel.

All except one. The one stood just to the right of us. He must be Kaloz. He's slightly shorter than Jyr, and thinner. His face, like the rest of them, has an ethereal, high cheekbones look, only his is more weasel than angel.

"You have mated?" He asks, insolence pouring out of him.

"Vivian is my mate." Jyr replies. I can feel the tension in the air. "We are blessed by Nisis with a female for our Legion. She will bear my young and make us stronger than ever."

His assertion makes me twist to look at him. His jaw is

set like stone and his clawed hand presses into my side. My desire to set him straight was weak to begin with. In the face of the other predators who are not entirely sure what to make of me, it dissolves completely, and I stay silent.

"Nisis," Kaloz spits. "A tale only fit for younglings. You address warriors, not idiots, Prime."

"And my warriors know better than to speak out of turn. You know the code, Kaloz." Jyr pushes me behind him and extends his claws.

If I'd remembered what he was harboring at the end of his thick fingers last night, there's no way I would have let him put them where he did. His claws must be four inches long, black and viciously sharp. He opens his wings, blocking the other Gryn from my view and a deep, evil growl reverberates in the air.

"We have more pressing matters to attend to Prime." Kaloz says in his nasally voice.

"Szent." Jyr says, his voice low and menacing. "I am taking my female to my quarters. I will meet you there."

There's a hand in the small of my back, and I'm being propelled along in a feathered fury. Dark eyes and one set of blue follow my progress as Jyr takes me into the building.

If that's what this is. The interior is quite dark, lit by the same lights as Jyr had in his cave, except not enough of them. More winged males appear in the corridors and all of them defer immediately to Jyr, not looking him in the eye. We pass by what look like barrack rooms, with Jyr length shelves sticking out from the walls up to five high. More of his kind are laying on these ledge like bunks, or sitting on them, conversing with their neighbor and preening their feathers.

Jyr keeps me moving, but I also spot a room full of steaming pools, like the one in his cave. More males are bathing, their wings splashing water about in great fountains, shouts of delight echoing, and which die away as they see us pass, their dark eyes full of interest and fear. I wonder how they get the water up so high in this building without any technology.

I loved my tech. Netflix kept me sane during my enforced isolation. But how any of it worked, that was a mystery to me.

Jyr doesn't stop; he doesn't slow down, so it's no real surprise when I catch my foot on something and go sprawling forward, landing on my chest and chin so hard I see stars. Before I can even groan, Jyr has me in his arms. I struggle against him.

"Let me go! If you hadn't been rushing me, I wouldn't have fallen." I snap at him.

"You should have been watching your step." He fires back, although his touch is gentle.

"I can't see, it's as dark as fuck in here." Jyr lifts me to my feet and a flash of pain spears through my ankle, causing me to cry out.

"*Eregri*?" He's gone from mad alpha to worried male in a nanosecond.

It pisses me off even more. I didn't ask for any of this, and now I've gone and sprained my ankle. In a building that's full of alien males, some of whom are obviously less than pleased I'm here.

Just what I need, to be the center of attention. Something I've been avoiding for a very long time. The insurance money from the accident meaning I didn't have to see anyone or do anything other than exist and wallow for the last three years.

"Do you need a healer?" He asks me, his voice still gentle and his dark eyes wide.

"You have a doctor? Here? Why, when you heal so fast on your own?" Jyr isn't even sporting a scar from those huge wounds he had yesterday. Jealous, Viv? Not much.

"Not all Gryn heal like me. I have been-" he hesitates, as if searching for the word, "-enhanced. There are a few of us seniors who can heal like me. The rest of my mercs, my warriors, and the youngsters, they require a healer if they damage themselves." From his tone of voice, I get the impression he doesn't suffer injury in the others well. "I could not return here when I was injured in any event. Any weakness will attract challenges." He says cryptically, his mouth buried in my ear as he tips me into his arms.

Great. As if I wasn't attracting enough unwanted attention, now all the aliens stop and gawp as we pass. Even Jyr's death stare isn't enough to chase them away.

We descend several crumbling ramps inside the building until we reach a quieter area. Jyr takes me through a set of double doors, and we're in a big room that has multiple shelves at waist height that are attached to the walls, sticking out like hospital beds. Bodies of Gryn males occupy a handful, their big wings draped over the edges of the shelves like limp blankets.

"Orvos?" Jyr calls out, swinging me around like a sack of potatoes.

"You can put me down." I push at his chest, and he reluctantly lowers me to the floor. I stand on my good foot, holding the other up. I steady myself on his arm but don't look at him.

"Well, well, if it isn't our glorious Prime." A strong and sarcastic voice carries through the room. A couple of the prone males groan and shift. "Come to see some of his handiwork."

A large Gryn walks towards us from a side room. His

hair is gray and his wings are almost black. The skin on his shoulders is bronze, the armoring polished like old leather.

"These mercs have only themselves to blame for their injuries, Orvos." Jyr says, confirming my suspicions. "I need you to see to my mate."

"You have found a mate?" Orvos cackles. "This I have to see."

My dislike of doctors deepens at his dark, interested gaze, reminding me of all that time in hospital. I thrust out my chin and hop out from behind Jyr. This time I'm not going to let myself be pushed around by so called medics, claiming to have my best interests at heart. What a crock that was.

"Not Gryn." Orvos raises his eyebrows.

"Your doctor is talented." I say over my shoulder to Jyr, trying to imbue the words with as much sarcasm as I can whilst I feel the sweat of fear slicking my body.

"Orvos is that, along with other things." Jyr gives me a hesitant half-smile. A flash of pain sweeps across his face and is gone.

He's suffered too, either at the hands of Orvos or others claiming to have medical knowledge. Odd for a creature that heals as fast as he does. My heart quickens and not in fear. His hand takes mine and I let him.

"Why don't you take a seat, mate of Prime." Orvos breaks into my thoughts, gesturing to a ledge.

Jyr reluctantly lets go of my hand, and I do as Orvos asks, shuffling my back against the wall and putting up my foot. My ankle has puffed up but there're no signs of bruising, so hopefully it's not as bad as it feels. Jyr drops to his knees next to me.

"My *eregri*, I will make this up to you, I promise." His

eyes are fixed on my swollen ankle. I suppose to him, this reaction to such a minor thing must be alarming.

"You certainly will." I reply. He deserves to be contrite, after all. It's not that I don't want to comfort him, it's just I want him to suffer a little too. "Later." I add with a hesitant smile.

"Don't you have somewhere to be, Prime." Orvos looms over me.

Jyr takes my hand again. "I have to meet with my seniors at szent, my Viv. I will return for my 'later'." The look he gives me heats the blood in my veins.

"You will take care of my mate as if she was me, Orvos." He booms at the doctor, his great wings opening, making him look even bigger than he already is. Orvos seems nonplussed by his display. Jyr growls, and it reverberates around the room.

"Of course, Prime." Orvos shrugs. Jyr looks at him for a long time, gives me a smile and is gone.

"Let me see what I can do about that ankle, and what I can do about getting you some footwear." Orvos rubs his hands together, and when he touches me, his touch is gentle and warm, like he actually cares. Like I'm not a piece of meat or a teaching instrument.

He retreats to the back room and returns with a bucket. He washes my feet then rubs in some evil smelling stuff on my ankle which works a treat. Tingling as the swelling subsides.

"Interesting."

"What is?" I baulk at the word. I heard it enough.

"That salve rarely has such a beneficial effect on Gryn anatomy. What species are you?"

"I'm human." I say, cautiously. The last thing I need is a doctor considering me to be a specimen for study.

"The mountain water baths normally cure most minor injuries for a Gryn warrior." He explains as he wraps my ankle in a bandage. "Except for Jyr and the seniors."

"Yeah, I've seen how he heals. What about these guys? Jyr calls them mercs." I point at the three bodies on the other ledges. "Why are they here?"

"Those two idiots took an experimental narcotic and are sleeping it off," Orvos says, dismissively at two mercs, who I can see have beatific smiles on their faces. "The other unfortunate came into contact with a joykill bot while on a weapons run," Orvos said. "My work is never done." He sighs.

Weapons run? My interest is piqued.

"What exactly is it you all do here?"

"We are the Legion of the Gryn, my dear. We provide the other tribes with what they need, our muscle, our weapons, and our drugs. We steal what we need and celebrate our spoils. Fear, fight, and forget. That's the Gryn motto."

JYR

W hen I return to the healing room, it is dark, save for the small light source in one corner, where Orvos sits, carefully inscribing something onto parchment.

The healer ignores my presence, knowing exactly which of my buttons to push every single time. It's not surprising, given that he knows everything about me. He was already in the lair when we arrived, desperate for sanctuary. He helped me and my seniors through the initial dark days, where we struggled with the changes Proto had made to us. His healing talents were welcome, then.

Even now, I can so easily recall writhing on one of these ledges, bathed in my sweat and vowing then that no Gryn would ever suffer as I was suffering.

Which is why I don't come to the healing room. It brings back too many bad memories. As for the mercs, if they don't know how to keep out of trouble, then they need to learn the lesson the hard way. There's no room for mistakes, not with what we do.

"Where is my mate?" I stride across to him, full of fire and fury.

Szent had not gone well. My poor temper causing me to take issue with every little thing my seniors raised. Kaloz had been difficult and it was only the worry that I don't know how far his rot has spread with the mercs that stopped me from ripping his wings off. The thought of his smirk makes me want to kill something. Or at least damage it severely.

"Shhh!" Orvos points to a ledge where a young merc lies, one wing draped over his chest, the other trailing on the floor. He's pale, his breathing ragged. "I put your mate in your quarters and made sure Fyn kept an eye on her." He puts down his pen, made from one of his own molted feathers. "She is an extraordinary creature. She is a worthy mate for a Prime of the Gryn."

"I don't need your approval, Orvos." I turn away to get to my mate, but my eyes fall on the injured merc. "What's wrong with this one?"

"The usual. On patrol, met a capture/kill bot. He got away but not before he took a bolt or two."

"Will he live?" I look back at Orvos. He shrugs.

"Since when did you care? Mercs, especially the younger ones, are expendable or at least that's how it appears, given how many you send down to me."

"No Gryn life is worthless." I bristle. "I'm mated, and I'll be bringing new life into this world. I know the value of life."

"You know the value of death. Mating and taking care of your own, you still need to learn, Jyr, and you have a lot to learn."

The fact that he is right does nothing to improve my mood.

"You stick to the healing, Orvos. I'll run the Legion as I see fit."

"As you wish, Prime." His voice drips with sarcasm.

Before I do something I will regret, I leave the healing room and make my way as swiftly as I can to my quarters. Fyn stands outside the door, watchful and alert. The thought of him with my Viv makes my blood boil over.

"Get out of my sight, merc." I snarl at him as I go to enter my quarters.

"Yes, *prime*." He retorts. I slam out one fist and pin him against the wall, the other hand gripping the shoulder of his wing.

"What was that?"

He stares into my eyes with his strange pale blue ones. Defiance rages there. "Nothing, Prime." He finally drops his gaze from mine.

The door to my quarters is partially open and I can scent my female. All I want is her. Mercs and legion politics can wait. I release him, pushing the warrior away. Without a second glance, I enter my quarters and close the doors behind me with a sigh of relief.

Viv is propped on my bed, her foot bandaged and raised on a smaller pile of furs. Next to her is a tray of thinly sliced maraha. Fyn's handiwork, no doubt.

I walk across to the bed and remove the tray with ill grace before lying down next to her, wanting to bury myself in her lush body. Her stiff posture reminds me I have some work to do before she will let me back between her legs, or anywhere.

"You're a criminal." She rushes out, her blue eyes brilliant but red rimmed. "You told me you were fighting against this Proto and you made it sound all so noble, but it's all a protection racket when you're not stealing from others and selling drugs on the side." Her little hands ball into fists and anger flows off her like steam from our mountain pools.

"My mate, how else did you think we survived?"

VIV

My bad angel really is bad. He's the leader of an alien crime syndicate, or whatever they call crime, on this planet. I'm not sure who I'm madder at, myself for conjuring up the concept that he was some sort of freedom fighter, or Jyr for not telling me exactly what he was before he brought me here.

For the time being, I've decided to be mad at him.

Now he lies beside me, looking like butter wouldn't melt in his handsome mouth. One that didn't even know what a kiss was until he met me.

"*Eregri*, we are fighters. It's all we know. The other tribes need us. If they want to pay us for our services, who am I to argue? It means I can rescue more Gryn from Proto and build the Legion. Yes, we used to take what we wanted, many turns ago, but now it's strictly in return for our services as protectors." He turns to me, flopping a wing over my body and grinning his sharp toothed grin in my face. "We are what we are."

I huff at him as his feathers tickle at me. Bad angel.

"What do you mean, 'rescue more Gryn'?"

Jyr rolls away from me, onto his back, his wings tucked underneath him. "After the great reckoning, Proto captured most of my kind. It experimented on us, some more than others. It was hardest on our females, most of them perished under the torture. Maybe all of them. I haven't seen a Gryn female in many cycles."

He puts his arms behind his head and stares up at the ceiling. Although I've not known him long, I'm recognizing when he's trying to hide his emotions. It's almost like I can feel them. Jyr wants to conceal his sadness at the destruction of his species, and he has no need. I am sad for him. I am sad for his species.

"Some of us managed to escape. Those that got free helped release others from Proto's camps. Now I make it part of our mission to find as many Gryn as I can and free them. The other species, the Mochi, the Kijg and the Zio, they were doing the same. The more Gryn I brought to the lair, the more supplies we needed." He gives me a sideways glance, as if trying to gauge my mood. "Yes, we stole from them. I'm not sorry about that, not when I had hungry mercs that needed feeding. As time passed, the other species wanted our protection from Proto and, as we needed their food and other things, we came to an agreement. You call it criminal. I call it surviving."

"And thriving." I sweep my hand at Jyr's suite.

I had a good look around while I waited for him, his scary blue eyed guard on the door. The separate bathroom has a large pool like the one in our cave and similar toilet facilities. There are two other rooms joined by a set of double doors, an inner room, where his bed is, and an outer, where there is a large table and a set of six chairs. The outer room was expressionless, but the inner bedroom was full of things. All neatly laid out, from sharp daggers and long swords to tiny pieces of crystal arranged in size and color on a small shelf.

My fearsome bad alien angel is very neat. And yes, I did have a look through his drawers, or a large chest where it turned out he kept his neatly folded clothes. Good thing he wasn't here, or he'd have seen me shove my head in and inhale the musk that smelled like him.

I genuinely don't know what's come over me. I've never felt this way about anyone, let alone a seven-foot predator that can eat me out like I'm dessert.

"We do what we do." Jyr says, unapologetically. "Don't humans?"

"I suppose. We're not averse to panic buying or looting when things go to shit." Or hunting down outsiders with pitchforks. "Sometimes I wonder if we've moved out of the Dark Ages at all."

"Dark Ages?" Jyr flips onto his side and his dark eyes study me. A slow smile spreads across his lips. "I want to know more about humans and your planet, Earth." He pronounces the word slowly, checking with me that it's correct.

"Is there much point? I'm not going to go back, am I? You're not going to help me find the other human women, so knowing anything about me isn't that big a deal, is it?"

He runs a finger down my arm as he looks up coquettishly. Reminding me of the Jyr who snuggled next to me while he recovered from his injuries. The kitten to his growly tiger. I know what he wants, and although there's a part of me that thinks this is all too quick, there's a greater part of me that has already dampened my pants with anticipation.

Who knew I would be this turned on by an alpha predator? Not me. Not Viv the recluse, the woman who decided she was too ugly to face the world.

"I can't get you back to Earth, my Viv. As for the other women, I can't risk my mercs in such an errand. It's too dangerous."

"And it's not for the humans? What does Proto want with them, anyway?" He has a point. That poor young warrior, shivering and struggling to breathe in Orvos's surgery, plays on my mind.

"I like to think we have saved at least one human." Jyr tucks his finger under the bottom of my shirt and runs it around the edge. "The one I've been thinking about all through szent." He extends his claw, and it slices through the material surgically as he draws it up over my breasts until the shirt is split from waist to top.

His huge hand pushes aside the ruined clothing and palms my breast.

"I'm supposed to be angry at you." My back arches as I lift into his touch, the tips of his claws toying with a raised nipple. "You lied to me."

"I would never lie to my *eregri*." Jyr leans forward and swipes his tongue over my breast. "I will always tell her the truth. You are my family, my savior. I want you. I want all of you." He latches on to me, suckling wildly as I clutch at him.

Are we doing this? With a further slicing sound, my trousers disappear, the air cool on my naked form. My anger dissipates with my clothing. We're definitely doing this. He stares down at my naked form, his eyes dark with lust as he drinks me in.

My predator is hungry. For me. My damaged flesh doesn't bother him in the slightest. As he moves alongside me, I can feel his enormous erection pressed against my thigh. He tentatively touches my lips with his, exploring this new experience. I want him too. He sparks something deep within me. His total acceptance of who I am, what I am. That unconditionality, it's gotten under my skin. I respond to his kiss, teaching him what a tongue can do as my hand snakes down to palm him through the leather like trousers he wears and which leave little to the imagination, especially now.

Good god, he's big. And a second bulge reminds me why. This alien has two cocks. A frisson of delight and fear sparks over my body. I've no idea how this is going to work, but I want to find out.

Jyr's desire washes over me, like his leathery musky scent that mixes with the spice from his wings. Wings that flare as he pushes himself into my hand with a groan. In no time, he has dispensed with his trousers, and I'm in his arms as he lavishes attention on my breasts again, hands that are strong and supple touch my scarred skin with infinite care. He teases each nipple into a tight peak and makes me pant with want.

"I need to be inside you, my *eregri*." He murmurs in my ear as he uses his tongue to lap down my neck, even while he inhales my scent. "But only if you want me."

"I want you, Jyr." I hear myself saying in a voice I hardly recognize, it's so thick with lust.

"Good." He descends swiftly and buries himself between my legs.

His tongue only needs to touch my clit, and I'm exploding into his mouth. He's set me on fire, as if I've been waiting all day for this moment. I hold his hair and squirm as he wrings another orgasm from me, hands holding my thighs apart as he guzzles at my pussy. He raises his head and wipes at his mouth with the back of his hand, a wide grin splitting his face, he grasps at my hips and pulls me towards him, up his muscular thighs until the tip of his thick cock nudges my folds and I lie helpless before him.

"Jyr-" I'm breathless. "You've got two cocks."

He grins down at me, badness written all over his face. "You want my cocks?"

"Human men don't have two cocks. Just the one. And certainly not the size of yours."

Jyr pushes against me, his main cock breaching my entrance.

"Relax, my *eregri*. Gryn are made for pleasure. Let me pleasure you."

And I feel his second cock, slippery with pre-cum pushing at my anus.

"Are you ready, my mate?"

"Yes. Please." I pant, breathless. He impales me easily, and the fullness removes my breath for a second time.

JYR

"Are you ready, my mate?"

"Yes!" She says with a breathy moan. "Please!"

I already know her channel is tight and, as I breach it, it's clear she is much tighter than I'd thought. Inch by inch, I slide in my primary cock panting with the effort of not taking her in one thrust. I have to let her get used to my size. My secondary cock weeps copious amounts of seed, lubricating itself and her perfect little pucker, before gliding inside her bottom hole. Her eyes are rounded with surprise and desire as I penetrate her with infinite care.

"Jyr!" She breathes. "So full!" It's all she can say as I slowly, slowly seat my cocks inside her, both holes hot and ready for me.

She ripples over my cocks, and I withdraw with a groan, easing her body into acceptance of my lengths. She moans as I plunge back inside her. I pull her to me and set up a demanding rhythm. She rocks against me, lifting her hips and wrapping her legs around my waist, allowing me to sink even deeper inside her. I feel my shafts rubbing close to each other through the thin skin separating her channels. She is ripe and perfect. I want this moment to last forever; me taking her thoroughly, our bodies as one.

Viv throws herself back, her entire body going rigid. She cries out my name and her pussy convulses, squeezing me so hard I cannot stop my seed rising. My wings open wide as I clutch her to me and release with a groan that shakes the bed, filling her in both holes over and over until I must be empty and the precious liquid leaks out, covering the furs beneath us. Her orgasm rolls, her tight pussy continuing to clamp over me long after I am spent.

"Jyr, that was incredible." She whispers, her head buried against my neck. "I've never - I don't-" My mouthy female is lost for words. "I've never had a cock in my -" She sighs. "I think I might have missed out."

I lap at her forehead as she cuddles into me, sleepy, her scent mingling with that of our sex.

"Hang on!" She suddenly jerks back from me, "I don't want to get pregnant." She clamps a hand over her mouth. "If that's even possible, but we didn't use anything and I'm not on any birth control." Water hovers in her eyes at her incomprehensible statement.

"A Gryn can only impregnate a female if both cocks release in her main channel at the same time." I explain. "I will never make you do anything you don't want, my *eregri*. Until you decide you want my young, I will enjoy taking you in both of your tight, glorious holes."

Viv settles back in my arms, placated. "Well, there's no way you're getting both of those monsters in there, honey." A satisfied smile crosses her lips.

"Sounds like a challenge." I curl around my mate, tiredness flowing through me. I want nothing more than to take her again, but I can hardly keep my eyes open.

Viv's breathing deepens, and I let sleep overwhelm me. She's safe in my arms, and I will ensure she's mated again before morning.

LIGHT STREAMS in through the shutters covering the outside entrance to my quarters. Viv is warm in my arms, and my cocks are already hard for her. She stretches out luxuriously, nestling her bottom against my crotch.

"Female." I moan, thrusting myself against her soft, fleshy behind.

"Woah there, you're going to have to give me more time to recover. You're a big guy, and it's been a long time for me." Viv laughs sleepily. The sound is simply one of the best things I've heard.

"Then we should cleanse you." I leap to my feet with her squealing in my arms as I carry her through to my private pool.

"Wait, Jyr-"

I pay her no heed and wade in until we are both submerged. She wriggles against me, one arm wrapped around my neck. I release her, and she floats comfortably in the water, her breasts bobbing temptingly.

"I could get used to having a hot tub on hand." She grins up at me. "I always wanted one when I was back on Earth."

"Why did you not have one?"

Her eyes drop from mine, and she looks across the pool, out to the hinterland that surrounds our lair.

"I probably could have, I just - it wasn't high on my priority list." She stutters. Pain squeezes at my chest, strong enough that I think it's my own, until I realize it's the thoughtbond.

"Are you hurting?" I ask her, swirling in the water to bring her close to me.

"No. My ankle is as good as new thanks to your doctor. Why?" Her eyes are on me again. I could drown in them.

"I felt your pain."

She laughs, throwing her head back, her slippery body flicks out of my grip. "Of course you do, angel." Her lip curls with disdain. "We had sex, Jyr, that's all. You don't get access to my innermost thoughts after sex." Her blue eyes flash defiantly. My little human is still not quite prepared to let me in.

And I love a challenge.

"We are bonded, my *eregri*. I feel what you feel, and you can do the same. In time, we will share more than simple emotions."

"Yeah, right." She snorts, heaving her glorious body onto the side of the pool, water running in rivers over her, beading on her pert nipples. "I know what you want. Now what does a girl do to get her teeth cleaned around here?"

VIV

No tech means no toothbrushes. I might have made a smart remark about the Dark Ages, but these aliens are living in a form of dystopia. They can see the tech, but they can't get to it.

To clean my teeth, Jyr opens a cupboard in the wall of the pool room, which I hadn't seen before. Neatly arranged are pots of varying size. He brings out a white one that looks like it once had some sort of alien writing on it. Inside is a gray powder. He licks his finger, looking very naughty, until he dips it in the powder and scrubs at his sharp canines as a demonstration.

Those teeth were in a very sensitive place last night and given the squirming I did, I'm stunned he didn't do any damage.

Not that his teeth were what I should have worried about. Two cocks. Both of which were impressive. Porn star impressive. My lady parts needed a good dunk in that pool to recover. I've never been into anal either, but with Jyr, it seemed natural. Providing he's right about the whole pregnancy thing, I expect I could get used to it.

I certainly hope he's right. The last thing I want is to get knocked up with some alien baby. Not while there's any chance of escape from this planet, and not while the other women are still out there. I give Jyr a sideway look, then follow his example with the gray powder. It's gritty but has a slightly minty taste that is familiar enough not to make me gag. We stand side by side, working our fingers around our mouths like an old married couple.

I wonder what our children would look like.

"Huhm?" Jyr says, his mouth full of clawed finger.

Shit! Did I say that out loud? I take my finger out of my mouth. "Nothing, just wondering what you've got in store for me today?"

Jyr scoops up a massive handful of pool water and rinses it around his mouth, spitting it out into a shallow depression carved into the wall with a hole in the center. He follows it with another handful of water, and I copy him.

"You are to meet my seniors, I want to show you my lair and then we have a celebration to plan." Jyr wipes his mouth with the back of his hand and the action causes heat to pool exactly where it shouldn't be pooling. He scents the air. "Or we could spend the day mating?" He adds, hopefully.

"Find me some clothing. You ruined all mine last night." I sweep past him into the bedroom and hide under the furs before my treacherous lady bits can give him any more ideas.

Until I have a plan, I have to try to keep my feelings for Jyr under control. That shouldn't be hard for a woman who'd hid herself away from everyone for years. He strides past me, all feathers and acres of deliciously muscled flesh. My core squeezes again.

Might be a tad more difficult than simply pretending you don't exist.

"Hang on, celebration?" My brain moves away from below my belt as I register what he said.

Jyr opens the chest in his bedroom and frowns at it. I might not have been as neat about putting things back as he obviously is. I give him my most innocent look.

"I want my Legion to celebrate my mating."

"You what?" I gape at him. "You celebrate having sex? Is it that rare an occurrence?" I let rip with a snort of laughter. It's not very fair, but I'm fed up with always being on the back foot.

"My legion demands that a mating takes place publicly, to confirm the union." Jyr starts to sort through the clothing in his chest.

My heart stutters. "You're kidding me!" I gasp out. "We have to have sex in front of all of—" I wave my hand towards the main door. "Them?"

"Not all, just my seniors. They will brief the mercs on the details of our mating. Intensity, positioning and so on." Jyr seems suspiciously interested in what is at the bottom of his chest. One wing is concealing his face from me. I can't think of a single thing to say, and my jaw works frantically.

A deep guffaw erupts from behind the mass of feathers.

"You complete bastard!" I pull a fur out and hurl it at him, he bats it away with his powerful wing, his face wreathed in mirth. "You *are* joking, right?"

In half a second, one downstroke of his massive wings means he's on the bed, caging me in his arms.

"Would I do that to you?" He traces a knuckle down the side of my face.

"I don't know, Jyr. I don't know you." His dark eyes

sparkle with life, an image of young Gryn playing games in the evening light fills my mind.

"I think you do, my *eregri*. Our mating is our business and ours alone." His lips are tantalizingly close to mine. I arch my neck to reach him.

BANG!

A knock that would wake the dead has Jyr on his feet as quick as he was on the bed. His wings flared. He grabs a pair of trousers and pulls them on, clipping together an ornate buckle at the waist. The knock comes again, and I dig myself deeper under the furs. Jyr strides over to the doors, throwing them open.

"What the vrex do you want, Kyt?" He bellows.

Another impossibly handsome face peeks through the doors, dark questioning eyes, cheekbones you could cut yourself on and a full mouth quirked into a half-smile. This Gryn is shorter than Jyr and nowhere near as bulky.

"You need a party planner, Prime, and you know how I like a good party." Kyt shoots me a smile.

"Get out of my chamber and leave my mate alone." Jyr growls, the words almost inaudible, but the threat hangs heavy in the air. Everything about him looks dangerous.

Kyt holds up his hands and backs away as Jyr slams the doors closed. "Wait there. I'll give my orders shortly." He bellows through the wood.

Crossing back to me, he puts his hand in his chest and hands me a small pile of clothing.

"These should fit you for the time being. I see Orvos found you some shoes," he indicates the pair of soft boots that the doctor conjured from somewhere. "We will go to a trading post soon to get you more suitable clothing."

I shake out the shirt and trousers he has given me. They are much smaller than his own clothing. Part of me wants to ask why he has human sized garments in his chest, but the wall of silence I feel indicates that this is something that can wait until later.

"When you're dressed, join me. If Kyt survives the next few minutes, we will discuss the celebrations."

JYR

My mate is complex. One minute she's prepared to take every inch of me, the next she's complaining she doesn't know me.

She knows me more than any Gryn. She has my everything; she is my everything. I let out a growl of frustration as I stomp through to Kyt, who sits with his feet propped up on the table, picking at his claws. Why does mating have to be so hard?

"Your mate is not Gryn?" Kyt asks me, it's obvious his question is genuine.

"Were you not at the landing yesterday?"

"I was otherwise engaged." Kyt grins. Which means he was presumably in his cave, trying to find a workaround against Proto.

"No, she's not Gryn. She's a human that Proto has stolen from her world and brought here." I look over my shoulder and lower my voice. "I'd like to find out why. Have you had any luck?"

His smile fades. "It's like I'm almost there, there's just something not quite right. If I can break the algo that Proto has stored in every piece of tech, we can bypass it and make use of the weapons at the bare minimum."

"You'll get there, Kyt. I have faith in you. If Nisis can bring me my *eregri*, then we must be due a break with Proto." I clap him on his wing and his smile returns.

"This is going to be a mega celebration." He says, enthusiastically. "All the mercs are talking about your mate." He cranes his neck to look at the closed doors.

"She will be joining us shortly."

Kyt hums and taps his teeth with his forefinger. I can feel his mind working. The door to my chamber opens and my beautiful Viv appears. Her scent intoxicating. She has got the clothing I gave her to fit her luscious curves well. Maybe too well, given the way Kyt looks at her. I immediately throw an arm around her shoulder and draw her into me. She makes a frustrated sound in the back of her throat.

"Viv, this is my quartermaster, Kyt." I introduce the grinning warrior.

He steps back and sweeps a bow like I've never seen. "My lady Prime." He lifts his head to check our approval. Viv looks horrified.

"It's Viv. Call me Viv." She stammers.

"Get up, you clown." I order. "We have a celebration to plan. What's the status on the var beer stocks?"

For all his irritating habits, Kyt can plan a party, and his parties are legendary. Viv remains quiet during our discussions, and I feel her reticence through the thoughtbond. She believes she isn't worthy of any celebration.

"Are we done?" Kyt asks, a small scroll of parchment in front of him covered in his scratchy writing.

"We're done for the time being. I will summon the seniors shortly to meet my mate."

Kyt rises and is half out the door when he turns back. "Does that include your Command?"

"Yes, of course it includes Kaloz. Why?" I'm hungry and I know my mate will be. Our next stop is the food hall.

"He went out early with a division of his mercs. From the way they were loaded up, I don't think he'll be back anytime soon."

Music to my ears.

"I'll speak to him when he returns." I say, trying not to show that, while I'm pleased not to have to deal with Kaloz in front of my mate and my seniors, I'm irritated he is going on supply runs without discussing it with me first.

"Bye, Viv." Kyt takes the opportunity to wave at Viv as he leaves.

"See you later, Kyt." She smiles at the warrior as I suppress a growl. Kyt looks far too smug at my mate's attention.

"What?" She looks up at me. "You're going to have to get over this alpha jealously thing. You brought me to a building stuffed full of males." She taps her foot at me. "How many of you are there, anyway?"

"I have a hundred warriors to serve my bidding and around fifty juniors." I say, proudly.

"Juniors?" Her brow furrows. "I thought you said you didn't have any females." She narrows her gaze.

"We don't. About half a turn ago, we found a camp full of young Gryn, between thirteen and fifteen turns old. Most of them remember their mothers but said they had not seen a female for a long time. They were raised by older Gryn males who had recently been removed from the camp."

The shard of distress that ached through me when I found these youngsters still burns.

"They were frightened." Viv says, slowly. "You saved

them." Her frown returns, but it is at the memories she is accessing, and these are not her own.

"I save any Gryn I can. They are not old enough to be warriors, so they serve in other ways. They have a home and a family now." I say proudly.

Viv doesn't reply, looking more thoughtful before her expression clears.

"What about breakfast? I'm starving."

I take her hand and lead her, carefully this time, through the lair, down to the food hall. A few merc stragglers are still finishing their morning meal. Most scramble to their feet, wolfing down the remains hastily as I enter, ushering her in front of me. I grasp the wing of one mercs as he attempts to get away.

"What's your assignment today?" I say, my voice gruff as I tuck Viv into my side. The merc is brought up short, and I increase my grip on his feathers.

"I'm on patrol for the Mochi." He gulps, trying not to look me in the eye.

"Find out when and where their next trading post is taking place. Find me after you finish and let me know."

"Sure, Prime. Anything you say." He says, raising his face to look at me and gives a curious glance at Viv, a hint of a smile curling his lips.

"Go!" I fire out, shoving him away from us.

"Yes, Prime." He hurries away, shooting glances over his shoulder, and nearly barreling into another merc, who gives him a playful shove.

I can't help but smile a little, even as my jealousy simmers down. I remember being a young merc once, too. It was fun. No responsibilities, all fun and fighting. We made our own fun in the camps. It was only when first the females started to disappear, then the older males followed, that life became more of the fight and less of the fun. That's why finding the camp of youngsters was at once joyful and sad. I want them to have some fun and joy in their young lives, which is why they only have light duties and plenty of time to themselves.

"Let's see if the mercs left us anything." I steer Viv towards an empty table near the large fireplace. She is looking around her in wonder at the food hall.

"This place is amazing, like something out of a movie." She says, cryptically. She sees my quizzical look. "Humans used to live a bit like this, hundreds of years ago. They lived in big buildings called castles with great halls where everyone used to eat."

I nod, pleased she's sharing something about her species, even if it's out of date.

"Let me get you something." I head over to the spit. A maraha is roasting, although, as I expected, there isn't much left of it. I carve off a couple of reasonable cuts from its flank and pile up a couple of plates with meat, piir sticks, and some fresh alag. The vegetable being the only thing that is plentiful, given that most of the mercs avoid eating their rations of greens, despite my orders.

"Here." I put the plate in front of her.

"Woah! Do you think there's enough here?" She chuckles. "Don't worry," a genuine smile in my direction calms my stomach, "I'm sure you'll eat what I leave, a big guy like you needs all the calories he can get."

"I'll need more than ever with you in my furs." I slide alongside her and wrap and arm around her waist, pulling her glorious body into mine and burying my head in her hair.

"Behave!" She admonishes me with good humor and eats her meat.

For a female who claimed she didn't like to eat in the morning, she manages to consume a decent amount. As predicted, I happily polish off the rest.

"Are you going to show me around?" She asks, swiveling towards me on the bench.

"So you want to check out the criminal's lair, do you, female?"

"May as well see what I've got myself into." Viv looks around the hall again, a hesitant smile playing over her lips.

A couple of the young mercs on food duty are tidying away the remains of breakfast. Two more walk in with a maraha carcass ready for roasting and set it on one of the five spits in the hall. By mid-afternoon, there will be a dozen cooked maraha, ready for the returning patrols.

"And maybe we can discuss how to free the other human women." She adds, quietly. "After all, stealing them from Proto won't be adding much to your criminal enterprises."

VIV

O kay, I got a dig in about what Jyr does. I watch as
several emotions flit over Jyr's handsome
features. Annoyance being the main one,
followed by something that is akin to confusion. It's the
confusion that gets me. He really doesn't know what to do
with me. And that's rather...sweet?

Orvos told me that the Gryn, such as they are, have not
seen a female for a very long time. Some of them, the more
senior ones, interact with females of other organic species
who attempt to make this destroyed planet their home.
From how Orvos described them to me, these other species
are cat people, lizard people and, just what I was hoping to
avoid, insect people. I felt a little queasy at the thought of Jyr
getting together with any female as apparently, they have
not lost their females in the same quantities as the Gryn did.

Because of this, Jyr has no females in his lair, and Gryn
females are, in essence, an unknown quantity. He might like
to pretend that he's all big, brutal and in control, but deep
down, he hasn't a clue how to deal with a female of any
species, even his own.

I could use that.

I could use it to get to the other women, to get off this planet. Maybe convince the machines that brought me here we should be returned. The thing is my stomach squirms unpleasantly at the prospect of interacting with anything that created the evil that was the robot I've seen. You can't reason with machines. Anyone who's encountered the 'unexpected item in the bagging area' self-checkout knows this.

I don't want to use him or the Gryn any more than I want to be stuck here. I've gotten used to not having to think, to hiding away, not considering what I was to do with my life because my life was over, this situation is testing me far beyond anything I've dealt with before.

All I can do at the moment is to be swept along with it until I get a grip and work out a plan. Until I can figure out exactly what my feelings are for this big predator who ate me out like I was the last meal he would ever have, and made love to me like I was his everything. He doesn't do anything by halves, and a primitive part of me quite likes that. To be taken, to be wanted, and to be needed. It's not a terrible existence.

"That's not going to happen, my *eregri*." Jyr says, finally. "I told you-"

"I know what you said. Doesn't make me want it any less."

He cocks his head on one side, his dark eyes contemplating me. My trousers dampen a little as I remember his gaze on me last night.

"I'll speak to my seniors at szent about your request." He concedes. "Can I show you the lair?" He adds, with a slight hint of pleading.

"Go on then." I give him a smile. His face lights up. He's

pleased me and his entire posture changes. His wings are held high and feathers bristle with life. He leads as we make our way down the building, with Jyr explaining enthusiastically what each layer is.

The vast lair is remarkably well organized for a bunch of males. There are huge areas for supplies, in and out. Crates piled high with all sorts of things I don't recognize. One massive room contains a fenced off area with a dozen six legged blue creatures. They have three eyes in the center of their big, long heads. Basically, they are alien cows and must end up as the carcass I saw in the food hall. I'm not entirely sure whether to be pleased the Gryn don't actively hunt them or not. I'm not a vegetarian by any means, but I'm used to the disconnect between what's on my plate and where it comes from.

There are levels that contain areas for training, for food preparation, and for the cultivation of the bioluminescent plants that light the lair.

Another level contains a pool where a couple of Gryn stand stirring the water with several large paddles. As I watch, they fish out items of clothing and furs. Slopping them onto the side where a couple of smaller Gryn squeeze out the water. These are presumably the juniors that Jyr mentioned, given that they are slender compared to the more heavily muscled warriors. They scamper away with arms full of fabric.

"It's a laundry!" I exclaim to Jyr.

"Of course." He looks puzzled. "Do humans not clean their clothing?"

"We do. It's just that human males are not generally as keen to have their clothes cleaned."

"All Gryn in my lair are expected to keep themselves and their clothing in good condition. We have finite resources."

Jyr says, eyeing his mercs. "If things get damaged, it's not easy to replace them."

"So, you have a laundry, but no one to do any mending?"

"Mending?" Jyr queries.

"Sewing, fixing clothing, you know?" I mime sewing and his forehead creases. "Maybe I should show you how sometime?"

Jyr grins at me. "You are the most remarkable female. Far more worthy than this Prime deserves." He sweeps me up in his arms, planting a kiss on my lips.

"It's just mending. No need to get carried away." I grumble, pushing at him, acutely aware of the staring mercs in the laundry.

With some reluctance, he puts me down and continues with his tour. I recognize the floor with the hot spring pools from yesterday. This time they are empty of Gryn.

"How do you get the water up here?" I ask him.

"Up?"

"Yeah, to this level."

"The water comes straight from the source."

Now I wish I was paying attention when we came into land yesterday, rather than praying he didn't drop me.

"We're in a skyscraper, right?"

Jyr laughs. "You have some funny expressions, little human. Why don't I show the lair properly?"

Before I can say anything, he's scooped me up in his arms and with several long bounds, we reach an opening in the side of the building. I don't even have time to scream as he jumps clear, his wings unfurling as we plummet.

"*Eregri*, open your eyes, for me." I hear his voice, deep like velvet, in my ear.

He hasn't dropped me yet.

I manage to unstick one eyelid. Jyr has tucked me under

one arm and I'm facing the ground. It's a very, very long way away. It's also a blasted wasteland. Ruined buildings, like the one I tried to hide in when I'd first arrived, are scattered like broken toys beneath me. I open the other eye. Dark clouds hang heavy in the sky, making the scene that unfolds look even more dystopian. Like the images I've seen of German cities after the Second World War, or Hiroshima. There's nothing living down there, not a fleck of green, not like the bomb sites that bloomed after the wars.

This place is dead. It's amazing anything survives here, even the Gryn.

"Your home, my mate." Jyr turns tightly and my stomach lurches at the G-force.

As we wheel in the sky, the wind rushing past my face, my heart leaps into my throat. Not in fear this time, but in exhilaration. I'm close to death, yet very much alive. In the warm, muscular arms of a creature that can defy gravity as he holds me to him.

A monolith rises ahead of us. The entire building is set into a huge cliff wall. It looks like it was once part of a huge complex, but it's the only one left. The rest are gouged out, only a hint of what they once were remains. The entire structure is set into the rock, ledges protruding to allow for landing. Smoke, presumably from the fires I saw in the food hall, vents from far below us. Further down still is an enormous waterfall, steaming as it churns.

The entire place must have been beautiful once. Now it is a fortress.

I feel Jyr pumping his wings as we fly directly at the cliff face and shoot upwards at an incredible rate until we burst free of the wall and are above the rock, still climbing, higher and higher. I clutch at his arm, gripping with all my strength, but I don't close my eyes, not this time. Because I want to see what he sees. I want to feel alive, just like he does.

This is all for you.

The words echo in my mind. They are not mine. I know my own thoughts. This is Jyr. He's in my head.

How did the damn alien get in my head?

JYR

A sharp pain pierces my temple and I spiral quickly down to a landing ledge, setting Viv on her feet as gently as I can.

"What the fuck, Jyr? Why are you in my head?" She shouts at me, taking several steps away from me. Her anger is blistering. I massage my forehead, the pain from her diminishing, but not dissipating.

"Thoughtbond."

She puts her hands on her hips and continues to stare at me, this time tapping her foot. She looks deadly, as if she might spring at me. Small but fierce.

"And that is what, exactly? Because if you can't give me a good reason for it, you can get the fuck out!" She says through gritted teeth.

It is the way true Gryn communicate with their mates.

She opens her mouth, closes it again and takes a further step back.

"What did you just say?" She whispers, her anger turning to fear.

"You heard that?" We've only recently mated, the thoughtbond shouldn't be this strong, not yet.

"I felt it." She swallows, still retreating from me. "I don't like it, Jyr. Don't do it." Her confusion radiates through me. "I've enough problems with my own thoughts in my own head. I don't need yours as well."

"I'm sorry, Viv. Thoughtbond is part of the mate bond, it is, or it was, welcomed by mated pairs."

"I don't know what this is," she points between us, "not yet. I'm human and you're an alien. I'm—" She hesitates. "I can't be anyone's mate."

The sudden sadness grips at my heart. She believes she is unworthy. She thinks her injuries make her ugly. No, she doesn't just think it. She believes it.

I close the gap between us both, taking her by the shoulders, needing to have her close to me. I have to make her understand what mating means, what it is to the Gryn.

"The mate bond is true, my *eregri*. It only forms where it is right, never where it is wrong. My parents were a mated pair. Their bond survived until the very end. If Nisis has chosen us to be paired, then it is to be." I brush back a lock of her long golden hair. "I don't believe Nisis could have chosen any better than you, beautiful mate."

She stares up at me, not moving, not trying to get away anymore.

"I want to believe you, Jyr. I really do. It's been a long time since I was close to anyone. Perhaps I just need time." She looks away, shaking her head. Her emotions are unreadable.

"Then let me show you my lair. We have time in abundance." I grin at her.

It's not strictly true, I need our thoughtbond to be strong by the time of the celebration, to show our unity to the rest of the Gryn. To prove to them we can mate and produce young. To show my strength in taking a fertile female.

"Take me to the heart of your criminal enterprise, great leader." She lifts herself on tiptoe and presses one of her kisses to my cheek, her hand lingering on my skin. She averts her gaze from mine, as if embarrassed by her show of affection.

It makes me long for a time when she will show all the Gryn our pairing. I feel my wings lift and feathers puff at her touch. My cocks swell in anticipation of what we can do once I have her all to myself. This might just be the swiftest tour in history. I'm more than ready to take her back to my quarters and bury myself in her soft curves and sweet pussy. Viv takes in the rest of the tour with a quiet interest, not speaking much other than to ask the occasional question as I show her Myk's forge, the labs, and finally the merc's barracks.

"Can we go back to Orvos?" She asks as we walk back up the ramp from the empty barracks.

"Are you unwell?" I'm seized by a fear that I've never felt before.

"No, it's just that there was a young merc." She hesitates over the unfamiliar word. "When I was there. Orvos said he was very poorly, and I'd like to see how he is doing." She twists her hands together.

I feel jealously roaring through my body. My mate should care for no one but me.

"No one came to see me." Her voice is very small. "Not after the first few weeks. I know what it's like to be all alone when you're sick."

She asked me not to do it, but I can't help feel out the thoughtbond. Her sadness for herself is mingled with her concern for the weak, young merc. A kindness that she is afraid of. I straighten. It is a kindness that I should be feeling.

"I saw him, too. As Prime I am responsible for the welfare of all Gryn. We will go and check on him together." I'm trying to impress her. I know I am, but the smile that crosses her face is worth it.

Even though the feeling in my stomach tells me I've been neglecting far more about my warriors than I am letting on. Maybe that's why Kaloz is gaining some ground against me.

We reach Orvos's surgery, and the medic is sitting behind his desk. One ledge remains occupied, and Viv heads towards it.

"Never had this many visitations from you, Prime. Your mate must be having an effect." He says without looking up.

"She wanted to check on that merc from yesterday. How's he doing?" I look across at Viv. She's perched on the edge of the ledge.

"He'll probably pull through. Very weak at the moment. His healing will take time, if you let him."

"What do you mean, 'if I let him'?" I query.

"Your standing order, all those who can fly must work." Orvos looks up at me from his parchment, his dark eyes flash with anger.

"There's no such standing order, Orvos!" I reel back. "I need my warriors to be healthy and able to work, not half-dead. Why do you think I spend so much of my time arguing with the Mochi and Kijg over supplies? We need meat, good meat, or no one works and the lair fails."

My hands have balled into fists and anger rises from the pit of my stomach. Why would any Gryn think that I could treat them badly? I provide a home, a refuge, food, and the fight for all my warriors. We party hard whenever we can.

The minute we get word about one of Proto's camps, I'm there, freeing my kind. My every waking moment is about the Gryn and their survival. I wouldn't order anything that would risk their health.

Orvos hums his disapproval. "Someone gave that order, Prime. I've been patching them up and sending them out as quickly as I can. Why didn't you notice?"

His disapproval resonates down the thoughtbond. Orvos isn't one for the senior bond, preferring to keep himself to himself, however it seems that this occasion demands it.

"Consider it countermanded. The merc can take as long as he needs to recover. Ensure he has the best food and the best care. I will send down some of my furs for him." I stride across to where Viv sits next to the youngling without a backwards glance at Orvos.

He knows I wouldn't do something so cruel and I'm livid he didn't come to me with his concerns.

VIV

The young Gryn warrior looks a little better than yesterday. His eyes are open, and he stares at me as I sit next to him.

"Hey." I smile, "good to see you looking a bit better."

He eyes me with something akin to awe.

"You're a female." His voice is weak and scratchy.

"Last time I looked," I laugh. "How are you feeling?"

He struggles against his thin blanket, wings flopping uselessly, and he winces in pain.

"It's okay, you don't need to move. Just stay still." He gives up and lies back down with a low groan. "What's your name?"

"Pytr," he peers around me and his eyes widen as he sees Jyr talking to Orvos. "Is that Prime?" He whispers.

"That's Jyr. We came to see you."

"Prime came to see me?" He starts his scuffling again in earnest, and gets rapidly weaker.

"Hey," I put my hand on his arm. "It's fine. We both saw you here yesterday and wanted to check on you."

"I'm getting better, I am. I'll be back on patrol tomorrow." He scrambles out as the blanket falls away, and I see the blood-soaked bandage beneath. I put my hand on his chest, trying to stop him from moving.

"You will remain here until you are fully recovered, under Orvos care, merc. That's an order." Jyr booms from behind me.

Pytr stops moving immediately, transfixed by Jyr.

"You're not to go anywhere until you're properly better. I'll come and check on you to make sure." I add, attempting to sound as masterful as Jyr.

It doesn't have quite the same effect. Pytr's eyes dart to me and tears form. "You will?" The words come out as a soft sob.

"I will." I grab the fallen blanket and cover him over as he shivers. "Rest now, sweetheart. Orvos will look after you, Jyr will look after you." He gives me a weak smile.

Orvos appears next to us and holds a small sponge under Pytr's nose. Within seconds, the young Gryn's eyelids droop and he goes limp.

"I need to change his dressings. Tranqued warriors are easier to deal with." He shrugs. "They squirm too much otherwise." He adds by way of explanation.

I look at the relaxed and sleeping youngster. "Why did he think he had to be back on patrol? He's far too sick."

"There seems to have been some misunderstanding." Jyr interjects. "Something I need to take up with my seniors." He puts a hand on my shoulder. "Speaking of which, it's about time they met my mate properly."

It's my turn to shiver. Once I would have relished meeting new people, or in this case, aliens. My self-imposed exile from humanity has dulled my abilities more than I'd care to admit.

"I promised Pytr I'd come back and visit him, is that okay?" I ask as he takes hold of my elbow.

Jyr looks at the sleeping merc and I see his eyes soften a little. "Yes, my *eregri*. I am having more furs sent down to make him comfortable."

For an instant, I see how much he cares. He doesn't want anyone to know because he doesn't want to get hurt. But the responsibilities of running this operation weigh on him. One merc is nothing in the grand scheme of things and at the same time, Pytr is everything.

I follow Jyr through the fortress, up multiple levels, each one is reached by a ramp up that runs around a central shaft. As we continue to climb, warriors, presumably the lower level mercs, that seem to make up the foot-soldiers of the Gryn, fly past us, zooming up the shaft, whooping with glee as they pass, their shouts ceasing when they spot their Prime.

I'm toiling up the ramp behind Jyr when a body lands with a thump and a flurry of wings in front of us. I recognize the blue-eyed warrior who had accompanied me back to Jyr's quarters yesterday and who had eyed me suspiciously the entire time.

"Fyn?" Jyr opens his wings protectively.

"I understand that you wanted to know about the next Mochi trading post, Prime." He says, planting his feet firmly apart. He folds up his wings close to his body. He's trying not to appear as a threat.

"I did." Jyr hasn't changed his posture. Even as I try to peer out from behind his wings, he subtly shifts to block me.

"There is one happening tomorrow at the edge of our territory, at the old bot factory. There should be a good range of traders, depending what you want."

"Good." Jyr steps forward, but Fyn still blocks our way.

"There were multiple joykill patrols today, Prime. Proto seems interested in something we have." He leans to try to see me.

"Proto is my problem. But if you're so interested in helping protect my mate, you can join my security detail tomorrow."

Fyn takes a step back, gaping at Jyr for a brief instant before he composes himself. Jyr grabs hold of my hand and sweeps past him. I hurry to keep up with his pace, and once we reach the top of the ramp; he turns left into a dimly lit corridor. I find myself pushed up against the wall, with a big, muscular alien male pressing against me. He smells divine, leather, spice and his own peculiar musk that sends my core into overdrive.

"We have to get to szent, but I need you." Jyr breathes, closing his liquid dark eyes and inhaling. "You are mine." He growls.

What is it with this male? How the hell has he managed to get under my skin? All these years of pretending I didn't need anyone, pretending I was done with intimacy, and within moments of meeting, he has me in his bed and underneath him, begging for more.

I press a kiss to his lips. The unfamiliar touch stills him. I wrap my arms around his muscular form, my fingers entwining with his soft, strong feathers. He's like my personal hot water bottle, all hard heat. Jyr hesitates, his body vibrates with emotions I can somehow tell he doesn't know how to process. He might be in my head, but I'm also in his. I slip my tongue between his lips, carefully exploring his sharp teeth and then withdrawing to bite down on his full lower lip. The iron rod of his erection—or should that be erections?—is pressed against my stomach.

"Are we really needed at szent?" Jyr's eyes roll in his head as I palm his lengths through the leather of his trousers. He gasps, lost for words momentarily.

I've never had this effect on anyone before. He melts into me, arms gripping, feathers closing over us like a protective blanket. His fingers pull at my clothing, wanting to touch skin and my hands are already on his belt, scrabbling to free him from the confines of his trousers.

His mind touches mine, all desire and longing. And fear. Fear for our future.

JYR

Viv pulls away from me, her eyes searching my face as she places her hands squarely on my chest. I can still feel the touch of her lips and my cocks ache for want of not being inside her.

"If we're going to do this, Jyr. We're going to do it properly."

"What?" My lust fogs my mind. All I want is to mate and impregnate my female. My hips jerk at her uncontrollably, my legs trembling.

"Me and you. I can't be left in the dark. You have to tell me everything." Her insistent tone penetrates my deep desires for her body. She's found something.

The thoughtbond.

I expected her to be able to use it, eventually. But as she isn't Gryn, I wasn't expecting her to be able to see into me, not yet, not with all the walls I put up. Could it be that a human is more receptive, more perceptive than a Gryn?

Whatever is happening, she deserves answers. She does deserve to know the truth because it involves her, however hard I try to deny it.

"Kaloz is the trouble." My shoulders slump as I let her slip out from my grasp, lust giving way to the tiredness that often infuses my very bones. She leans against the wall next to me and folds her arms, her intelligent eyes taking everything in. "He and his mercs were part of a separate legion for a long time. We were rivals, of sorts. When Proto found their lair and there was a massacre. It seemed that all that was sent was joykill bots. There was no attempt at capture."

Viv frowns at me. "You mean that Proto still tries to capture you? Why?"

"We don't know the answer to that. We don't know why it kept us alive in the first place. It has no need for organic life-forms. As far as its algorithms are concerned, we are a pest. But it still tries, except in Kaloz's case." I lean my head back against the wall, staring at the crumbling ceiling and wondering if my lair would stand up to a joykill bot onslaught. "He came to me with what was left of his mercs and begged for sanctuary. What could I do? I've dedicated my life to saving the Gryn from Proto."

I drop my chin onto my chest. I never thought I'd rue the day I offered my home to another Gryn.

"Why make him your second in command?"

"As a former Prime, he couldn't be anything less."

Viv makes a hissing sound. "Then he should have been grateful."

"He was, for a long time. Until he started making suggestions about our processes. At first, little tweaks which didn't seem unreasonable. Then he wanted to get back into narcotics." I see Viv's face harden. "We didn't bother with drugs, but Kaloz's legion was a master at providing all sorts of narcotics. The Mochi, Kijg, and even the Zio paid a good price for his stuff. We were finding and releasing more and more warriors at the time, and I needed the income."

"And now?" Viv isn't letting me off the hook. "What about now? Do you still have to run drugs? On Earth they cause nothing but misery. I can't believe it's not the same here."

I can't help but let out a harsh laugh. "You've seen what remains of Ustokos. What do you think?"

"I think that it's always possible to rebuild. Humans did it, many times over due to natural disasters and manmade ones. I don't think that running drugs, weapons, and protection has to define you or your kind."

"Our kind." I can't help myself but catch her up in my arms.

Her eyes are flashing with fire as she berates me, and it is all kinds of gorgeous. I capture her mouth with mine, wanting to prove to her how much I've learned about her kiss. Wanting to taste her sweet, glorious taste and scent her until nothing else matters.

"Jyr!" She breaks off the kiss, pushing me back with some urgency.

"My *eregri*." I murmur, trying to get to her again.

"Jyr!" She shoves harder. I hear a cough behind us, one I couldn't mistake for anyone else.

"Ryak, you vrexing bastid. Can't you see I'm busy?"

"Prime." He does a little bow that would be comical if I didn't know he was annoyed. "You requested us at szent."

"Ryak, this is my mate, Vivian, a human from Earth." I stand away from my mate so that he can see her beauty. "Viv, this is Ryak, my head of security and expert in sneakery."

"Oh, a spy." Viv smiles brightly, stepping forward. She holds out her hand towards Ryak. "Pleased to meet you, Ryak. You can call me Viv."

Ryak stares at her and her outstretched hand.

"Not Gryn." He says to me, and I roll my eyes in

response. "It is a pleasure to make your acquaintance, Viv, human of Earth." He proffers her the shoulder of his wing in the age old Gryn greeting and it's Viv's turn to stare.

Without any prompting, she reaches up and runs her hand over his feathers before stepping back to my side. Ryak nods curtly.

She is unusual. But acceptable.

I consider whether or not I could get a punch in before the slippery warrior has the opportunity to dodge me. From Ryak, that is praise rather than disrespect. I still make it clear to him down the senior bond that he's hovering on the edge of what is acceptable as I wrap my arm around Viv's waist and walk her up the final path to the szent chamber.

I'm trying to work out why Jyr is so pleased with himself until we walk into a room that almost takes my breath away. An enormous table, constructed with incredible skill from metal that could only have been taken from those terrible robots, dominates the room. Ranged around are six chairs, like in Jyr's outer chamber. The biggest and the most imposing is the one at the head of the table. Throne-like, it's also constructed from parts of robots, but these pieces have been fashioned to look like feathers. Iron feathers on an iron throne. Jyr strolls up to it and sits, beckoning to me to join him.

An iron throne for an iron ruler. Figures.

There's nowhere for me to sit on his spiky throne, he gestures for me to sit on his lap, his face a beacon of smugness. He knows exactly what he's doing. I launch myself at his lap and suppress a silly giggle at the 'oof' sound he makes.

Other Gryn make their way into the room. Ryak and Kyt sit either side of the table, facing each other as a further three join us. The last to enter has a long leather apron covered in burns. He's as tall as Jyr, with incredibly muscular arms. A long scar runs down the left side of his face, causing his lip to hitch and expose a sharp canine. I notice he also holds one wing stiffly. He takes his seat to the right of Jyr.

The Gryn that takes his seat on Jyr's left has to be Kaloz. I remember him from when we'd first landed. Even though Jyr didn't introduce us properly, the way he sits and stares insolently, it has to be the Gryn that Jyr described.

"Szent is in session." Jyr intones. "My fellow seniors, I wish you to meet my mate. Vivian, a human from the planet Earth."

Four pairs of dark eyes turn to me, and I feel myself turning bright red. I'd rather be anywhere than here, especially perched awkwardly on Jyr's lap. I'm horribly exposed like this, and I hate it. I feel my natural defense, anger, rising inside me.

"Vivian," Jyr fills the silence with his deep gravel of a voice, "this is Kaloz, my second in command, known as Command." Kaloz inclines his head to me, although his eyes glitter unpleasantly as he appraises me. "Kyt and Ryak you have met." Kyt offers me a silly salute, a big grin on his face. Ryak nods solemnly. "And this is our slayer and swordsmith, Myk."

The big, silent Gryn on Jyr's right turns to look at me. There's something haunting in his eyes.

"I am pleased to meet you, Vivian, mate of Prime." He rumbles. His presence, although scarred and twisted, comforts me. The others accept him, despite his outward appearance.

"It's good to meet you too, Myk. And all of you." I reply politely, his sweet acceptance quashing my need to snap.

"Myk is one of the best and most talented weapons

manufacturers in Ustokos." Jyr says generously. "What he can't do with metal isn't worth knowing."

"Did you make this?" I put my hand on the table. It's cold to the touch but completely smooth.

"I did, my lady Prime." He answers, but his eyes show he doesn't want to. He'd rather be anywhere except in this room right now. I know exactly how he feels.

"We will be attending the Mochi trading post on the outskirts of the old bot factory tomorrow." Jyr announces. "My mate requires clothing and other essentials." I lean away from him, trying to work out what he thinks the 'essentials' might be, although underwear would be pretty high on my priority list. The girls aren't doing well without a bra. "I will require a security detail. I have already picked Fyn, as he seems to be at a loose end. Ryak, please pick the rest for me."

"Why does she speak funny?" Kaloz queries, his brow drawn low over his gimlet eyes.

"She is human. She speaks-" Jyr looks at me.

"I speak English. I'm from England, it's a large island in the northern hemisphere of my planet."

Kaloz's brow furrows further.

"Since when did Proto start giving creatures like her language downloads?"

Ryak lets out a bark of laughter. "I could say the same about you, Kaloz."

Kaloz sits back with a huff of annoyance.

"Not that your language download is much good anyway, given you're always having to shout when we go to trade with the Mochi." Kyt joins in with Ryak's laughter.

"I speak Mochi just fine." Kaloz snaps.

"Good enough to end up balls deep in one of their whores." Kyt retorts.

Kaloz leaps to his feet, wings held out and a snarl on his lips.

"Quartermaster is an easy post to fill, Kyt, if you want to repeat that." His claws are extended, although no where near as long as Jyr's, they are still fearsome weapons.

Kyt is also on his feet, stepping purposefully towards Kaloz. The air crackles with the Gryn equivalent of testosterone.

"Enough!" Jyr roars, lifting me bodily off his lap and jumping onto the table in one fluid movement. "I choose my seniors, Kaloz and don't forget it." He snarls. "And stop vrexing about, Kyt." He fires at the other Gryn. "What is the code?" He bellows at the room.

"The Gryn is all. Prime's word is law." They chorus, although Kaloz is reluctant to join in, his eyes dark with anger, he adds his voice to the rest.

Okay, so I'm not going to lie. Seeing Jyr like that, all predator and all in charge, is an enormous turn on.

Perhaps I should just embrace the fact that he picked me. Whatever his reasons, being in the room with a male as powerful as he is, that I know wants me, is entrancing. My mind goes back to earlier in the corridor, when wanting him seemed natural and right.

"Very good." Jyr descends from the table with one swift beat of his wings, hardly even stirring a feather on the others. "I don't expect that I will be needed tonight, but I am taking my mate back to my quarters and should only be disturbed if we get a full on attack from Proto." He looks down at me. "One final thing. I have heard there is an order that mercs work as long as they can fly. This has resulted in young ones being sent out before they are fully healed. These are not my orders, and this practice will cease." He stares around him, daring anyone to contradict him.

The room is silent, but from the look on Kaloz's face, I'm pretty sure I know where the order came from. What a twat.

Jyr grabs my hand and hauls me up from the seat, pulling me behind him as he races out of the door. Once we are in the central shaft, he tosses me into his arms and with a few hard downbeats, we're in the air, flying until we reach a level I recognize.

"You will be the death of me, my *eregri*. Your arousal, it drives me wild." He races through the first set of doors and the second into the bedroom, kicking them shut behind him, he has me on the bed in seconds.

"Wait, Jyr." He pulls at my clothing, his claws making a ripping sound on the fabric, which for some reason I feel I should try to leave intact.

He moans, his eyes half lidded, desperation pouring off him. In a flash, my clothing has gone again, and he has me at his mercy. I press my lips to his, enjoying the feel of his mouth on mine, luxuriating in the touch of our bodies and the spicy smell from his feathers. He is insistent, his tongue sweeping my mouth, his fingers feeling for my nipples, circling the tight peaks with the tips of his claws and making me shudder.

Jyr pulls back, and I whine as I miss his warmth and touch. He stands at the end of the bed, his eyes tracing every inch of me as he undoes his trousers. They fall to the floor, and he fists his cocks.

"Beautiful female." He says, his voice filled with wonder.

I see that his lower cock fits neatly into the grooves on the underside of the larger one, presumably to allow entry of both at the same time. Seeing him work at his enormous members and how he licks his lips gives me an idea. I sit up in front of him, reaching out for his cocks. He watches me with interest as I take hold of him, my hand not able to encircle the girth of both shafts, but I can still stroke him easily. He is already slippery with pre-cum and his hips buck at me as I run my hand over the tips.

Tentatively, I lean into him, my tongue touching the broad head of his main cock. He tastes salty sweet with a hint of the spice that infuses his feathers. I take as much of him in my mouth as I can, separating out the second cock so that I can pay it special attention with one hand as I suck on his main cock and work it at the same time. Jyr moans in delight, one hand on my shoulder and the other in my hair, the sharp points of his claws just pressed lightly into my scalp.

I like to think that blowjobs were my thing. Not that I've had much practice in recent years.

Jyr is very much enjoying my attention. His groans are coming thick and fast and he thrusts himself into my mouth and hand with increased fervor.

"*Eregri*, I wish to spill my seed." He has both hands on my head.

"Where do you want to spill it?" I release his cock long enough to see he can't possibly make a decision.

I smile to myself and redouble my efforts on my alpha alien who, by now, can hardly see straight. With a grunt and a low bellow that seems to come from the bottom of his feet, he releases. Hot cum runs down my throat and over my chest as he pumps at me. I work at both cocks, wringing every delicious drop from him, until I'm able to look up at Jyr, swallowing the last mouthful and wiping delicately at my lips.

His eyes flare as he sees me covered in his cum and he topples forward, spouting nonsense, as he hits the furs face down with a muffled sound. One arm snakes out and grabs at my waist, pulling me into his warmth.

"You will pay for that, my mate." He murmurs, his voice muffled and sleepy.

"I hope so." I snuggle against him.

After everything I've seen and participated in today, Jyr feels like home. I don't yet know what to make of the mate thing or the 'he's in my head' thing. He might be a criminal, arrogant and stupidly alpha, but the soft center that he hides, like when he spoke to Pytr, it melts my ice heart just a little. He is determined that I am his 'mate', no matter what. He has accepted me, scars and all.

He says I am beautiful.

I can't deny that there's something inside me that wants to be with Jyr. Maybe not enough that I want to stay on Ustokos or give up on the other humans. But enough that leaving wouldn't be as easy as it should be.

JYR

What Viv did with my cocks was spine-shatteringly good, even if it didn't involve me mating with her. The feeling of bliss spreading through my entire body is nothing short of a miracle. I'm not sure I've felt this relaxed before. Sure, after a good fight, relaxing with other warriors in the healing pool, that was always enjoyable. A decent amount of time to preen and sort my feathers after a long flight. It usually helped me. If another Gryn could assist in the preening, all the better.

But Viv's tongue lapping over my cocks. Her hands working me. Her face as she drank me down.

Indescribable.

I try to move, but I'm boneless. I should help my mate cleanse and pleasure her like she pleasured me. Instead, my brain turns off and sleep, blissful, dreamless sleep claims me.

Something snorts loudly, and I'm awake. The room is dark. We've missed the evening meal, and my stomach is not thanking me for it. I flop my arm out, searching for my mate.

Nothing.

She's not in the bed. Instantly, I'm on my feet. My eyesight is as good in the dark as in the light, but she is not in the room. Panic grips me until I remember the thought-bond. I reach out for her.

Outside

I pull on my trousers and pad across to the landing ledge. The shutters look closed until I get nearer and see there is a human sized gap. I open it wider to allow me and my wings through. Viv leans in one corner, keeping her distance from the edge. She stares out over the remains of the great city of Kos. The clouds have cleared and the depression in which the ruins lie is illuminated by the light of the moons.

"This was an incredible place once, wasn't it?" Viv says as I join her, sliding an arm around her waist to ensure she stays safe and close to me.

"It was. I don't remember it. The great reckoning leveled it long before I was born." I inhale her scent and I'm pleased to feel her little hands entwining with my feathers.

"But you chose it for your lair?"

"I needed somewhere large enough that I could expand the legion as we found more Gryn. It wasn't my first choice, but when we first came here, none of us were in good enough shape to find anywhere else. It sort of stuck."

"You really care about them all, don't you?"

"Kyt, Ryak and Myk? We all escaped together. I couldn't imagine being without them."

The emptiness in my head would be unbearable.

"I mean your young ones - the mercs. You care about them too," She says like it's a statement of fact.

"I try to. We're a family of sorts. Dysfunctional but functioning. I care more about you though." I nuzzle my nose into her hair. "My mate." The concept fills my heart to the brim, even as I hold back my concerns.

I have to deal with Kaloz, only then will she be safe.

But dealing with that vrexer is easier said than done.

"I-I trust you, Jyr." Viv stutters out. "I can't remember a time when I trusted anyone. The doctors, they did things to me without my consent after my accident. All I wanted to do was to be left alone. I pushed everyone away, my family, such as they were. My friends. No one wanted to know me. I'm difficult." She turns her face up to me, her eyes shining with liquid. "But I trust you."

I take her hand and gently run my tongue over her sweet tasting skin.

"I am honored, my *eregri*. Trust is not easily won."

"Humans don't do mates. Hell, humans often can't even stay with one person more than one night. The concept is as alien as this planet." She waves her hand vaguely out at the moonlit scene spread beneath us. "Shame. Maybe it would make things easier if we did." She adds, seemingly to herself.

"Without females, no one, especially me, ever thought we could take a mate again. But you—" I trace a finger over her collarbone. She's wrapped a fur around her body, and the thought that she's naked underneath causes my cocks to wake. "You are the key, *eregri*. Organic life has to survive on Ustokos. We cannot let Proto win."

As if in answer, far in the distance, a phalanx of capture-bots zips across the night sky. Their blue glow eerie in the moonlight. Viv takes in a breath.

"They are heading to Mochi territory. We have night patrols that should keep them safe." I dip my head towards her, tipping her chin to me. "That's what we do. In return, they help us with food and other things we cannot produce."

"And the drugs? How does that fit in?" Viv has captured me, as usual. Razor sharp, she has slipped her blade right down the center of my world.

"If we didn't produce them, one of the other species would. It's a hard world out there. Not everyone wants to see it as you do."

"No excuse, Jyr. On Earth, drugs only cause misery." She ruffles my feathers again, and it relaxes me. She's right, of course.

"I've no desire to cause injury to anyone. What we produce, it's limited and as non-addictive as it can be."

"Not everyone is as strong as you or the Gryn." Viv says, looking away from me. "I know all about weakness. I don't want this to define you."

"It doesn't. I will speak to Kaloz about our production, for you. And you will see soon enough what defines us." I wrap my arms around her. My feathers itch for her touch again. I want to drop into the healing pool with her, mate her and preen together.

Sounds good

Her blue eyes are almost as dark as mine in the night. A smile plays around her lips. She is a master at getting what she wants but giving me what I need.

We slip back into my quarters, and Viv drops the fur to the floor, the pale globes of her ass swinging as she walks through the pool, looking over her shoulder at me. I scramble to kick off my trousers and join her.

VIV

Have I really done this? Jyr rumbles a snore next to me under the furs. One wing covers me, and I run my fingers through the soft, steely struts. He might appear like a bird of prey, but he dissolved into a little chick after he showed me how to work my way over his wings and ensure they were clean.

The evident pleasure that the simple action in helping him preen settled in my stomach like a warm meal after a long walk. I felt it heat me from within.

What is he doing to me? There's no such thing as a fated mate, not for me. I can't risk getting hurt. I've already had a lifetime of pain and my life is nowhere near over. Except my stupid heart seems to think I'd risk anything for the male who slumbers next to me. The bad angel who came to me when he was hurt and alone, even though I'd rejected him.

You could do worse, Viv.

And he could do better.

Jyr lets out a snort and flips over to look at me.

"Did you say something, my Viv?" God! I love how he says my name.

"Nothing. But what does a girl have to do around here to get some breakfast?"

Jyr chuckles. "I'm one step ahead of you today." He rises, his body lithe and muscular as he walks towards the doors to the outer chamber, allowing me to enjoy the view of his edible behind. He disappears for a few seconds and returns with a tray piled high with the foods similar to the ones we had yesterday.

The Gryn diet is not exactly adventurous. But given the size of these guys, it's got to be nutritious, even if part of me would kill for some fruit right now.

"For a human that doesn't eat breakfast, you certainly put plenty of it away." Jyr comments, his cheeks bulging.

"I guess being abducted by aliens and spirited away by a massive predator changes your view on breakfast."

Jyr hums and I catch his uncertainty. It hovers in my mind like a gray cloud.

"I'm joking, hun. I guess it must be the air or something, but I'm starving." The cloud dissipates and is replaced by a frown.

"Hun?"

"It's short for honey, like the ambrosia you have." I try not to think about how nice that stuff was, or lament the lack of it at breakfast, given how much shit I gave Jyr for peddling his artificial drugs.

The frown deepens, and it only serves to make him look cuter.

"Perhaps it might be an idea not to call me that outside of our chambers." He says, feeling his way with the words.

I hop onto his lap and grin up at him. "Would it damage your street cred, Prime?"

He oscillates between enjoying me being on his lap, and his desire to be masterful.

"I don't understand 'street cred', female, but I doubt my mercs would like to hear their Prime referred to as 'hun.'" He tries his best to scowl before a wonderful smile creases his cheeks. "Although I don't mind it when we are alone." He adds.

I'm so going to call him 'hun' at some point today.

Breakfast finished, albeit slightly weirdly, as Jyr insisted on feeding me various pieces of food I was perfectly capable of putting in my mouth without his help. I let him because I enjoyed the pink cloud of pleasure that formed in my mind as he put each carefully selected morsel in my mouth. Yep, I've ended up with this alien in my head and between my legs.

And, as a shock to my system, I don't seem to mind either option. Since he accepted me for what I am, it's as if my brain is prepared to accept him lock, stock and barrel. Or seven feet of winged muscle in Jyr's case. Not to mention the drop-dead gorgeousness that is the Prime of the Gryn.

Jyr grins at me when he sees me appraising him, arrogantly puffing up his chest and setting his wings high to make himself look bigger. Not that he needs to.

"I'm going to need more clothes, given that you shredded what I was wearing last night." I say as we stand next to each other, naked, cleaning our teeth.

"As much as I'd prefer to keep you as you are." Jyr's eyes glow with lust. "I cannot have you distracting the other Gryn." He returns to the bedroom and comes back with a pair of trousers, Jyr size, and another shirt.

Once I've dressed, I join him in the outer chamber. Waiting for us is Myk, leaning on the most enormous sword, and the younger Gryn that Jyr collared from yesterday, Fyn.

"I have your security detail ready, Prime." Fyn announces.

"Handpicked, no doubt." Jyr flashes a smile at Myk.

In the back of my brain, I feel their connection. Myk gently acknowledging the young warrior's enthusiasm with familial amusement.

"I'm not too late to join the expedition, am I?" Kaloz leans against the door frame. Jyr stares at him for a beat. It's a look Kaloz returns with no fear, and the silence that follows could be cut with a knife.

"I would have thought you had more important things to do than tag along to a trading post, but if you wish." Jyr says, finally.

"I believe it's important we are seen together, Prime. Gives the right impression to the mercs and to our prospects."

"I'm not going to sell any more of your products this month, Kaloz. There's enough of your vrexing drugs out there already."

Kaloz steps into the room, hands held up, claws sheathed. "We've made more than enough on the shipments I have been able to get past Proto. No need to drum up any more business."

"Let's go." Jyr turns his back on Kaloz, reaching for my hand, and we walk through the darkened corridors of the lair until we reach a ledge. Half a dozen warriors stand ready, bristling with daggers and what appear to be miniature crossbows.

Reverentially, Myk hands Jyr a soft hoop of leather and he puts it over his head, looping it under one arm. I can see that it is tapered, the lower part of the leather being wider than the rest.

"Come, my *eregri*. This should make your flight more comfortable." Jyr beckons to me.

He tucks me against his chest and slips the loop over my

head, tucking the larger section under my bottom. I can sit on it like a swing, able to grip him and the leather. Thank god, no more spider monkey impressions.

"You ready?" He calls over at Fyn.

The warrior nods and, without any warning, Jyr launches himself into the overcast sky.

With a few strong beats, he's higher than the other warriors, who battle to keep up, all except Fyn, who swiftly joins us. Even with my extra weight, he's still stronger, faster and better than Kaloz. I guess that's why he's Prime, and this little show is to put Kaloz in his place.

JYR

The flight to the trading post is uneventful. My security detail keeps in the proper formation, and my *eregri* seems much happier in the sling we use to carry injured warriors. She isn't clinging to me like I might drop her, which of course would never happen. She seems far more relaxed, and the flight is even more enjoyable.

Our cohort circles the camouflaged stalls set up in the remains of the old bot factory. There's plenty of life and plenty on offer. I presume that this is one of the Mochi's large trading meets. The furry creatures throng the market place, tails twitching with interest as they see us circling. Ranged around the place are the total of two Gryn patrols. I note with satisfaction they are all correctly positioned to keep watch for Proto, and they are concentrated on their jobs. Even our arrival has not caused any of them to ignore their duty.

I can't say the same for those on the ground. We descend for a landing as one, hitting the ground at the same time with a loud and resounding thump that draws looks from almost all those attending, our wings stirring up dust and debris. It never hurts to remind the other species who provides their protection.

With the security detail taking up a defensive position behind and in front of us, I walk Viv through the market stalls.

"What is this place?" Viv stares around at the stalls, and her eyes nearly pop out on stalks when she spots a Mochi trader speaking with a Kijg female. The brightly colored Kijg female is arguing, apparently over a cooking pot of some kind. As usual, the furry Mochi has the appearance of not caring, but the slow flicking of his long tail indicates his rising anger.

"The risk that Proto poses to all organic life forms means we can only trade like this. Nothing permanent."

"Like a pop-up supermarket?" Viv smiles, unable to keep her head still as she tries to take it all in.

"If you say so." Her expressions are odd, but then she is an alien to this planet.

Kaloz has already disappeared, and I breathe a sigh of relief that I can show my mate something good about Ustokos, given that all she's seen so far are the ruins left behind after the great reckoning. It sounds like her planet had some semblance of technological sophistication, and I'm anxious that she understands we were once a great species, and that Ustokos was once a great planet.

Even if our over-reliance on tech was ultimately our downfall.

Fyn leads as we move into the trading area. Our presence is noted, but not enough of a distraction to stop the bartering going on.

"Clothing." I bark at him, and he turns a sharp left,

heading towards several stalls that have strips of fabric fluttering from them in the light breeze.

"I wish you to outfit my mate." I announce to the Kijg stall holder, ushering Viv forward. "She requires—" I hesitate, not entirely sure what a female needs. All I really remember of my mother was her unique smell, and that she wore soft, slippery material that felt nice under my fingers.

"Clothing suitable to her status as mate of the Prime." The owner suggests. She is a multi-hued female and is well dressed. She casts a practiced eye over Viv.

"I'm not sure about this—" Viv turns to me, attempting to get behind one of my wings.

"Nonsense. You cannot wear my clothing any longer, female." I bark and push her at the Kijg.

"Come through my dear." She takes Viv by the upper arm and drags my reluctant mate through the stall and into an area at the rear that is part of the original building.

I extend the thoughtbond, probing to ensure that Viv is safe. Her alarm fires through me like a joykill laser. I don't even think further, racing through the stall until I reach the back, claws extended and ready to kill anything that threatens my mate.

Viv and the stallholder stare at me. Both are entirely unharmed, and there's no sign of any bots.

"This will take much longer if you insist on being present, Prime of the Gryn." The Kijg levels her beady gaze at me.

"She wants me to undress, that's all." Viv says dully. The dawning realization of what she is afraid of hits me between the eyes. "I've not been shopping for clothes for a long time. I bought things off the internet."

I'm beside her in an instant, arms around her waist,

holding her to me. She doesn't look up, liquid hovering on her eyelashes.

"You do not need a t'inter-net, not when you have me. No one is judging you, sweet *eregri*." She places a hand on my chest. It's hot and dry. "But you don't have to do anything you don't want to do." I give the stallholder the benefit of my best stare. "You can fit clothes without my mate having to undress, can't you?"

"Well—" The Kijg begins. I feel my claws extending, and she swallows hard. "Yes, I can do that. It'll take me a bit longer, but I can." She concedes.

I nuzzle in my mate's hair. "Will that do for you, my Viv?"

"Yes." Her voice is small but strong.

"But it'll take even longer if you don't put her down!" The Kijg recovers her composure and shoos me out.

"I'll leave Fyn and security here with you. I have some other purchases to make." I call over the irritated Kijg's head to my mate. "They'll be right outside if you need them."

I need something for my mate, for our mating ceremony, and I know the perfect stall for what I want.

"Fyn," I call to the young warrior, who is carefully scanning the crowds and sky for any threat. "My mate will stay here. I have other business to attend do. Remain with my mate at all times." I indicate that half the security detail is to come with me.

"As you wish, Prime." Fyn responds with all due respect and a swift nod of his head.

Maybe I have underestimated him. It might be the case that he's only been trouble since I brought him back from the capture camp, but his behavior today indicates he has taken on board some of the training we have provided him. He should be more senior than he is by now, and it's only because he's prone to hot tempers and unsanctioned fighting that he has not risen higher in the merc rankings. With some more training on how to control himself, I can see him shaping up for great things.

I feel a much more relaxed Viv down the thoughtbond, and I head into the traders, attempting to keep the spring out of my step and present our usual demeanor to those surrounding us and who depend on the Gryn to keep them safe.

VIV

I was never one for trying on clothes in the shop before my accident. The relief that I feel when Jyr steps in to stop the bossy lizard lady making me strip is unreal.

Instead, she walks around me, holding out her strange, scaly hand to show she wants to touch me. I let her run her hands over my body. She clicks to herself as if she's taking measurements. In a whirl of activity, she's pulling out boxes and fabric from everywhere, and a pile of clothing grows before me. Now and then she holds something up against me, with further rapid clicks, and it goes on the pile, or slow clicks and it's thrown to one side.

Finally, she seems to have finished her clothes tsunami impression and sorts through the pile.

"I have some everyday outfits here for you." She puts several sets of dark red leather-like trousers to one side along with a couple of matching tops, made of a similar material and long-sleeved. "And something for your mating celebration."

"Mating celebration?" I sound like an idiot as she holds up a dark green dress that's covered in gold embroidery.

"The Gryn are planning a celebration, are they not?" She cocks her head to one side, and I'm reminded of a chameleon, especially as her scales seem to shimmer to a different color. "They have doubled their food requests and have increased their var beer production."

"There's going to be a celebration, but just to introduce me to the rest of the Gryn."

Lizard lady shakes her head and makes a hiccuping sound.

"You are already mated, but it will not be confirmed until he has shown you to all the warriors in his lair." She presses a hand over my stomach. "And you are impregnated with his young."

I jump back from her. "He already knows that's not going to happen."

She hiccups again. "The mate bond is strong between you. You cannot deny what your body wants."

"For fuck's sake, is every species on this godforsaken planet fucking telepathic?" I fire out. I had more than my fill of humans thinking they knew what was best for me, and I'm damned if I'm going to let a bunch of aliens do the same.

"I only say what I see, my lady Prime." The lizard lady takes a step back, her forked tongue flicking in the air. "We Kijg have known Jyr a long time, and I have never seen him like this."

"Like what?" Jyr doesn't seem to be any different from when I first met him, big, self-assured and as arrogant as fuck, especially when I heard him barking orders at the warriors outside.

"So in love."

I gape at her, working my mouth like a goldfish at the fair. All this talk of fated mates, of thoughtbonds and mating celebrations.

My mind was already reeling. But love...it had never occurred to me that all of this was about love. That love was at the heart of what Jyr feels towards me.

That my heart could love.

I'm hot and cold at the same time. All I've done is hate for what seems like forever. Myself, the world, everything. This fluttering in the pit of my stomach, is it? Could it be?

I'm desperate to dismiss it, to find something that would tell me that love doesn't work this way. That it's not possible for me to know already that I've fallen for a dark angel who could devour me in an instant.

Or make me feel like the only being in the universe.

"I don't think it's like that at all." I babble. "He thinks he's found a fated mate in me, that's all. He can't control it. He has no choice but to take me." All at once I've laid bare the terrifying truth that forms ice inside me.

Lizard lady starts hiccuping wildly. She throws her arms around me, hugging me to her cool skin. She smells like mint, which I find a little odd, but not unpleasant.

"Little one, the fates are not everything. Jyr has a choice in who he chooses. We all do. Any life-forms on Ustokos can choose their destiny. Fate simply presents it to us. Believe me, if Jyr didn't want you, you would not be here now, with an entire phalanx of Gryn warriors to wait on your every whim."

"Really?" My cheeks are wet, and I hadn't even realized I was crying. "It really works like that?"

She holds me at arm's length. "I think you need to ask your mate that question. I have told you what I know, and I've rejected a mate or two in my time." She leans in and her tongue wipes away my tears before I have a chance to say 'uhg'. "Now let's get you ready for your mate."

There has to be something about a heart to heart, but

my concerns about taking off my clothes in front of the lizard lady, or Siliza as she introduces herself to me, have disappeared. That and discovering that aliens do underwear also helps.

Alien underwear. It's different. Knickers? Check. A not exactly sexy gray color, but functional. Bra? Nope, corset.

Alien planet meet medieval Earth. The short corset is surprisingly comfortable and does a good job of containing my generous bust. As an added plus, it covers most of my scarring. I find myself feeling sexy for the first time in I don't know how long. The rest of my outfit comprises the dark red leather trousers, a pair of soft black boots that reach just up my calf, a soft gray leather t-shirt, and a neatly fitting jacket that's almost tailored for me.

Siliza packages the rest of my clothing up into neat rolls that I see will be easy for the Gryn to carry.

"Come back for your winter wardrobe at the next trading post." She says cheerily. "I have a coat lined with pix fur that would be perfect for you."

"You mean this isn't winter?" I had assumed that the heavy overcast skies were Ustokos winter, like back at home.

She makes her hiccuping laugh again. "What species are you? From the southern continent perhaps."

"I'm not from this planet at all. I'm human from Earth."

She stills in her mirth. "Proto?" It's a whisper, the threat all too real.

"Jyr seems to think I was brought here by Proto. There were other humans too."

Siliza chitters nervously. "That does not bode well for us organics."

"*Eregri*? Are you finished?" I hear Jyr shout from outside.

Looks like males the universe over find waiting outside a shop boring.

"I'm coming." I call over my shoulder. "Thank you." I return to Siliza. "How much do we owe you?" It's a strange feeling, being reliant on another for something as simple as paying for clothing, but I have nothing that would even vaguely pass as money, so I hope Jyr does.

Siliza waves her three fingered hand at me and makes a hissing sound. "Nothing. Jyr deserves something good in his life. He's done enough good for others, including my species." Her scaly lips ripple, and I see that it's a sort of smile. "I wish you a good mating. Unless you've already mated." I get the impression she'd be raising her eyebrows suggestively if she had any.

"Maybe," I say slyly. Something about her demeanor makes me comfortable with my new alien friend.

"The Gryn are legendary for their mating." She hiccups a dirty laugh.

"They certainly have anatomy that's different to humans, in many ways." Her amusement is infectious.

"I see younglings in your future." Siliza's eyes glitter. "As you didn't wait until the mating ceremony, you'll find out sooner rather than later."

"What do you mean?" My blood chills. If it's even possible to get pregnant by an alien, it's the last thing I want or need. "Jyr told me they have to use both of their—"I lower my voice. "Cocks to get a female pregnant."

"If that's what he told you." Siliza says, and it's impossible to tell from her lizard like face whether she's agreeing or not.

And my blood is no longer cold. Instead, curiosity curls in my stomach, settling like the warmth of a cat.

"I'd better go, before you have another Gryn explosion in your shop." I put my hand over hers briefly, not knowing if it's appropriate or not, but not caring either. I'm human and that's what we do.

Siliza follows me with all the packages. Outside, Jyr stands waiting, muscular arms crossed. He strikes an imposing figure. Behind him stands the rest of the security detail. Predatory stone statues.

Jyr's eyes widen as he takes in my new outfit. His jaw doesn't exactly drop, instead his tongue peeps out, and he licks his lips while swallowing hard.

"Your Lady Prime looks well, does she not?" Siliza asks him, and this time I hear a note of amusement in her voice.

"She looks amazing." Jyr half whispers, leaning towards me as all the Gryn eyes turn in my direction. He hastily stiffens. "You have done well. You have my thanks."

He reaches for me, running an arm down mine, his eyes dark with desire. I have a flash of what he intends to do with me on our return to the lair and my new underwear dampens considerably. He gestures to Fyn and wraps a wing around us.

"You look beautiful." He breathes in my ear and nuzzles at my neck. "My *eregri*."

This time the word is filled with new meaning for me. I run my hands through his strong, soft feathers to release their scent. I still don't know about love, but I do know that my body wants him more than anything.

JYR

A chill wind lifts my feathers. A wind that should not be at the trading post. It's tinged with a metallic smell that bodes no good for any organics.

"JOYKILL!" A shout up above us.

Whistles fill the air as my warriors shift seamlessly into action. The security detail, led by Fyn, is already in the skies above us as the stallholders scatter, heading for any underground space small enough to hide from the oncoming bots. They trust us enough to know we'll deal with the situation.

That just leaves my mate. She stares up at the wave of bots that are buzzing down towards us; her face a mask of horror. I don't want to risk carrying her, even with the sling, but I have to get her to safety. The joykills are already firing their laser weapons, and the air heats. I can taste the fizzing ions.

A brief cry reverberates around the ruined factory, and my warriors let rip with the first volley of crossbow bolts. Myak's finest work takes out a dozen of the blasted bots, which drop out of the sky and impact hard enough to shake the surrounding ground.

I look around for a place where Viv can wait out the battle. Just across from the clothing stall is a small hatch in the ground, no doubt originally for conduits that would have supplied the factory. It's too small an opening for anything other than my tiny human. I shield her with my wings and rush her across to the hatch, wrenching it open. A smell of long decay emanates from the hole, but there's no scent suggesting that there's anything dangerous down there.

"Get in, my *eregri*. I need to deal with these bots, and this is the safest place for you."

"Jyr!" She pleads. "I don't want to leave you."

"I've been fighting Proto for a long time, my mate. This is nothing, just an irritation. Let me handle it and we'll be back at the lair in no time."

She pouts at me, her protruding lower lip too much of a temptation. I sneak in a kiss. It's as if they are made for these moments, then I push her down into the hole. She squeaks in protest but allows me to close the hatch.

The cackling whine nearby alerts me to the presence of a joykill searching out organics, having broken from the rest of its battalion. I have to draw it away from where Viv is hiding before I can join my warriors in the sky above. I creep around behind the empty stalls and once I'm far enough away from her; I kick over a pile of rusting parts.

"Hey! I think I just found your mother!" I holler across as the bot swivels towards me. The grating artificial cackling getting louder.

"Remain still, organic, and you will not suffer."

The voice it projects is harsh and artificial. Joykills are not programmed to take prisoners. They kill like any machine, without mercy and without fear. These bots have something else that makes them feared throughout Ustokos, as well as lacking compassion. They appear to enjoy their work. The pseudo laughter that emanates from them as they go about their job makes them sound as if they take pleasure in their killing.

"Very true, I will not be suffering today." I laugh in its direction and with a couple of beats, I'm up above it.

The bot fires up its thrusters and lifts off the ground, a laser whip narrowly misses me as it narrows the gap between us. A clunking sound shows that it has deployed its laser bolt gun, the new weapon that caused me such injury not that long ago.

"Prime!" I look up to see Fyn above me. He holds swords in both hands, tossing one to spiral down and which I dive to catch.

The bot is almost on me as I grasp the sword, swinging the feather light, super strong blade through the air and cutting the machine in two. The halves tumble back to the ground, sparking until there's no power left.

With the bot that was too close to my mate for comfort dealt with, I can take control of the battle raging in the skies. I signal to Fyn to land on a crumbling wall top.

"Pincer formation. We've destroyed enough that if we mount one final attack, they will enter preservation mode and retreat."

It's the one thing we have on our side as organics. Proto doesn't want to lose too many of its precious bots. Once we damage enough of a battalion, they retreat swiftly. By my count, we're close to that number.

"No." Fyn states.

I extend my claws further as I look at him. His pale blue eyes bore into me with defiance. "There's a second wave. We have to get everyone out of here by drawing the first phalanx away."

"How do you know there's a second wave?" I growl.

For an instant, his stare falls away, and a frown appears.

"I feel it." He snarls, thumping a fist on his chest and baring his sharp teeth, daring me to contradict him.

I know where I found Fyn, and if I don't trust his instincts, we're in a whole load of trouble.

"Alert the mercs. Use half of them to get the traders to vacate and the other half to concentrate on holding back the bots. I need to get to my mate." I look down on the battle raging as Fyn springs into action. "Where in Hyddar is Kaloz?" I add to myself.

A long way off in the distance, I spot the cloud of ionized air that spells out the second wave Fyn 'felt'. They are far enough away that we should be able to neutralize the rest of the bots already here and get the vrex out of their way, but it's going to be tight. I watch as Fyn drops into the thick of things and begins directing the mercs to their tasks.

Since when did he decide to make a decent warrior of himself? All I can recall is him engaging in unsanctioned fights for as long as he has been with me. He seems to attract the wrong kind of attention or go looking for it. But his instinct is strong and his change in demeanour only serves to strengthen the lair.

Is his instinct strong enough that he has similar abilities to me and my seniors? Could it be possible that Proto made more of us? I push the concerning thought to the back of my mind. Explanations and questions can wait until the situation is under control.

VIV

The drip, drip, drip sound somewhere off in the black distance is beginning to get on my nerves. I wrap my arms around myself and shiver. The dripping is nothing compared to the way the ground underneath me shakes from time to time and my rising terror for Jyr the longer I stay down here.

I've already tried to push up the hatch, to see what's going on, but it's enormous and far too heavy for me even to move. What's beginning to bother me, the longer I wait down here, in the dark, is whether anyone is going to come for me at all. What happens if Jyr dies? Or is injured? What would I do then?

What would I do without him?

I can't be thinking this way. I know dark times, and this isn't one of them. Well, okay, it is literally pitch black down here, and I'm certain something just ran over my foot, but I've faced worse than this and made it out the other side.

Sort of.

Not that I was the same person after the accident. When the car in front of me swerved out of control, the driver drunk at the wheel, there was nothing I could do to avoid the collision. My car span around and around until it came to a stop on the roadside. There was nothing I could do other than watch in horror as the other three cars piled into the first in the dim, foggy morning light. It was only when I saw the flames lick up from underneath the first car that my brain started to work again. I don't remember much after that, only being loaded into the back of an ambulance, searing pain down one side as the paramedics looked at me in awe.

I still feel the heat sometimes. I can always smell the charred flesh. My charred flesh. I can smell it now.

I want Jyr. I want the big alien to carry me away, up into the sky of this planet, and never let go. Abduction changed nothing for me, but he has changed everything. He did not judge. He only loved.

"Jyr!" My voice comes out hollow and echoey in the dark, damp hole.

It's a whine, and it's a desperate cry for the male that stole me and then got under my skin.

"You called?"

A sliver of light cracks above me, opening wider until I see the grinning face of Jyr, his elongated canines exposed. I'm found in the darkness of his eyes.

"I thought you were never coming back. Talk about keeping a girl waiting." I grumble as he holds out his arm and helps me out of my hiding place.

"I just had a few things to take care of first, my *eregri.*" He looks around dramatically.

Laid on the ground behind us is a pile of smoldering parts that was once a joykill bot. I'm pleased to see it out of action, but as I look up there is a tremendous battle over-head between the Gryn and some more bots. The cackling and shrieking emanating from the machines makes them sound like they are alive. And psychotic.

"You missed some." I point upwards and he grins even wider.

"I have mercs for that. My job is to keep you safe." He spans my waist with his huge hands and slides down over the curve of my bottom as he leans into me, inhaling deeply. "Among other things."

Despite the destruction going on around us, it's as if time stands still. Even the smell of a burning robot isn't triggering me, not while I'm in Jyr's arms and his lips are on mine.

Our tongues are entwined in a kiss that could, literally, be the death of both of us. Red light bolts zip past and I close my eyes. Wanting to only ever be in this moment with Jyr.

"That one was a bit close for comfort." Jyr pulls away, leaving me panting.

He extends a wing and checks his feathers. Presumably he must have felt the heat of one of those lasers. He unwraps the sling that I used on the way here and pulls it over my head.

"What about everyone?"

"The mercs are in the process of clearing out the trading post. Everyone will be safe, don't worry, my mate. I'll send some back later when this is over to retrieve your clothes."

"Literally the last thing on my mind right now, Jyr." A shrieking bot flies overhead, stalls and descends, cackling insanely.

"Let's go. Hold on."

He doesn't need to tell me twice. I entwine my hands in the soft leather of the sling and press close to him as he lifts into the air with several short, easy beats. One arm is wrapped around me and the other holds an enormous shining sword. As the bot nears us, he puts on a turn of speed, shooting straight up and the thing follows. I don't want to look as the ground disappears at a tremendous rate, but I can't help myself. The bot is gaining even as Jyr flies higher. Suddenly, he stalls and falls back. I scream and my voice is lost to the rushing wind. He flips, wings pumping hard as he stoops towards the bot. At the last possible second, just before we collide, he brings the sword forwards and rakes the blade down the side of the machine.

It lets out a mechanical groan and splits in two; the pieces tumbling away from us as the laser gives out one last blast, and I feel a searing pain in my leg.

"Are you okay?" Jyr says into my ear, urgently.

"I'll be fine." I reply, teeth gritted. Of course, I'll be fine. I'm always fine.

I DON'T PAY much attention to the return journey, although the relief that washes over me when the cliff that holds the Gryn lair looms up ahead is new and welcome. The cool air has done some to reduce the burning in my leg, but as we come into land, the pain starts up again. Jyr sets me on my feet and I hop, still holding onto him.

"You are injured?" He says, a look of horror on his face. He holds me at arm's length, scanning down my body.

"It's not that bad." I extend my leg in front of me and there's nothing.

I crouch, the sensation of burning all to real and roll up my trouser leg. Reddened flesh greets me. I've certainly seen worse. Somehow, the blasted bot managed to actually fire up my trousers.

"Orvos. Now." Jyr's jaw is set tightly, a muscle flickering

in his cheek. Yet again, I'm scooped up, and he's thumping through the corridors to a central shaft. A few beats of his wings, and we are on the level of the surgery.

"My mate is injured. Heal her." Jyr demands as soon as he enters.

Orvos is standing over Pytr, who I'm pleased to see, looks much better. He strolls over as Jyr deposits me gingerly on a ledge.

"I'm fine, Jyr." I attempt to tell him he is so desperately trying to hide behind a mask of stoicism. I can see his anguish as a cloud of dark blue emotion. It settles around my heart so deeply I'm not sure it can keep beating.

Orvos rolls up my trouser leg.

"Ah, a joykill laser burn. I have just the thing for that." He bustles off in a flourish of feathers.

Jyr stands over me like a statue, hands balled into fists.

"How are the others?" I ask him as a distraction. He stares down at me, uncomprehending. "The other Gryn. The ones fighting the bots?"

He hesitates, brow furrowed, until a spark returns.

"My warriors are well trained. All will be well." He says, some imperiousness returning.

"And for those of us that don't speak Prime?" I tilt my head and look up at him.

"I don't expect any major injuries. Fyn spotted the main threat, and they are well trained to deal with Proto." Jyr relents.

Orvos returns with a pot of evil smelling gel and smears it on my leg while I beg him not to get any on my new clothes. The salve has an immediate cooling effect, and I lean back against the wall. It's hard not to compare my last experience in the burn unit with this one. Given that I have the chiseled gorgeousness that is Jyr to look at, rather than fully masked up doctors and nurses, this is already infinitely better.

"You'll need to reapply the kenos once this layer has dried. After that you should be as good as new." Orvos says, handing me the pot.

"That's it?" Jyr asks incredulously.

"Yes, you can go."

Without another word, I'm back in Jyr's arms, and we are ascending to the top level. He strides through the first chamber and into the bedroom, kicking the doors shut behind us before he gently lowers me onto the bed of furs.

"Sit." I tug at Jyr's wing. He's staring at the wall and his entire being radiates with anger. It's beginning to piss me off.

He looks down, his head swiveling and eyes alighting on me as if I'm some tasty morsel he's just found.

"Jyr, it's okay. Look." I shove my leg forward. The red is already reducing.

He blinks and sways, then sits down heavily on the edge. His wings droop and he puts his head in his hands.

"If anything had happened to you, Viv. I don't—"He lifts his head and fixes me with a piecing gaze. "I can't be without you." He finishes, angrily thumping a fist on the ledge.

I want to comfort him, to take him against my breast and soothe the savage beast. But I can't let this go.

"Life is fatal, Jyr. I don't have to tell you that death lurks around every corner. We have to live in the moment, that's all we can do."

Listen to me, Ms. Philosopher all of a sudden. Like I took my advice, hiding away from everything all this time.

And look where that got me.

Anguish floods from Jyr, and it's as if I can taste it. His fears twist around my heart like tendrils of ivy. In return, I try to make flowers bloom, red roses, my favorite, their scent filling my head.

"Your thoughtbond. It's not like any other." Jyr murmurs, his eyes closed. I pull him into me and plant a kiss on his cheek before unfolding myself from the bed.

"What are you doing? You need to rest that leg." He exclaims.

"It's fine. What I need is to have a nice long soak." I tell him as I take off my jacket and lift my top over my head.

Jyr's dark eyes almost pop out of his head when he sees the dark red corset. It pushes my boobs up, and they spill over the top. I'm not sure I've ever felt sexier than under his gaze, especially when I see what's tenting his pants. I turn my back to him as I push my trousers down, carefully, over my injured leg and step out of them. This is swiftly followed by my new knickers. I make a show of bending over to pick up both garments. Holding them to me as I look over my shoulder at Jyr. He makes a low growling sound at the back of his throat.

"You can join me if you want, it looks like you could do with a bath." I say playfully.

Jyr looks down at himself, holding out his arms. His naked torso is streaked with black from the battle, although it only serves to make him look more like a bad angel. He spots his arousal and looks up with a mixture of anguish and lust. I turn away and walk off towards the pool, dropping my clothing and undoing my corset as I go.

I hear him pad behind me, feathers rustling, like the predator he is. I know there's only one thing on the menu tonight.

It's me, and I've never felt more alive.

JYR

I stare open-mouthed at the delicious globes of Viv's retreating ass. If I thought seeing her unclothed was erotic, seeing her partially undressed, biting her bottom lip with a hint of a smile at the corners of her lips, sent my cocks into overdrive. I could have spilled my seed then and there with no hesitation. The only thing that stopped me was remembering how delicious it was to be sheathed in her tight, wet channel.

My skin is covered in the day's filth, and my feathers itch. I don't need any more encouragement to follow my mate through to the pool. She discards the rest of her clothes and stands on the edge of the water, slightly turned towards me, displaying a full breast with its rosy nipple pert for my pleasure, as she dips her toe in, testing it.

"It's always warm, my *eregri*." I pull off my boots with indecent haste.

Viv has her back to me again. She has crouched down on the edge, presenting her rump, and my cocks weep with pre-cum. My trousers swiftly follow, but not swift enough as she has dropped into the bubbling waters, constantly refilling from the source somewhere deep in the mountains behind the lair. For an instant she drops out of sight under the surface, but bobs back up facing me, breasts bouncing.

"Are you coming in?" She asks as she lies with her back to me, propping her injured leg on the side.

Like she needs to ask. My cocks are rock solid, jutting out in front of me obscenely as I wade into the waters. The touch is like silk and only serves to make me hornier. My mate wants me. Viv eyes me over her shoulder, the curve of her breasts just visible. I wade over and move behind her, luxuriating in the scent of her skin matched with the water and the slippery sensation as I get in close, pressing my cocks up against the glorious cleft of her bottom.

"You should cleanse." I take up a cleaning cake from the side of the pool and work up some lather.

I start at her shoulders, rubbing the fragrant suds into her, moving up into her hair. It's long and the strands flow through my fingers as I tease out the dirt of the day. When I'm finished massaging her scalp, I gently pull her back so that I can rinse away the cleanser, allowing my hands to drift over her collarbone and down to cup her breasts. She lets out a soft moan.

My Viv thinks she can tease. Two can play at that game. I withdraw my hands and spend some time working up another mountain of bubbles. She wriggles against me, rubbing herself over my cocks.

"Not fair." I murmur in her ear and run my tongue around the sweet shell. "You started this."

I begin again on her shoulders, lifting her arms to clean carefully over her skin, marveling at its beauty. She moves back onto me, trying to get at least one of my cocks into her pussy. I pull my pelvis back from her, and she makes the most gorgeous sound of annoyance.

"I'm going to take you so slowly, so hard and so long." I add, pushing down over her breasts, flicking at her tight nipples with the tips of my claws. Viv arches her back, shoving her breasts into my hands.

"And I'm going to ride you until you fill me to the brim." She breathes. It takes a moment or two for her words to penetrate, and when they do, I'm only just able to stop my climax by thinking very hard about smashing joykill bots for a few seconds.

"Wicked mate. You want me to paint your back with my seed?" I shudder as I take in air, continuing with my work, ensuring she is very, very clean.

"I'm sure you'll save some for my pussy." She throws over her shoulder.

"I always have seed for your tight, pretty pussy." I run my hands down her back, around her waist and down towards the little wisp of fluff that guards the entrance to her delectable channel. I toy with her slippery folds, knowing it's not just the water that makes them slick.

I need her. I have to be inside her. With a quick motion, I have her turned towards me, one arm underneath her back. I spread her out in the warm water.

"You are so beautiful, spread for me like this." I run my fingers over her breasts, down her abdomen, marveling that Nisis would let me have something as perfect as Viv for my mate.

She is ripe in every sense of the word. Bending over her, I lap at her nipples, circling each one and sucking until it peaks with deliciousness. Viv hisses in pleasure, her hands in my hair and in my feathers, pulling and pushing at the same time. She moans my name, lifting herself to press against my abdomen. I want nothing more than to be inside her, but she needs to understand how much I worship her.

She can't keep everything from me. The thoughtbond betrays her. She still holds back, unsure of whether I have accepted her, all of her.

There is nothing I want more.

I grasp her ass in my hands and lift her out of the water so that I can explore her cunt, specifically the peak that nestles like a jewel at her entrance, with my tongue. Viv squeaks once as she comes out of the water, and I lift her onto the edge of the pool, and again when I bury my head between her thighs, her legs draped over my shoulders, heels just touching the base of my wings. I swirl my tongue into her ambrosia laden channel, eating up as much of her goodness that I can until she bucks in my arms and floods my mouth with more of her perfect moisture.

Semi-boneless, she lifts her head to fix me with her deep blue eyes.

"My turn."

VIV

Jyr is an absolute master at eating me out. My climax shakes every atom of my being.

But I want more.

I want more of my handsome bad angel. The one creature in whatever universe this is that accepts me for what I am. I certainly want to ensure that he gets what's coming to him. His desire has finally made its way into the deep, dark recesses of my being. It's awakened the part of me I hid away. The part that wasn't angry at everything. The part that wanted to have fun, to be a woman, to be free.

Jyr makes me free.

I kick back against the side of the pool and take him by surprise with my speed, pushing him into the center of the pool, I wrap my legs around his muscular waist and press my lips to his. He slides his tongue into my mouth, and I can taste myself on him. The thought makes me wetter than ever. With a bump, we come up against the side of the pool again. I know exactly what I'm going to do with him and I put a hand on his chest, gently pushing until he is sitting on the edge, leaning back on his elbows, watching me with interested dark eyes. His two enormous cocks are rigid against his six-pack. As the water runs off him, I can see that they are both oozing a pale pearly pre-cum.

A spongy sort of moss surrounds the entire pool, making a comfortable bed for my next activity, and I lift myself up, straddling him, my pussy at his head height. He grasps at my bottom and tries to pull me into him. I slap his hands away. I promised I would ride him, and those cocks are crying out to be ridden.

I lower myself down astride his slim hips until I'm kneeling over him. Taking both cocks in my hand, I can hardly get my fingers around their girths as I stroke him, feeling each nodule, each ridge. Playing with their strange bony texture that I know is so very good inside me.

"*Eregri.*" The name is a plea. He needs me.

I pull his cocks between my legs and lower myself onto them. The broad head of his primary cock breaches my tight entrance. Then, with some considerable pressure, the second one enters the same hole. I'm stretched to my limit.

"I'm not sure I can take you." I pant.

Beneath me, Jyr grins wickedly and thrusts upwards. There's an instant of pain and then he's buried inside me as I descend the rest of the way on my own, taking all of him. As I hit his pelvis, he groans, his wings beating against the soft floor.

"Too much." He breathes.

"Never. If I can take you, you can have me."

I lift up, each node on his ridged primary cock bumping against my g-spot and my walls ripple in pleasure. I plant my hands on his chest as I rock my hips, building up a rhythm and watching his gorgeous face as he tries to process what I'm doing. Soon he takes over, pumping up as he holds my hips, grinding himself into me. His pace is demanding, and the friction is intense. My climax builds and I come adrift as my pussy pulses, flooding us both with my juices. His cocks have separated inside me, and the feeling of fullness increases as he continues to pound, hard.

"I'm close, my *eregri*," he labors, sweat sheening his skin, his hair stuck to his forehead in the warm air. His fingers dig into the flesh of my hips as another orgasm sweeps through me. "I'm so close." He groans and shoves me up and off his cocks. The sudden loss of all that dirty muscle is aching. My channel pulses at nothing.

Then Jyr is drawing me back down again. His main cock slipping easily back where it belongs, I feel the pressure of his second cock at my tight ring. With its natural lubrication and everything I've covered it with, it pushes easily inside my anus, burning and stretching my underused channel.

"Fuck!" I can't help but exclaim as I'm impaled on his enormous members. Jyr wastes no time in returning to his previous pace, each cock riming me, filling me, pounding at me. I'm in a constant state of orgasm, unable to stop my convulsions, even if I wanted to.

"By Nisis!" He roars and I feel a hot stream of his cum firing from each cock, painting my walls as they ripple violently around his lengths. He fills each hole over and over, continuing to thrust into me until he is finally still, and I fall forward onto his chest, breathless and sated.

JYR

My limbs are imbued with an incredible lightness as I comb my way through my flight feathers. I hear Viv humming to herself as she attends to her needs. I woke early from a sleep that seems to have refreshed my soul. Viv and I didn't stop after we got out of the pool, not in any way. We spent the night entwined in each other, our bodies as one, while we explored the thoughtbond. My cocks rise again at the remembrance of being buried in her tight cunt.

I've already sent off a couple of mercs to retrieve Viv's new clothing. All returned unscathed from the trading post, thanks in most part to Fyn and his newfound ability to determine what Proto is doing. I smile to myself. He reminds me of when I first arrived at the lair. Full of piss and fire, with nowhere to direct my energy. It was only because none of others wanted to lead that I became Prime. The responsibility weighs heavily on me, but I'd never want to be without it. It centered me at the time. Viv centers me now.

She wanders back into the bedchamber, wearing only

the short pants and strange contraption that binds her breasts. Yet again, seeing her partially clothed has a further effect on me. I want to remove them violently.

"Don't you even dare!" Viv waggles a finger at me. "Siliza gifted me this stuff and you're not ruining it, however alpha you feel." Her blue eyes flash as I swipe at her with claws outstretched, and she dodges out of my way, laughing. "Anyway, until I get the rest of my clothes, this is all I have, so don't touch!"

"Never!" I mock growl, lunging at her until I get her in my arms and have her pinned against my chest. She squirms and pants, her hair falling in her face until she finally realizes I'm not going to damage her precious clothing, and she melts against me. I feel the warm, wet circle of her lips pressed against my chest. "I'm going to keep you like this. No clothes and no complaints."

"That could be awkward around the others." Viv throws her head back to look up at me.

"You don't have to be around the others. You are mine, Viv." This time my growl is deeper, as if I'm drawing the words up from Hyddar itself.

"How very caveman of you, Jyr. But I don't think that's going to be possible. Besides, if this is going to be my home, I'm going to have to learn some more about it." She pushes her way out of my arms and, to the disappointment of my cocks, she dresses.

My confusion at the term 'caveman' is countered by the squeeze in my heart that she might think of my lair as her home. She must have given up on the idea of going back to Earth and her notions of rescuing more humans. A thought nags at me, however. If Viv can be my fated mate, what it there to say that other Gryn might also find their mates with human females? If there aren't any Gryn females left, perhaps this is our only chance at breeding.

Except I don't even know if Viv and I can make a child. Plus, she still isn't very keen on the idea either, so I may never know. I push the thought to the back of my mind. I've neglected lair business for too long. Today I have to get on top of things and there's a vrex load of work to do. The last thing I want to do is pass Viv off to another Gryn to keep her entertained, but as she's asked about knowing more about the lair, I don't see any harm in her shadowing me.

I already know the other seniors will back me on having my mate participate. The sticking point will be Kaloz. The Gryn who disappeared as soon as Proto attacked yesterday. I can already hear Ryak's warnings echoing in my head.

"You hungry, my *eregri*?" She is bent over, pulling on her boots, her sweet ass begging to be bitten.

She straightens, flicking her hair back.

"After the night you've given me, you bet!"

She links arms with me as we walk down to the next level towards the food hall. Due to my early rising, the place is packed with warriors and full of noise. A cacophony of calls, wing beats and arguments fills my ears as they jostle each other for food and for the perceived best seats nearest the open hearth. The air is thick with the scent of many males in an enclosed space, smoke from the fire and the scent of roasting meat that makes my mouth water. Mating is a hungry business, after all.

I check on Viv and she stands, mouth slightly open, taking in the chaos that is my lair and my brother warriors. It's her first time seeing so many Gryn together at once, and I know we are a formidable sight. Her intelligent eyes take in everything.

A long, loud whistle has heads turning as one in our direction.

"Prime!" The shout goes up. Drinking vessels are raised, along with hunks of meat in salute. A drumming begins, and it runs around the room like a wave. They are high on the battle yesterday, the one we won easily. I spot the source of the whistle.

"Fyn!" I thump my fist over my heart to show my respect at the way he acquitted himself, and a roar of approval echoes around the chamber.

Warriors scramble to allow us to take the best seats and, without asking, steaming cups of cala and platters piled with select cuts of maraha are placed in front of us.

"Eat, my mate." I grin at her. "You have enchanted the Gryn as it's unheard of for any warrior to give up his meat ration." I say out loud, and a ripple of laughter spreads through the warriors surrounding us. We have not had to ration our meat for many cycles.

I see that they are keeping a reverent distance from us, trying not to crowd in on my mate, but many pairs of dark eyes are watching Viv with awed interest. She takes a bite of meat, chews it slowly, and nods.

"Delicious. My thanks to the warrior who sacrificed his meal for me." She grins at me as a buzz fills the air.

I might not have a thoughtbond with all my warriors, but I can pick up on their collective emotions. They are happy to have this tiny female in their midst. Which is understandable. So many of them would have been taken from their mothers as younglings. They won't have seen a female since, let alone been this close to one.

With a single beat of my wings, I stand on the table.

"We will shortly celebrate the arrival of my mate, my *eregri*." A hushed whisper runs through the warriors at the mention of the fate bond. "She is to be welcomed like any new warrior, and more because she is the mate of your Prime. The celebration will be in a few days, and I intend it to be one of our best!" I punch my arm in the air, filled with the joy of Viv and that my soul is complete.

From the roar that erupts at my words, not only do my warriors agree, but they are going to make this a celebration to remember, or not, depending on how much var beer is drunk. I look down at my little mate. She regards me with interest, half a smile quirking the corner of her mouth. She raises her cup of cala in a toast and my heart swells in my chest.

VIV

I can see why Jyr built a nest for us. Since he announced the celebration, we've not been left alone. First there was a stream of rather over excited mercs wanting to congratulate us and have a good gawp at me. Feathers rustling, swaggering as they approached us. Then tucking their wings hard behind them, curiosity and something I can't quite put my finger on, any alpha posturing forgotten in an instant as they stand next to me. Their dark eyes filled with wonder and their mouths filled with nothing but promises of assistance and 'anything the Prime or his lady needs'.

A lifetime ago, this attention would have been my worst nightmare, but I bear it with as good grace as I can until finally Jyr claps his hands and shoos them away, dissipating any grumblings by pointing out we are not going anywhere and will be back in the food hall later.

Like we're some sort of rock star couple.

Jyr's certainly got the bad boy vibe down perfectly, even if I'm the silent bass player. Once he's gotten rid of most of the room, his seniors appear like mist, all except Kaloz, and take their seats next to us.

"Celebration time." Kyt rubs his hands together enthusiastically. I get the impression he's a bit of a party animal, given any opportunity. "The brewer says we should have plenty of Var beer ready. I've already primed the Mochi for more maraha."

"Excellent." Jyr smiles. "We'll do the mating ceremony in two cycles."

"Wait, what?" I interject. "Were you going to ask me if I wanted any of this, Jyr?" I know I shouldn't be speaking to him like this in front of his seniors, but, even if I accept that this place is going to be my home, it doesn't mean that he can make all the decisions. I fold my arms and give him my best death stare.

Jyr rubs at the back of his neck, his wings drooping back. "Do you want to get mated, Viv?" He asks.

Broad grins appear on the faces of Kyt and Ryak. Even Myk has a hint of a smile.

"It's not the most romantic proposal, I suppose," I grumble.

Although the food hall is like a medieval castle, with the huge fire burning in the hearth, fragrant wood smoke filling the air, and I do have an extremely handsome bad angel sitting in front of me, bare chested as always. I guess it's not completely unromantic. Jyr's chiseled form looks like it's been sculpted in the flickering light. An alien angel who's asking me to be his equivalent of a wife.

It's not like I had any proposals before, of any kind. So, it could be said that this is *the* most romantic proposal I've ever had. Still, I'm going to leave my alpha mate squirming like a worm on the end of a hook for a little longer.

"What do humans do when they want to have a mating

ceremony?" The taciturn Ryak asks, his eyes, dancing with mirth, betray him.

"We call it marriage, although it's not the same as a mate bond because humans don't always bond for life." Jyr huffs at my words. "Not all humans though." I add hastily. "My parents were probably what you call bonded. They were devoted to each other." I say, trying to make my species sound a bit better than we actually are. That I didn't just abandon them after we argued.

"And if humans want marriage to each other, do they follow a ceremony?" Ryak is not going to give up and at least it stops my babbling.

"It's traditional that when a human man wants to marry a human woman, he gets down on one knee in front of her and gives her a ring." And when I say it out loud, it sounds pathetic.

Kyt snorts into his cup of brown stuff. The liquid was hot when I first tried it, but savory, rather like gravy. Not unpleasant, but given the amount of meat piled up on my plate, not what I want first thing in the morning. As it cooled, it tasted a little more like coffee and was reasonably palatable.

Three dark pairs of eyes fix on Jyr and the air becomes heavy with anticipation. Myk delves into a pocket and shoves something across the table. He pushes it into Jyr's hand and Kyt gives his Prime a firm shove with one wing, grinning from ear to ear.

I watch, half horrified, half amused as the huge Gryn warrior rises above me, wings slightly open, then sinks down onto his knees in front of me.

"Will you..." He hesitates and clears his throat, looking nervously at the surrounding warriors. "Viv, will you be my mate?" He looks up at me under long dark eyelashes, his handsome face nervous as if this is a big deal. He proffers up a purple metal ring that is bracelet size and I realize that to the Gryn, a ring is not jewelry. It's just, well, a ring.

The three other warriors lean forward in anticipation of my answer. It even looks like Jyr is holding his breath.

Here goes nothing.

"Yes, Jyr. I will be your mate."

After all, what choice do I have? And how could I possibly say no?

JYR

I slip the ring that Viv said she wanted over her hand, which she holds out to me. It was lucky that Myk had a ring with him, then the swordsmith always seemed to have an assortment of items in his deep pockets. Humans have some strange customs, it appears.

Kyt lets out a whoop of joy and punches the air at Viv's answer. Ryak chuckles and Myk claps his hands on his thighs, a hint of a smile twitching at his mouth. All three radiate down our thoughtbond of their pleasure at my mate's acceptance.

Viv is smiling too. I lean into her, capturing her mouth with a kiss. It's the natural way to conclude this strange ceremony, with an action that is entirely human. When we part, all of my seniors are fascinated.

"It's a kiss." I tell them, trying not to sound smug. "Something else humans do and which I think is a great idea."

Kyt nods, sagely. Ryak and Myk give nothing away. I don't pay much attention to what mating my warriors do, providing they take care what they mate. Even so, I'm not sure if Kyt has ever mated with any species. Ryak and Myk are different. Myk lost his mate many turns ago. Ryak is a closed door. He can even conceal his feelings regarding mating from me.

"I need to see Fyn." I announce. "He did a good job yesterday, and it's about time he was given some more responsibility."

"Might keep him out of trouble." Kyt grumbles.

"Why, what did he do now?"

Kyt looks shifty, clamping his mouth shut.

"More fighting?"

"A Gryn only has to look at him the wrong way and he's in there." Ryak says. "Luckily there were only two of them that needed Orvos's attentions this time."

I breathe out a hot sigh and feel Viv's hand on my arm. Looking down, I see my ring encircling her slim wrist, and my chest swells with pride.

"Don't be too hard on him, like you say, he did well." She says softly.

"He's on a rest cycle today." Ryak inspects his claws. "I'll send him up to your chambers." He turns to Viv, "I have delivered your purchases from yesterday, my lady Prime. I hear you made some excellent choices."

I never knew Ryak was capable of charm, but he smiles a secret smile for Viv, and she giggles, tossing her hair over her shoulder. Red sheets my vision and she's in my arms even as my growl rends the air.

"Hey!" There's a pulse of discontent in my thoughtbond that rapidly turns to something pink and fluffy filling my brain.

A small hand touches my cheek and my mind stills as I drown in the blue eyes of my mate. "You can put me down, hun. I'm not going anywhere."

"Hun?" I hear Kyt behind me, dissolving into laughter. I

treat him to the benefit of one of my best Prime snarls, but he's not put off, not in the slightest.

"See what you've started?" I grumble at my mate, taking her hand in mine as we leave the food hall and return to my quarters.

Viv squeals with delight when she sees the slightly scorched packages laid out on my table. She piles them into her arms and rushes through into the bedchamber, where I hear further exclamations of delight as the wrappings are removed.

"You wanted to see me, Prime." Fyn slouches insolently in the doorway, his strange pale eyes baleful.

"I hear you've been fighting again." I admonish him.

"So?" He really is full of fight, even after yesterday, when there was more than enough battle enough to go around.

"I have clean knickers!" An exclamation comes from my bedchamber. "Clean knickers!"

I stare at Fyn and he stares back at me. Eventually, he cracks.

"What are 'knickers'?" He asks.

"I've no idea," I sigh, sitting down at the table and indicating for Fyn to join me. "This is as new to me as it is to the lair."

Fyn's serious expression softens slightly. "I think having a female around might be a good experience."

"You do?" I try to keep the growl out of my voice. Viv is my female and no one else's.

Fyn cocks his head at the sound of feminine squeals of enjoyment as further ripping takes place. "I think we all miss females." He says wistfully.

I see the image of a Gryn female, large above me. Fyn is thinking of his mother, presumably the last female he remembers.

"Before I found you, did Proto do anything to you?" I ask him, carefully.

"The usual experiments." Fyn replies dismissively.

I drum my claws on the tabletop. "Okay, Fyn. This fighting of yours has to stop. I can't risk mercs being injured, and we need everyone fit for work. We're stretched thin as it is."

"I can't help it. When they wind me up..." He blows out a breath, folding his arms and sitting back in his seat.

"Wind you up how?"

"My eyes. I'm not a 'proper' Gryn. I'm not a warrior." He mutters, not prepared to meet my gaze.

"Vrex that!" I fire at him. "You are more warrior than most of them, especially after yesterday, which is why I'm promoting you. Enforcer status. See Myk for your marker." All the more senior Gryn have a metal band that sits above their right bicep. "Ryak will be your direct senior, report to him."

I stand, wanting to check on my mate, as it's gone suspiciously quiet in my bedchamber. Fyn scrambles to his feet.

"Thank you, Prime." He gabbles out. "I won't let you down." He looks over my shoulder and executes a small bow. Viv is standing in the doorway, holding an item of clothing in one hand. "My lady, Prime." He greets her, formally.

"Be sure that you don't." I tell him sternly. "One more thing," I call out after him. He flares his wings and comes to a halt. "You are to make yourself available for my mate's personal guard whenever needed."

I might want to keep Viv all to myself, but if all Fyn sees in my mate is the mirror of his long-lost mother, I can trust him. He flashes me a grin that seems out of place on such a serious warrior, and then he's gone.

"Looks like you've won over another warrior, my *eregri*." I stalk back to my mate. "You're still always mine, however."

Viv's eyes dance with mirth and lust as she puts a hand on her hip, watching my every movement.

"And how can any woman resist you?" She laughs, throwing her arms around my neck as I lift her off her feet and carry her towards the bed.

VIV

The scale of Jyr's operation becomes clearer as the days pass. I still can't claim to be completely happy about some aspects of what the Gryn do, but having seen them in action at the trading post, and hearing from Siliza that the other species are grateful for what the Gryn offer, I can accept the protection part better than the other things, such as the stealing and, in particular, the drugs.

Jyr has been careful to keep me away from the labs at the base of the lair. I think because he knows how I feel and he's keen that I don't say anything that might annoy Kaloz.

That particular Gryn has been at pains to avoid me. Unlike the rest of the lair, it seems. As I get to know my way around, we fall into a rhythm of work and play. I try to help where I can. Pytr, who has appointed himself as unofficial spokes-gryn for the younger mercs, many of whom are a similar age to him, finds me various mending tasks that I rather enjoy.

I should run a mile from all this attention, but with Jyr by my side, the big Gryn glowering at every merc that approaches me to ask a question about humans or to simply be near me, it doesn't seem so bad. They don't know what I was on Earth. They can't see my scars. Their curiosity is endearing, and for a bunch of fearsome predators, they are actually rather sweet.

Not that I dare tell Jyr that I could scoop up his supposedly terrifying warriors and cuddle them, especially the really young ones. Every time I make one smile, for instance, they walk away with little springs in their steps, feathers all puffed up.

So fluffy I could die!

The interest does get a bit much, and we've taken to eating at least one meal a day in Jyr's chambers for a bit of peace, although we're often joined by Kyt and Ryak. Kyt is highly entertaining, and I don't mind his company at all. Ryak likes to project an image of a brooding warrior, but he's as giddy as the mercs inside. I can feel his delight through the thoughtbond. He misses females.

Myk lets me watch him making the weapons. His ability to craft just about anything out of metal is a true skill. I get the impression he tolerates my presence in his warm workshop, even if he doesn't say much. His thoughtbond pales from his usual dark swirl to a lighter blue when I'm near his furnace.

Most of Jyr's day is spent checking up on the various patrols, barters, and supply runs. I'm struggling to contain my inner organizer when I can see ways to improve their operation. It's not for me to interfere, and part of me doesn't want to be tainted by the illicit, at least on Earth, work that they do. The other part constantly reminds me that the Gryn have to survive. As it turns out, Jyr was exaggerating about the stealing. They don't take anything from the other species, only raiding Proto for stores.

I've seen some of the young mercs under the influence of the drugs that Kaloz peddles, and it wasn't pretty. Jyr clams up entirely when I raise my objections, closing off his thoughtbond as far as he can. The only concession he has made has been to ban any narcotics from our celebration.

"Do all Gryn have the thoughtbond?" I ask him as he is working through scraps of ancient paper, scribbled with Gryn hieroglyphics. The paper is incongruous, looking like it was torn from long forgotten pads, till rolls and the backs of books. It's mottled with age and every part of it is covered in writing, nothing is wasted.

"Most Gryn develop the bond with their family, and later, with their mate." He says absently, scratching at the paper with a feather quill.

"But Kyt, Ryak and Myk aren't your family, are they? Why do you have the thoughtbond with them?"

Jyr's head jerks up, his dark eyes swirling. "How do you know I have a thoughtbond with them?"

"I feel it between you all when we're together. I feel their emotions too. How far does it work? Can you feel them when you were at your nest?" I have so many questions. The more time I've spent around Jyr and his seniors, the more confusing things have become.

"You feel them too?" Jyr's voice is a low growl. "You have a mate thoughtbond with my seniors?"

"No. No!" I cry out. My bond is nothing like that with Jyr. Even now, his anger sheets red across my vision, and I desperately attempt to soothe him.

Jyr stands, suddenly, all seven feet of him looming over me, his dark wings unfurling and becoming the deadly weapons of the predator he is.

"You are my mate, mine alone! If my warriors turn your head, I will take you to my nest and claim you until you grow ripe with my child, to prove to them you are my mate. Any that dare look at you will lose their wings!" He roars, papers flying everywhere, as he claps his wings together thunderously.

In a single bound, he is over the table and has my chin pinched between his clawed thumb and finger. "Your thoughts are mine, little female. All of you is mine." There's a blackness that has descended around us, like a veil. "Mine." He growl-mutters, his eyes fixed on my face as if he is about to devour me like a plate of raw maraha.

And I can feel his heart beating in his chest as surely as my own. His desire to keep me to himself, the one I witnessed just after I'd dropped out of a spaceship, it rears up, all-encompassing. I'm struggling to see my way past it, and I know Jyr can't.

I jerk my chin out of his grip, retreating a couple of steps. I've faced my mortality and just because this big handsome alien male has said a few nice things and smells divine, it doesn't mean he owns me, or control me.

"Fuck you, Jyr! This thoughtbond, it's your doing. Humans have nothing like it. If it's not working as you expect, then that's not my fucking fault."

My expletive laden speech has him blinking in surprise until his brow furrows and the bad angel returns. "You are here for my benefit and mine alone. Don't forget that, female." He spits out, turning on his heel and sweeping out of the chamber in a flourish of feathers. His great wings beating as he descends the central shaft.

"I'm here because I want to be and nothing else." I call after him, pathetically. A lie.

I've always been good at lying to myself. Even better at hiding the truth from others. A Jyr shaped hole appears in my life and the emptiness he leaves is worse than anything

I've experienced. I retreat to the bedchamber, sitting beside the bed and hugging my knees to me.

I don't want to be alone anymore, and Jyr just did what he does best.

Fly away from a problem he can't solve by growling.

JYR

ow can Viv have a connection with other Gryn? Anger seethes through my veins, boiling and removing any vestige of civility. I need a fight, and I need one with an immediacy that has my claws extending and my nostrils begging for the tang of blood.

The training pits are where I should go. There's always a merc prepared to try his luck, maybe earn a favor or two from another Gryn, whether that be a better cut of maraha, a flagon of Var beer, some assistance with preening, or, more of late, some of Kaloz's blasted relaxants that have become more prevalent in the lair. The unfocussed gaze of a warrior, reclining anywhere he can as the drugs course through his system, greets me too often.

This is not what I agreed to when Kaloz and the others from his lair joined us. It's yet another reason I should heed Ryak's warnings. Kaloz corrupts us and he corrupts the lair. We might have been 'criminals' before he arrived, as my mate put it. But the various tribes of the Mochi and Kijg requested our protection more often than not. It's been a long time since we had to 'suggest' it was available if they knew what was good for them.

Another thing that I cannot ignore is why my Command disappeared during a fight with Proto at the trading post, something else that shows his lack of respect for me and the lair. Something else that boils my blood.

I land on a darkened ledge, some way from the training level. All this thinking has dissipated my anger and now I feel drained. I'm not proud of how I started the lair, by forcing my presence on the other species in return for food and supplies, but the mercs that I gathered in the early days needed more help to recover from what Proto had done to them. These days, the mercs are relatively unharmed by Proto. Kept for fighting and then healed. Still, not a single one had ever asked to stay in the camps. I drop my head into my hands, trying to force out the thoughts of the torture Proto inflicted on me, amplified by the thoughtbonds that linked me to my seniors.

And the days after when we writhed and shuddered in Orvos's care.

There's the sound of footsteps and feathers rustling in the corridor behind me, and I freeze in the shadows.

"Why don't you ask Pytr to ask lady Prime to look." There are two mercs stood not too far from me. Young ones by the color of their wing feathers, only just old enough to take part in the patrols. I must be on a barrack level. "She knows about things like this."

I lean forward, craning my neck to see why they are talking about my mate and what they want her to look at.

"I heard she helped Lynd." I see that one merc holds a piece of fabric, torn nearly in two. "But—" His breath hitches. "It's just it was my mother's...it's all I have of her."

His voice tails off. The second youngster puts a hand on his shoulder.

"She's good at helping. Did you not hear that Fyn got promoted? He's on the Prime's side, and he's already made sure we all get more maraha and proper rest cycles. Lady Prime did that."

I know Pytr was in my outer chamber not that long ago, speaking with Kyt. He's often around, but as he's deferential, I tolerate his presence. I got caught up in the lair business and as long as Viv's by my side; I didn't pay much attention to what she was doing. Now I come to think about it, she's been working away on something the last few cycles and my curiosity overtakes me.

"What's going on here?" I boom out, revealing myself as I stride towards the two mercs. The first shoves the fabric behind his back, scrubbing at a cheek. He puffs out his chest, making himself look bigger and braver than he clearly is.

"Prime." They both execute a bow and remain silent.

"Names?" I snap.

"Ryn." The merc without the fabric, says, quietly. "This is Oly."

"What do you have there, Oly?" I lean to one side, trying to see behind him. His breath stutters in his chest and with some reluctance, he brings his hand from behind his back.

"It was his mother's. It got damaged." It's a scarf, once brightly colored, now faded with age.

"How?" Ryn and Oly look at each other, then down at their feet.

"Fine. You don't have to tell me. Why do you want to take this to my mate?"

"Pytr says she knows how to fix things, things that we have and that she's already fixed stuff for Lynd and this was

Oly's mother's. He only wants it fixed, Prime. That's all. Lady Prime is kind, Pytr says. He says she does these things because she wants to." Ryn's stream of consciousness finally tails off in the heat of my glare.

Rest now, sweetheart. Orvos will look after you, Jyr will look after you.

Viv didn't have to do anything. She could have never glanced at a single merc, and I wouldn't have been bothered. Instead, she's been watching, taking it all in and becoming part of the lair under my nose.

Not only that, but she has become a good part. A part where the mercs care about her. Where they think her kind and approachable, unlike me. But I have to be aloof and dangerous, or the lair would cease to exist. There was no room for softness in my existence. But Viv? She's gained the trust of the younger mercs. Maybe of more. And she's done it all in such a short time.

Perhaps I've underestimated what this lair is, and what it needs. I can provide food, shelter, and training. I can provide an outlet for male exuberance. I can provide gainful employment. But have I provided a home? One where they want to stay, and grow and be part of our family? Have I even provided a family?

I want nothing more than to see my mate grow ripe with my child in her belly, but if I can't even help my own kind have a comfortable, secure existence, how can I provide that for my young? My stupid, mate bond induced jealousy has blinded me to what Viv is to me, and to my warriors.

"Come with me. Let's see if Lady Prime can help." I say, turning away and heading back to the shaft, two eager young mercs trotting behind me.

VIV

J yr stands in front of two mercs, arms folded across his permanently bare chest. Other than Myk, who wears a heavy leather apron and Kyt with his long coat, none of the Gryn bother with clothing on their upper half. Their heavy, leathery skin providing them with enough protection from the elements.

The pair of youngsters look around the outer chamber with terrified eyes, their wings drooping behind them.

"What do you want?" I mirror his pose, leaning against the doorframe to the bedchamber. "How can I be of *benefit* to you?" I parrot his words back, their taste ugly on my tongue. I hate he made me feel bad earlier, and I've done enough hating to last a lifetime.

Jyr reaches behind him, grabbing one of the young mercs and pulling him forward.

"Apparently, you've been helping a merc called Lynd fix something. Well, this one needs something fixing too. Show her!" He demands of the warrior.

A couple of emotions flit across the merc's face. Terror,

pain and finally bravery. He holds out a tattered piece of material to me.

"Oh, and how is this of benefit to you?" I don't move. Jyr's features soften slightly.

"It would please me if you helped this merc with his problem." He says, still imperious. I turn my head away and look at the wall. "It was his mother's." Jyr adds.

I look back at the three of them. The two mercs continue to look terrified to be in the presence of their Prime. Jyr has unfolded his arms, and he holds the palms of his hands towards me.

"If you could fix it for Oly, it would only be for his benefit."

"And you're okay with that?" I hold out my hand for the material, keeping my eyes on Jyr.

"If my mercs are happy, I'm happy." He says, some of the old bravado returning.

"As long as you're happy." I mutter, inspecting the torn fabric. "Yes, I can fix this, Oly." I give the young merc a smile. It's not his fault his Prime is a jerk of the highest order. "Are you okay to leave it with me for a few turns?"

Oly looks over his shoulder at his friend, who nods.

"Yes, Lady Prime." He says to me, although he looks longingly at the bundle in my hands.

"I'll take good care of it for you, sweetheart." I say quietly.

"Right, that's taken care of," Jyr claps his hands loudly, "now vrex off the pair of you."

The two mercs don't need telling twice and they scramble to get out of Jyr's quarters, although not before Oly has one last look at the material.

Sometimes I want to strangle Jyr, and this is one of those times. Except while my attention has been on stowing the precious material safely, he has moved beside me, strong arms wrapping around me and a head nuzzling in the crook of my neck.

"*Eregri*, my *eregri*." He murmurs. "I underestimate you at every turn. I am a fool. What have you been doing to capture my warrior's attention so?"

I breathe his strong spicy scent deep into my lungs. His wings surround us, blocking out the lair, blocking out everything.

"Pytr asked me to mend a few items for some of the younger ones. They don't have much and some of the things remind them of their families. I've always been crafty, and it was a way of thanking them for making me welcome." I explain.

Jyr lifts his head. "You like it here?" He asks, a hint of anguish in his voice.

"I like it when you're not being an alpha dick."

"But you like my alpha dick." Jyr exposes his sharp canines, and I feel a pulse between my thighs.

I didn't consider myself insatiable but having a gorgeous alien who loves nothing more than to eat me out has awakened a dormant sex drive in me which is becoming impossible to contain.

"Don't think you're forgiven, Jyr. You were the one yelling 'mine' and stomping off. But I don't mind it here, not that I have much choice. I think there are some things that could be changed, for the better. Still, it's okay and I could get used to it."

Jyr's grin fades. "Just get used to it?" His skin looks pale. "I'd like you to stay."

"Because I'm going to go where? Back to Earth? You've already told me that's impossible." And from what Kyt's told me, the chances of the Gryn moving from the Dark Ages to something that resembles the twenty-first century is unlikely to happen anytime soon.

"I'd like you to want to stay." Jyr says, his shoulders dropping. "Because—" He hesitates, clawed hands twisting together with his discomfort, "The lair needs you. I need you."

He drops his head back onto my neck, his tongue already lapping at my skin. His hands slipping under my top, claws scrabbling at the catches on my corset.

He needs me.

I didn't think anyone would need me ever again. I resigned myself to not being close, or intimate, or anything with anyone. But on this strange, dystopian planet, I have found an alien who can't get enough of me. Who wants me in his bed without a trace of disgust at my damaged body. An alien who wants me by his side as well as in his bed.

I allow him to strip off my top and corset without shredding them. He falls on my naked breasts, devouring my nipples hungrily. I palm his huge lengths through his pants and his hips snap towards me. He pushes me back towards the table, leaning me back onto the warm wooden surface, he releases a nipple from his mouth with a soft pop in order to prop my legs up against his chest and he pulls off my boots, one by one, grinning as he throws them over his shoulder. My trousers follow suit. Jyr stares down at me.

"So beautiful. Do you need me, my *eregri*?"

Do I need him? Do I need a male that yells that I'm his and calls me beautiful? Do I need one that brings me his young proteges because they have a problem? Do I need this leader, this Prime?

"I want you, Jyr. Inside me. Now." I demand as he parts my legs, rubbing his huge hands down my thighs. He puts a foot on each shoulder.

"But do you need me?" He asks again. I'm pinned by him, one hand pushes aside the crotch of my knickers, a clawed finger toying with my folds. The tip touches my clit, and I shudder, my core clenching at nothing, at the emptiness I want filled by Jyr.

I need him to fill me.

"I need you inside me, Jyr. Take me, take me now." I mew desperately. With a flick of his hand, his trousers are undone, and he's stroking both cocks.

"You need both my cocks? Inside you?"

"Yes, please, please, Jyr!" I beg, pushing at my knickers, attempting to free myself, to be entirely naked in his presence.

He chuckles as the panties are spirited off my body, tossed over his shoulder to join the rest of my clothing.

"Spread for me, my *eregri*. Perfect for my cocks."

He delves a thick finger into my channel, curling it as if beckoning me and he hits my g-spot perfectly. I convulse over him, milking at his digit for all I'm worth, panting his name in ecstasy. He raises his hand to his face and laps my juices from his soaking hand. I feel a further pressure at my entrance. Looking down my torso, I see his thick cocks pushing at me, slipping in easily. They might be large, but my orgasm eases their passage until he's buried deep in me.

"Look at my cocks, stretching your pretty cunt so wide." Jyr marvels. "Stretching you for me."

He grasps my ankles and withdraws to thrust back into me, his pelvis circling as he picks up the pace. I spread my arms out, my breath short with his invasion, with the fullness both his cocks provide. Jyr is pounding at me, and I feel my climax rising. How can he get my body to sing like this? Every nerve ending is both blunt and alive at the same time. I can't close my eyes or I'd miss his stupid, alien handsome face, his lips curled back as he drips with sweat and his wings rise, open and beating every once in a while as he takes me, hard and fast.

"Do you need me?" He grinds his hips against my clit and I see stars. "Do you want my seed, my *eregri*."

"Yes! I need you!" In that moment, I want nothing but Jyr and the joining of our bodies, the heat and the fire, the obscene sounds as he works at me. The explosion in my loins as my orgasm crashes over me, lifting my hips up and up so that he can plow me deeper, so he can take me completely.

Jyr splits the air with a roar, thumping into me with irregular thrusts as he comes, his hot cum filling me, heating me from the inside. A sharp pain hits as something hard forces its way inside me. Jyr stills, only his hips shifting slightly. He lowers my legs from his shoulders and drops forward over me, his breathing ragged.

Too late, I realize what I've done. The one thing I said I wouldn't do. I've let him come with both cocks. Panic sets in and I squirm away. Except I can't move. Jyr is still in me and it feels like he's stuck.

"Jyr!" I exclaim. His head is drooped, his eyes closed. "What's going on?"

"My second cock has swelled with my seed, my *eregri*. I cannot move until it subsides."

"We're stuck." I wriggle again, but it hurts, and I stop.

"It will subside soon. It is only to keep my seed inside you. To better ensure it takes root." Jyr raises his head, eyes half lidded with the aftermath of his climax.

"How long?"

"I've never experienced it before. My second cock never stirred until I met you. But that was glorious, so good." He sighs with contentment.

"Jyr, I didn't mean for this to happen. I still don't know if I want a baby." I say, keeping my voice even.

My initial panic dissipates as I contemplate if that's still what I believe. I feel stupid for getting carried away, like some silly teenager. I'm so used to being able to control myself, to control every aspect of my life, that giving some of that away seems...

Liberating.

"Viv," Jyr gasps, "I'm so sorry. I-" There is an audible pop, and he withdraws, his seed spilling out of me onto the table. "I should have thought."

I sit up. He stands in front of me, head bowed. His lust and confusion warring in a gray cloud on the thoughtbond. He thinks he has wronged me. I wrap my arms around his slim waist and press my cheek against his hard abs.

"What's done is done. I guess it has to be your fault."

"Yes, my *eregri*." He says, his voice weak.

"Because you're so damn sexy, you make me want you. You take my thoughts and toss them away. I forget myself around you." I grin up at him, and his face slowly brightens.

"I didn't do wrong?" Realization dawns and a very naughty smile appears.

"We don't know if I can even get pregnant by you." I say as Jyr frowns, "Yes, I know you think you have super sperm or something." I shrug, *like every male ever,* I add silently. "But we are different species after all."

"Does that mean we can try again?" He asks, like an eager puppy.

JYR

"Is everything set for the eve?" I finally catch up with Kyt, who is currently working through the recent supplies the mercs have delivered inside the huge cavern that we use for our stores. The live maraha low to each other in one corner. The big, six legged blue beasts blinking their three eyes and chewing at the grass that the Mochi deliver with them.

"We're all set, Jyr." Kyt is wreathed in smiles. "This is going to be one Hyddar of a celebration. Most of the mercs have been hoarding their var beer rations and," he lowers his voice, "I've got the Kijg to part with some of their cizz wine."

"Vrex!" I exclaim, and Kyt hushes me. "What did that cost us?" I ask, quieter.

"Nothing, they are happy with our patrols and wanted to help with the celebrations."

I stand back and fold my arms. Nothing comes for free on Ustokos, not anymore.

"Okay, well." Kyt rubs the back of his neck. "They said they would like some additional patrols on their eastern border. Apparently, they've been having problems with joykills."

That seems more like it.

"Looks like you've got everything in hand. I'm going to see to my mate. She's a little nervous about the mating ceremony."

"Tell her she's nothing to fear, the lair loves her almost as much as their Prime." Kyt calls after me.

A few cycles ago, that comment would have made my blood boil. But recently lair business has never seemed as interesting. I feel renewed, reinvigorated after my mating with Viv. The lair feels different too. The atmosphere lighter, virtually no fighting outside of the pits. Training sessions are better attended, and Ryak has reported that tardiness for patrols and supply runs has decreased. For once, in a long time, it is as if the Gryn is the unity all over again.

Surely this isn't because of Viv?

She has shown me the work she has been doing for the young mercs, and, as it turns out, some of the older ones. In the main, it's been mending scraps and small toys. Orvos has also asked her to make regular appearances in the surgery when there are casualties as, he claims, they get better faster. Her presence is a benefit to us all that I didn't expect.

Her insistence that we all try to consume more vegetation is less welcome. At least tonight it will be all maraha and var beer. And no narcotics, by general order.

A merc is leaving my chamber when I arrive, clutching something in his hand, he gives me a terrified stare, but I clap him on the wing as he hurries away. I can hear Viv muttering to herself in the bedchamber, and after making sure the doors to the outer chamber are fastened to avoid any more merc visits that will disturb us, I make my way through.

She stands next to the bed with her back to me, dressed in nothing but her underwear. As usual, it causes my cocks to rise as I take in her creamy skin on display and think about what is underneath the skimpy pieces of fabric. I'm not sure she is aware of me as I stalk up behind her and wrap my arms around her warm body in a pincer movement. She snuggles back at me with a happy hum.

"Looking forward to the eve, my *eregri*?"

"As long as you're there." She says as I bring my wings around to cover her and envelop us. Viv combs her fingers through my flight feathers. "Because the whole lair is going to be at the celebration, isn't it?"

"The lair is waiting for us to announce our bond, my mate. It's been a long time since any Gryn was able to take a mate, let alone find their *eregri*. This is a special moment for them."

Viv takes in a shuddering breath. "I guess." She hesitates. I drop a couple of her kisses to her bare shoulders.

"There is no guess. The lair loves you nearly as much as I do."

Viv twists in my arms to face me. "You love me?"

Her eyes shine bright and clear, liquid hovering in them. I lean into her, ensuring that we are entirely encompassed by my wings.

"Of course, I love you. You are my fated one. Without you, I have nothing. You are mine. I am to protect you, care for you and our young. Should anything attempt to take you from me, I will destroy them. That is my vow to you and my pledge." I whisper in her ear.

Viv's entire body vibrates. Her eyes close, tracks of two tiny droplets running down her cheeks.

"That is the most incredible thing anyone has ever said to me," she says, pressing her wet face against my chest. "I always thought I was unloveable, even before my accident, before I was marked out as different. I'm difficult." She looks back up at me. "You mean it, don't you?"

I find it hard to believe that any species wouldn't want to claim my *eregri*. Her perfect face tilting up and her long golden hair hanging down her back. Why she is concerned that a small part of her beautiful body bears the mark of an act that meant she saved two of her kind, I don't know.

"I mean it. You are the most beautiful creature I've ever set eyes on. My heart is yours, if you want it."

"Oh, Jyr." She sighs, her arms around my waist and her cheek against my skin again and then lets go. "What do you think of this to wear tonight?"

She twirls away from me, not answering my offer, and picks up a long gown from the bed. She drops it over her head and the featherlight material descends over her curves, clinging in all the right places. The embroidery around the collar is reminiscent of ancient Gryn text. I hadn't thought she could look any better, but the gown completes her.

"I think I'll be the envy of all the Primes that the Gryn have ever had tonight."

I just hope I have her heart, too.

VIV

I take Jyr's hand as he leads me out of his chambers. The whole lair is lit by tiny, dancing lights that look like fireflies. It's almost magical. Jyr smiles when he sees my reaction and tips me into his arms as, with a single beat of his powerful wings, he drops through the central shaft, and we land just outside the food hall.

He loves me.

My heart sings. It nearly stopped when he said the words, only restarting with a stutter when I knew I had to go on, to stay alive for him. To stay with this huge, winged alien. The leader of a gang of misfits and lost warriors. The leader of Ustokos' main protection racket, weapons trader, and drug empire. The male that has taken my heart and flown away with it.

So why couldn't I tell him how I felt? I saw it in his eyes, it was all he wanted from me. Something so simple it should have been easy for me to say.

That I love him, too.

He offered me his heart, and I could have given him mine. I still can. If I want to. Jyr looks at me as we stand outside the doors to the food hall, a loud drumming coming from within. He has furrowed his brows in a way that I know means he's trying to work out the thoughtbond. I put up a white wall to keep him from my swirling emotions, and to block out the emotions of all the Gryn in the lair. I've not told Jyr the extent of my links with the others, not after he reacted before.

The more time I spend here, the more I never want to leave. Jyr is everything to me and the rest of the Gryn are the sweetest bunch of bad angels a girl could hope to meet. And I still couldn't tell him how I feel. Because I spent too long not able to love myself. If I say the words out loud, what if he rejects them?

"Are you ready, my *eregri*?" He asks.

"Ready as I'll ever be." I reply, giving his hand a squeeze. He pushes at the doors to the hall, and they swing open to a roar that almost lifts the roof of the huge cavernous space.

"Gryn!" A voice splits through the sound. "Your Prime and his mate. Salute them, respect them and above all, show them your approval." It's Fyn making the toast.

I didn't think it was possible for the assembled warriors to make any more noise, but I was wrong. The shout that assaults my ears is incredible.

'THE GRYN IS UNITY! ALL HAIL PRIME! ALL HAIL LADY PRIME!'

I almost stumble back at the volume and at the sea of faces that are looking at me. This should be my worst nightmare, but with Jyr at my side, it's the complete opposite.

I am accepted.

Jyr holds up his hands, opening his wings wide.

"My warriors, my fellow Gryn. Today is a new chapter for us all. Today is the day you celebrate a successful mating, and I promise that this will not be the last." A ripple of feathers being shuffled fills the room. Jyr holds his hands higher.

"My *eregri*, my Viv," he addresses me. "You have accepted my ring, but I ask you to accept my mating lock to bind us for eternity." He takes my hand and Myk steps up next to us, holding out two bands, one large, one small. "Will you accept my lock?"

It's as if all the breath has been squeezed out of my body. His gesture is unexpected and with all eyes upon me, I should feel pressured. But I don't. I feel special, and I feel loved.

"I do." My throat is hoarse, but I can get the words out. I slip out of my jacket and allow Jyr to slide the banding up my arm and onto my bicep. It settles there, warm and almost glowing, as if it has become part of my skin.

I pick up the second band and inspect it. It is the same color as mine, a deep glowing red, and my fingers tingle as I touch it. Jyr's dark eyes meet mine and I push it over his hand and up his arm to place it on his huge bicep. Without warning, tears spring to my eyes and spill down my cheeks.

"My mate." I whisper and wrap my arms around his torso, inhaling deeply his delicious musk.

The room erupts around us, and I find I'm grinning from ear to ear at being with Jyr and accepted by the lair.

"She has chosen me!" Jyr crows. "Now, my glorious legion, drink, eat, enjoy. This eve, we celebrate!"

Jyr grabs me, and I'm lifted into the air as he does a circuit of the room with me squealing in his arms, before he lands at the one empty table. I see that his chair from the szent has been moved and next to it is a slightly smaller version of his, equally beautifully crafted. Jyr ushers me to sit, and the mercs fall over themselves to put two great flagons in front of us and platters piled with meat, along with several more piled with vegetables.

Not quite what I was used to on Earth, it's a sort of red and blue alien broccoli, which was always green when I was a child and more recently morphed into being purple and 'sprouting', so I can't exactly complain about the color. The entire hall is buzzing with laughter and noise. A huge fire crackles in the hearth as more maraha are roasting. I eat my vegetables and enjoy the scene.

I'm not sure I've ever seen this many Gryn together, but in the here and now they resemble a dysfunctional family brought together by Jyr. I look at my mate. He's currently downing another flagon of the ale he calls var beer and laughing with Kyt.

He is the biggest predator in the room, and he's mine.

"What did you mean about our mating not being the last?" I lean over the arm of my chair and into him, capturing his attention.

"I've talked it over with the seniors and they agree. We should see if we can find the other humans. If it is possible for me to find my *eregri*, maybe it will be possible for others. We have to do something to continue our species."

I take a long drink from my previously untouched flagon to moisten my dry throat. The ale is sweet, with a hint of the ambrosia I like so much, and not particularly alcoholic.

"You will?" I dump the vessel on the table and leap onto his lap, peppering his face with kisses. "Thank you, Jyr. Thank you so much!"

JYR

By Nisis, my head feels like it's about to fall off.

With a groan, I roll onto my back, clutching at the bed to stop it spinning.

Gradually the evening returns to me in snippets that flash by. Wing wrestling with Myk, even the taciturn Gryn got into the party mood. More var beer, more toasts. Some sort of race, which I won, although I don't think I could fly straight at the time. All the while, Viv by my side, her comforting sweet presence making our celebration perfect. Finally, she helped me back to our chambers, and I got to enjoy all of her delicious body. She made sounds I hope were heard throughout the lair. I wanted all my warriors to know what it is like to mate and be a mated Gryn.

Looks like I'm paying for all that with a sore head. Shame my rapid healing doesn't work on the morning after. I flop out an arm, searching for my mate. It takes too long to realize she isn't within reach.

"Viv?" I pry my eyes open and see that the bed contains only me. There's no sign of my mate. With some considerable effort, my wings not quite wanting to co-operate and rendering me unbalanced, I stagger through to my healing pool to see if she waits for me.

Nothing.

I feel out for her with the thoughtbond. She's mastered it quicker than I expected, and she's as good as Ryak at keeping it closed down, but on this occasion, I can't trace her and it's not because she doesn't want me to.

I drag on my trousers and stumble my way through the outer chamber into the central shaft. Bodies of sleeping Gryn lie where they dropped. If I didn't feel as groggy as I do, I'd have sworn there had been a massacre. However, the gentle snores that lift all around me tell me that these warriors are partied out. It doesn't stop me from giving the one nearest my chamber a kick to the ribs.

"Have you seen my mate?"

He looks up at me blearily, unwrapping a wing from around his body.

"No, Prime." He rubs his eyes and gets to his feet, stumbling a few steps down to the next prone warrior and shaking him awake.

In no time, there are more than a dozen warriors all looking for my mate. I make my way to the seniors' barracks and find Kyt flat out, lying across Myk, the pair of them dead to anything and anyone. Ryak gets to his feet when I enter, and I know he already has glimpsed my rising panic.

"She's gone." I tell him.

"She has to be in the lair, there's no way she would have got out without any warriors seeing her."

Can you not feel her?

"If I had a thoughtbond with my mate, do you think I'd even be asking?" I snap and immediately regret it. "We have to find her."

"We'll find her." Ryak places a hand on my shoulder and aims a kick at Kyt, who snorts awake, elbowing Myk.

"Viv is missing."

The words galvanize my two closest seniors, who are on their feet in moments, any ill effects of last night forgotten. Kyt is straight out of the door, whilst Ryak and Myk call in the enforcers to start a systematic search of the lair.

"Prime." Fyn is standing in the doorway. He places his hand over his heart, saluting me. His eyes are dark with anger, and I don't have time for any of his gak today.

"If you've been fighting again, Fyn. I don't want to know." I turn my back on him.

"No, Prime. I think I know where Viv is."

Before the thought has entered my head, I have Fyn pinned against the wall. My claws dug deep in the flesh of his neck.

"Where. Is. My. Mate?" I'm not even snarling. My voice is dry and hollow as my jaws drip with the desire to rip out his throat. I leave him in no doubt that he will live or die by his next words.

"Let him go, Jyr." Myk has an iron hold on my arm. Of all the Gryn, I know Myk is the only warrior who could best me. "He has information, he is not the enemy."

If Myk is speaking, I need to listen, the rational part of my brain tries to reason with me. Except my mate is missing, my one reason for being. Myk squeezes my arm and brings me back. I release Fyn, leaving him with a number of puncture wounds that flow with blood.

"One of my mercs told me he saw her in the food hall this morning, speaking with Kaloz." Fyn says, leveling a defiant gaze at me.

"Where is Kaloz?" I bellow as I stride out into the lair. "Bring me Kaloz!"

The entire lair fills with the sounds of beating wings. The central shaft is a blur of feathers and mercs undertaking a search, led by Fyn.

"There is no sign of either Kaloz or your mate, my Prime." He says. "But one merc found this in the passage at the rear of the food hall.

He hands me Viv's red coat. My heart all but stops. Kaloz took her. He saw what I had, and he took her.

"Find me Kaloz. All patrols out, now." I keep my voice even, but all I want to do is rend something, anything, into a thousand pieces.

"Prime!" A shout goes up and descending the shaft is one of Kaloz's mercs. A greasy-looking Gryn that I think goes by the name of Jos is flapping hard as he reaches me, landing with some effort and a nasty grin.

"Where is Kaloz?" I reach for him, but he dodges my fist.

"I wouldn't do that if I were you, Jyr," he deliberately doesn't address me by my title, "not if you want to see your pretty mate again."

It takes everything I have not to kill him on the spot, but I can feel Ryak in the back of my brain, and I'm grateful for his presence.

"Where is my mate, you vrexing piece of gak?" I take a step towards him, claws extended, and he takes one back. Coward.

"I will leave her co-ordinates at the old bot factory. If I see you before I get there, she's dead. Only you and your seniors. No other warriors." He beats at the ground, lifting off slowly. "Or she's dead." He grins a mouth full of brown and broken teeth at me.

It's not like I have much choice. And what's worse. I have to let the filthy creature go.

"Seniors and Fyn. With me." I say as I head to the armory.

I've already severely underestimated Kaloz. That's not going to happen again. I raise Viv's jacket to my nose and inhale her scent that lingers on the clothing.

"I'm coming, my mate. Hold on." I whisper under my breath, wishing that the thoughtbond could cover the distance between us and hoping that just this once, it does.

VIV

There's a roar in my ears, and I jerk my head up. First, I find I'm alone, second, I have a headache that is like someone drilling into my left eye, and third, I'm tied to a chair.

For a few, futile minutes, I fight at my bonds, while trying to work out how I ended up here, wherever this place is. Once I realize I'm not getting loose anytime soon, I try to clear my vision and look around. The place is as ruined as everywhere else I've been on Ustokos. It could have been anything, workshop, theater, bar. Now it's a shell, part of the roof torn away. The twisted metal and shattered concrete worn smooth by the passage of time. Outside, the sky rolls with dark clouds that mean business.

I remember Kaloz catching my attention in the food hall when I went to get Jyr some breakfast. He had so much fun last night. It was wonderful seeing him being himself. Not some serious leader but a Gryn that loved being in the center of his warriors. In turn, they loved having him play with them. I couldn't breathe for laughing when he was challenged to a race to the top of the shaft by one of the younger mercs. For an instant I thought he would refuse, but he looked at me, winked and off they went.

He won, of course. It made no difference to the youngster who looked fit to burst with pride that he had flown with his Prime.

And later when he made love to me, passionate and intense, it was glorious. I felt as if I had come home.

I left him slumbering while I went to fetch food for us both. I'd already made up my mind. I was going to tell him I loved him. Make sure he knew he had my heart too. Make sure he knew I wanted to have his children, if we can.

Because he made a broken thing whole, and I'd never thought that was possible.

Unfortunately, Kaloz was waiting in the food hall. He had been conspicuous by his absence last night. I certainly welcomed the absence of his particular specter at the feast as he's always given me the creeps. I stupidly stopped when he asked if he could speak with me, and in seconds, he had me in a headlock. I squirmed and kicked, but with his foul hand over my mouth, I was unable to scream, and all I succeeded in doing was lose my jacket. Shortly after, I felt a sharp prick on my neck and everything went dark.

"Awake then?" I hear his voice behind me, and I don't move. He appears beside me, thrusting my head back and pinching my eye open.

I ram my head forward and make contact with his nose. The impact hurts like a bastard. He lets out a thin cry as blood spurts from his nose. Totally worth the pain echoing around my head.

"Jyr is going to kill you for this." I fire at him.

"Ha! Your precious mate will not have the chance." He grins nastily at me. "He's not going to be Prime after today."

"So that's what this is all about, some petty power grab?

You've got no chance. The lair will never accept you. The lair is fed up with you and your drugs. They want rid of you."

I've spent the last weeks making sure every young merc I come into contact with avoids the stuff like the plague, with Jyr's backing.

"It doesn't matter what happens to me. All that matters is what happens to him and that's up to you." Kaloz picks at his teeth with a claw. "You are the only reason he will come and when he does." He draws the claw across his throat in a universal gesture.

I laugh without mirth and turn my head away. "Whatever." I say dismissively.

Kaloz is in my face, clawed hands gripping my shoulders, his foul breath invading my nostrils.

"I'm going to get what's due to me. The lair. Your mate will pay for his failure to invest in my business. You were the perfect little distraction." He growls. I jerk my head back again and he releases me, throwing himself out of the firing line.

Kaloz goes around behind me, and I feel my chair moving. I'm spun around with some force and tipped back as I'm dragged, chair and all, across the room, then I'm flung forwards, teetering on the edge of an open void. It's the rest of the building, or what's left of it. Lit dimly, most of it is open to the elements. In the center of the open space is another chair, containing another body, its head covered by a bag.

It's only after a moment of staring, I realize that the figure in the chair is supposed to be me. I giggle.

"What?" Kaloz is not amused. "What is so funny, female?" He asks as I continue to laugh.

"You don't know anything, do you?" I gasp out. Kaloz

growls low in his throat. "Jyr is never going to fall for that." I toss my head towards the figure. "You should have paid more attention to the stuff you called children's stories. If Jyr doesn't feel my thoughtbond he will know that's not me."

"Your mate is in no fit state to determine what is real and what is not. I added something special to the var beer last night, just for your celebration. All he wants is his mate." He grabs the back of my chair and roughly tips it up, causing me to fall back against the hard metal and look up. "Here he comes. To his doom." Kaloz intones.

I see some tiny, winged shapes high above us, descending rapidly like sickles. I open my mouth to scream, but Kaloz clamps a hand over it, claw tips pressing into my skin.

"This is on you, female. Whatever happens to him, it's all on you."

JYR

S he's close. The thoughtbond is weak, but it's there. I increase my speed, my seniors keep formation behind me, matching my pace easily. I have to get to her, there's nothing else filling my mind but the need to see her beautiful face and to hold her in my arms.

I always knew that Kaloz was planning something. The male has always been as slippery as they come. He should have been born a Kijg, then he could slough his skin twice a cycle and be done with it.

Viv told me that humans have a saying about keeping your friends close and your enemies closer. She also told me it didn't actually mean that you had to keep your enemies close, just have an insight into what they are doing. I already know that I've put the entire lair in danger because of my agreement with Kaloz, and my mate has paid the price.

Our alliance is no more. Once I recover my mate, Kaloz and his mercs will be on their own, banished to the badlands. He brought nothing but trouble to our lair and I'll be glad to be rid of him.

"There!" Fyn points down and I can see the low lights of

the former weapons factory just on the edge of our territory. I fold my wings and stoop as hard as I can to get down to the tiny figure I see in the clearing.

Out of nowhere I'm pulled sharply sideways, my wings flailing as I try to correct my course, except they can't move. I can't move. Looking up, I see the unmistakable blue lights of a capturebot. I'm caught in its silken net. To my left, I see they have also caught the others. Myk fights tooth and nail against his bonds, his roars reaching my ears. Instantly, the capturebot activates the netting and Myk goes rigid before his body curls into a ball and he is still.

My last thoughts are for the tiny figure below me. I failed her and in the process, I flew straight into Proto's trap. My net is activated and oblivion beckons.

———

"ONE GRYN MALE. *Wings and limbs intact.*" The smooth, easy voice seems to drop into my head.

"*Jyr. Prime. Rogue Warrior.*" The second bot voice makes me open my eyes to be assaulted by a wall of white.

"*Remain still, Gryn. You are restrained for your safety.*"

"For yours you mean, bot. I'll rip out your innards!" I snarl as I struggle uselessly against the laser restraints. All of my weapons have been removed, along with my boots. At least Proto left me with my trousers.

"*This one resists.*"

My eyes have become accustomed to the bright white light, and I see both of the medbots, long white tubes, they have lights that morph across their cylindrical surface in a semblance of facial features. Both appear to be smiling at me. There's no sign of the other seniors, and my thought-bond seems to be broken.

"*It requires further tranquilizers. For calming.*"

One bot leans over me, its rictus grin getting wider.

"*For your safety.*" It says, and I hear a hiss as they pump the drugs into my system.

I try not to let them take effect. I stare at the bots as if my gaze alone can disable them, but I cannot resist the pull of the powerful tranqs, and I'm dragged down into a healing pool that is warm and silky. Where Viv sits, waiting to wash my aching limbs and preen my feathers.

I watch, horrified, as the bots appear out of the clouds and fire long streams of what looks like energy at Jyr and the others. It immediately caught them up, as if in a soap bubble made of a spider's web and one-by-one they go limp. The bots buzz away with the Gryn hanging below them.

"You!" I twist so I can see Kaloz. "You did this. You're working with Proto." The nasty realization that Jyr welcomed this Gryn into his home, fed him and clothed him, even gave him a position of responsibility sours my stomach. And being angry at Kaloz means I don't have to think about my part in Jyr's capture.

"I've always been working with Proto." He looks over his shoulder and moves to one side. "She is here for you too, master. As I promised."

"Master." I snort. "Sounds like you did a good deal, Kaloz." My pleasure at seeing a flicker of pain cross his weaselly features is short-lived when the large, black robot slides into my view.

If I thought the joykill bots were the embodiment of evil tech, over and above that of the self-serve checkout, then I was wrong. This thing is so black it almost sucks in light. It has to be eight feet tall, hovering over the ground with no obvious means of propulsion, unlike the other bots I've seen. It's shaped like an upside down, three-dimensional triangle. At the top, the broadest part, it has a long oval slit that glows red, like the grin of a demon.

"*The Gryn will depart.*" The metallic voice booms out. "*If the Gryn wishes to remain alive.*"

This time Kaloz looks frightened. He backs away slowly, then takes off at a run.

"Fucking coward!" I yell after him, not that he looks back before he takes flight and in no time has disappeared into the clouds.

"*Human female.*" The bot looms over me and a red laser light fires out from the oval slit, causing me to flinch. It runs over me from the top of my head down to my feet.

"*Mated with a Gryn.*" It continues. "*To be returned to Proto for disposal.*"

A slim appendage morphs out of the side of the bot and resolves itself into a mechanical arm, tipped with a syringe filled with blue liquid. Whatever it is, I'm not being stabbed with it, and I jump up and down on the spot in my chair, hoping I can hop away from the thing and maybe find somewhere to hide. All that actually happens is I fall over, still completely immobile, and I'm stabbed in the arm, anyway.

"Fuck you," I slur as my limbs become weightless and the bot in front of me shimmers.

Further limb/arms extend from it, and my bonds are cut away. I want to struggle, but nothing responds. Instead, I'm tipped into a cradle of metal, clutched to the bot, as it ascends towards a huge spaceship I'm absolutely sure wasn't there before.

All I can think, before the light goes dark, is that not only did the bot know what I was, but that it knew about me and Jyr. An icy hand clamps around my heart as the fear for my mate takes root. This is all my fault.

JYR

I've been attempting to get free for hours. Writhing against the metal clamps holding me, spread out on the cold white surface in Proto's labs. I'll never forget what they look like, and this is definitely one. I've ripped my skin apart again and again against the metal, but each time it knits, and all I have is the pain.

But the pain keeps me focused. Viv and my warriors, they're all in Proto's grip because I didn't see what Kaloz was, and how he was poisoning the lair. Not just with his drugs, but with his very presence. I tried to pretend we were a family, and yet I didn't care at all.

I brought my mate into the midst of a silent war, and I've lost her to the one thing on this planet I should have been able to keep her from. What's more, because of my negligence, my lair is in trouble. All those mercs I saved are at risk of being recaptured and put back in the camps.

With a roar, I redouble my efforts, straining hard at the clamps and ignoring the burning pain. I'm certain that the restraint is about to open when a slot in the ceiling opens and a small round infobot drops to hover over me.

"*Jyr.*" It announces my name in a voice that has been programmed to be both soothing and authoritative.

"Vrex you!" I continue my twisting as the clamps press down.

"*We don't wish to tranquilize you again, Jyr. It is important that we can talk.*" A further swooshing sound and a further opening has a medbot hovering next to me, syringe in pincer.

"Vrex off! If you're going to tranq me, just do it. I've nothing to discuss with you." I spit, unable to move as the clamps have tightened to where my circulation is going.

"*You don't wish to discuss your mate or your warriors?*"

I've never understood how Proto was able to convey emotion, but this bot sounds positively smug. I know enough about the algo that I can't give the response I want, which would be to smash this bot back to its component parts.

"What mate?" I grit my teeth and say the words. They are only words, and Viv will forgive me.

"*The human female that you have mated.*"

I shake or rather roll, my head from side to side.

"Don't recall any mate. Must be the tranqs you gave me."

"*In that case, you will not care that we have disposed of her.*"

My blood turns to ice in my veins.

"What?"

"*She was defective. She had been damaged. She was of no use to our program and was terminated.*" The info bot says, this time emotionless. "*If she was not your mate, we can assign another, after you have provided us with the information you hold.*"

Proto doesn't lie. It's not capable of lying. Viv was hung up on the tiny part of her skin that wasn't like the rest of her, but that couldn't be why Proto had killed her. It can't be.

"She's dead?" I hear the question form on my lips before my brain can hold it back. "You killed her?"

"It is no matter. She was not yours."

I can't even breathe. There's no thoughtbond to bring her back to me. Without Viv, I am nothing.

The clamps release, but I don't get up until a guardbot is released into the room and it uses a stun laser to stir me into some form of compliance. My wings are bound at the shoulder to stop me from being able to fly and they bind my hands with the same restraints. I care not. My legs feel like I'm wearing shackles as I'm pushed down many sparkling white and metal corridors that go past in a blur, because all I want to see is Viv, and she is dead.

Finally, a door slides open next to me, and I'm pushed sideways. I fall onto the floor and lie still. There's no reason to get up. There's nothing left to do.

After a while, I take notice of the sounds in the cell. A shuffling of feathers and whispering. I don't want to move. My world is torn apart, the colors gray. Proto can do what it wants. The scuffling gets louder, and the whispers resolve into words.

"Do you think he's okay?"

"I don't know, there's a lot of blood."

I can feel a presence just behind me, and with a snarl at being disturbed, I roll over. Three young Gryn leap to the back of the cell, wings outstretched, their eyes terrified.

'What are you doing?" I add with an unnecessary growl. I want to be left alone.

"We wanted to help, that's all." One steps forward a pace, obviously the bravest of the three. "You looked like you were injured."

"I'm not injured, and you can't help me." I turn my back on them. "And I can't help you, if you thought that." I close my eyes, wanting to trace the image of my Viv in my mind. I have to remember her sweet face, hold her close, praise Nisis that I had her.

Because a moment in my life with her is better than never having met her at all. If my life is over, then it will have been finished in perfect harmony of a Gryn and his fated mate.

My Viv. My *eregri*. My boundless flight.

VIV

"Hey." An unfamiliar female voice penetrates the fog filling my skull. "Wake up, the robots will be back soon."

"Fuck!" I groan as I open my eyes to a light that's far too bright.

"She's awake!" A red-haired woman has her back to me.

"Whoop-de-do. Another one for the robots. Lucky her." A laconic female voice answers. She sounds as if she's from the north of England. Very Game of Thrones.

The redhead turns back to me. She has a sweet face that's peppered with freckles. Her green eyes are full of concern.

"Drink this. The drugs they use will give you a hell of a headache." She offers me a cup, and I push myself up onto my elbow to take it from her.

I'm in a room that is all white and silver horizontal stripes, almost painful to look at. The entire ceiling appears to be a white light. Arranged around the hexagonal walls are ledges, a bit like the ones in the lair, which presumably serve as beds. Two other women, one with dark hair streaked with shocking red highlights and one with long ice blond curls, sit side-by-side on a ledge. A further black-haired woman leans against the wall, her arms folded and an annoyed expression on her face. They are all wearing buff-colored jumpsuits that are too small or too large. One size definitely not fitting all.

"You—"I take a gulp of the water. "You're the women from the bags?"

They all look at me like I have an extra head.

"I mean, did you all arrive here together?"

The redhead looks around at the rest of them. "Yes, we did." From her accent, she has to be from the Midlands.

"We shouldn't speak to her, she might be a spy for those things." The black-haired woman says. "Why else bring her here now?"

"Because maybe they've just abducted her from Earth? Come on Sophie, she's as real as we are." The woman with the highlights walks over to me and kneels down. "I'm Emma. This is Lucy." She puts her hand on the arm of the redhead. "Over there is Bianca," the blond gives me a little wave, "and that's Sophie." The black-haired woman snorts in annoyance and looks away.

"Do you know how we got here?" Lucy asks, twisting her hands. "And if we can get back to Earth?"

"We're never going back to Earth, Lucy!" Sophie shouts across, "I don't understand why you torture yourself and us with that shit."

"I have my birds and I want to get back to them." Lucy shouts back, her eyes full of tears. "Just because you have nothing to go back to doesn't mean we all have nothing."

"I'm sorry, sweetheart." I push myself into a sitting position. "Unless Proto takes us back to Earth, we're not going home anytime soon, and from what I've seen, Proto has no intention of letting us go back."

Lucy lets out a loud sob and Emma wraps her arms around her, shooting daggers at me. They all do.

There's no way I want to hurt the first human I've seen in weeks. Looks like I'm already back in my old ways. Making myself so unpleasant that no one wants to get close.

"How come you know so much?" Bianca asks.

"I—"My reply is cut off by the only door to the room snapping open and the huge black bot from earlier zips into the room, stopping in front of me.

"Human females." It rotates to take us all in. *"Your number is complete. You will now breed with the Gryn to produce hybrid young for Proto."*

"Like hell!" Sophie cries. "I'm not 'breeding' with anything for anyone. And I'm certainly not having babies like some farm animal." She folds her arms in a gesture of defiance, but I see her step back away from the bot.

"We will assign you one of the rogue warriors that arrived with the new female. You will breed or you will be artificially impregnated." It does another one of its slow, menacing turns. *"It will not be pleasant."*

"I already have a mate, but these women should not be forced to do anything. You should let us go." I say with a boldness I know comes from my time spent with Jyr. If he's here, in Proto's complex, then there is hope and not just for me, for the other women, too.

"If you speak of the Gryn known as Jyr, because of his defiance, we have terminated him. We will assign you to one of the other Gryn." The devil bot does another turn, its red slit glowing with, what seems like anger. *"Your mating will commence in one cycle."*

Behind it, the door snaps open and it floats out backwards as if it's watching us all and the door slams shut again.

I slip off the ledge onto the floor, pressing the heels of my hands into my eyes, desperately pushing out through the thoughtbond to find Jyr or any of the others.

There is nothing.

I'm all alone.

Tears I've been holding back all this time flow. Huge sobs wracking my body as I curl up on the floor. When I had Jyr, I still held onto the idea of getting back to Earth, to going home. But he's gone and I know, with every atom in my body, that he was the best thing that ever happened to me and my home was on Ustokos, with him and the rest of the Gryn, my new family.

In one fell swoop, all of that has been torn from me and I have become Vivian Owens again, failed human being, damaged and irreparable. The woman who hid from herself and from the world. The woman I hated.

"What did you mean, you already have a mate?" Emma's posh southern English accent penetrates my thoughts. I look up to see all of them standing over me.

They all look pissed. Sophie looking the most angry, like she's about to punch me.

"What the hell are you?" She spits. "You are in league with them! I knew it! Well, you're going to make them give up this disgusting mating idea." She reaches down and attempts to haul me to my feet, but I'm a dead weight for the slightly built woman. Instead, she goes to give me a kick when Bianca puts out her arm.

"No, Sophie. Wait. We need to give her a chance to explain, she is human after all." Bianca holds out her hand, which I take as she helps me to my feet. Once I'm up she doesn't let go, her baby blue eyes glittering with menace.

"And it had better be a fucking good explanation." Her cockney accent shines through with her threat, even if she hid it before.

I sit down heavily on the ledge, eyeing them all as I'm the center of attention again. I gulp at the air, attempting to settle my thoughts, to try not to think of Jyr, and to be convincing to the four women who, by now, clearly despise me.

It's everything I dreaded, made worse by the loss of the one male who made me whole.

JYR

The three mercs rustle with fear at the back of our shared cell. I haven't bothered to move from my position on the floor. There's no point. Where exactly am I going to go? I can't return to the lair, even if I thought I could escape.

Even if I wanted to escape.

So, I lie on the floor and attempt to blot out everything, the sounds of the mercs, their whisperings, thoughts of my lair. Thoughts of my mate.

"You should eat something, Prime." One of the mercs says, far too close to me. My skin feels as if it's on fire, probably because of the tranqs, which never agreed with me.

"I'm not your Prime." I pull my wing further over me, unable to muster a growl. "I'm no one's Prime. Go away."

There is further whispering.

"We heard there was a Prime. One that came to save Gryn warriors from Proto. A Prime that came to the camps and freed us." Another round of whispering follows and one of them sets a cup of water and a ration block down in my eye-line, the merc quickly retreating.

"If there was, he's gone now." I close my eyes. "No one is coming for you, get used to it." The whispering mercifully ceases, and I'm left alone.

I must drift in and out of sleep for a while, or at least my mind ceases to function on and off. I should welcome these moments of respite, but when I'm back in the present, all I can see is the yawning pit where my Viv should be. The one precious jewel left on this Nisis-forsaken planet.

Blame settles around me like rain. I believed I was invincible and, as long as I was present in the lair, as long as I did what a Prime was supposed to do, rule by iron fist and soft wing, that would be enough. It would mean I could have it all.

I made my nest for her.

She allowed me to take her sweet body in the one place she would have been safe. In the place I wanted her to stay as she grew round with my young. Yet, her presence in the lair made the place joyous. She lifted everything up in a way I never could. The night of our ceremony, the happiness of the mercs and the smiles on the faces of my seniors, even Myk, it was all I could ask for.

But my arrogance knew of nothing. I should have dealt with Kaloz a long time ago. He remained as a thorn in my nest and in my lair. My strength on my own was nothing, not when I had allowed him access to everything that was good.

I once saw a mated pair ripped apart in the camps. In the struggle, the bots killed the female. The warrior lasted three cycles before he took his own life. At the time, I could not understand his reasons. Today I know how he felt. Without Viv, I see no reason to go on. I was bonded to her, heart and soul. Our thoughts were one. I need her as surely as I need my wings and feathers.

"*Gryn warrior. You will come.*"

I don't know how long the guardbot has been in the cell. It's one red eye stares balefully at me. The three mercs huddle together in a mass of limbs and wings. They reek of fear until one untangles himself from the others and steps forward.

"I will come. Leave him."

"*No.*" The bot intones. "*Gryn warrior. You will come or the rest die.*"

The mercs do their best, but I hear their whimpers of terror, and I can't accept that anyone else should suffer because of me. My limbs are stiff from the time spent on the floor, but I get to my feet with a groan and shake out my feathers, wanting to stretch my wings, but they are still bound together in an awkward position, as are my hands.

"Vrex you, Proto. I'll come. Leave them alone." My heart is not behind the words, but I'd rather offer my life than those of the youngsters huddled behind me. My life means nothing now.

The guardbot moves behind me, bumping at my rear until we reach a door only a short walk from the cell. I'm shoved inside to be greeted by the medbots from earlier, or different ones, it's impossible to tell.

"*The Gryn will lie on the specimen table. The Gryn will comply.*"

I'm hoping that they make it quick as I slide onto the table, unable to lie flat because of the way my wings are bound. A bright blue light hits me and I'm paralyzed by it. It rakes over my flesh and feathers as I stare up at it, willing for my life to be over. But no pain hits me. The laser doesn't even burn my skin. It winks out as quickly as it started, and I sit up to release my wings.

"*Jyr.*" An info bot buzzes out of a nearby alcove. "*You are in good health and you may now breed with the other human females.*"

"I won't be breeding with any other female, not for you or anyone." I mutter, staring at my bare feet.

"*In which case, we will milk you for your seed.*"

The guardbot flashes forwards, and I'm lifted bodily from the table and, before I can struggle, I'm being sealed in a chamber which has a clear cylindrical front. My bound hands are pulled apart with the cuffs still around my wrists as some hidden force pulls them back against the wall and some other restraints capture my ankles.

A humming noise begins, and I can smell burning, craning my neck. A red laser is traveling up my legs and as it does, the fabric of my trousers disappears, the edges glowing with fire. Shortly I am naked. The guardbot hovers outside of the chamber, attempting to look menacing. I've been tortured by Proto before and this is nothing new.

Until the clamp unfolds out of the wall containing a large metal cup and slams itself over my cocks with a force that is entirely unnecessary. This is new. Pain spears through me as the thing suctions itself against my exposed flesh. I feel something extending and pressing against the tight ring of my anus, it burns as it enters me.

"*This will assist.*"

The flash of a needle before it's plunged into my flesh and my entire body goes into a convulsion. My cocks feel like they are being turned inside out, such is the suction. I'm rock hard, unable to stop myself from thrusting at the cup. Unable to stop the groans escaping my lip as the thing in my ass pulses.

It turns out there are worse things than dying. There is living with the failures you have made. I can't conjure up my mate's face to keep the worst of this violation of my body from my mind. If I see her, it's only a reminder of what I lost. Yet I would give anything to see her again for one last time, to tell her I loved her, not because of fate, but because she was the peace inside me made flesh. She made a flawed Gryn warrior good.

Proto intensifies its invasion of my body and even though I believe I deserve this torture, my conscious mind gives up and blackness beckons.

VIV

Sophie taps her foot at me. She isn't buying any of my explanation. I don't blame her. If all you've seen are bots, you're hardly going to believe in seven-foot tall, winged aliens. Not that my explanation is up too much, given that I can hardly speak about Jyr without more tears and snots.

So basically I've snivelled my way through the worst explanation ever and none of them believe me. Even Lucy, who I feel would want to believe anything, is looking like I'm something she found on the sole of her shoe.

I was never any good at this sort of thing, even before I had my accident and withdrew from the world. I had few friends outside of work, even at work I'd avoid speaking in meetings. I was good at my job, so my bosses didn't care that I wasn't interested in contributing. They went the extra mile to get me back to the office after my job, but because I couldn't bear to look at myself, let alone them, there was nothing left.

"So, these aliens," Emma says.

"The Gryn."

"They were natives of this planet, but they lost a war against the robots?"

"There are a couple of other species, but the Gryn were essentially the soldiers."

"Isn't this just the plot of a movie?" Sophie says. "It all sounds like bullshit to me."

Lucy takes my hand. My first reaction is to pull away from her, but I don't. The touch of another person, for once, seems necessary. Something to ground me.

"You were with one of these Gryn, like a boyfriend?" She asks in her soft accent.

I can't stop the hollow laugh that escapes my lips, tilting my head up as my eyes brim with fresh tears.

"It was so much more than that. Jyr was—" I halt, wanting to put what he was to me in a way that these women will understand. Not just understand but feel as I feel. "Jyr was a gorgeous, handsome, arrogant jerk of an alien who treated me like a princess and worshipped the ground I walked on. I don't expect you to understand, but that was a big deal to me. He'd do anything for his fellow warriors, even if he didn't want them to know how much he cared."

I'm breathless, not with my explanation, but from my heart beating so hard I think it's going to burst out of my chest. All I want is Jyr to be here with me now. To prove to these women that I am worthy of love.

To tell him I love him.

"Why are you even believing those things that say he died?" Sophie stalks over to me and I cringe back, but all that happens is she crouches down in front of me. This time her pale blue eyes are soft. "This alien doesn't sound like one to give up on a fight."

"He wouldn't," I hiccup sob.

"It doesn't sound like he'd give up on you either." Lucy adds.

"I don't feel him." I put my free hand over my heart. "I can't explain it, but after I met him, I could feel his emotions and some of his thoughts, and he could do the same with me. But I can't feel him now."

"Uhg, creepy." Bianca says, making a sour face. "Can't imagine anything worse."

"It was beautiful." I say. My tears have dried, and I know I have to face up to our capture. "It was special. It made me special."

None of them look convinced, and I'm back where I belong. Back at the bottom of the pile.

Emma jerks her head at the other three and they retreat to the opposite side of the cell, talking in whispers. Like being back at school, I sit in the corner while the popular girls ignore me. The gaggle reaches a conclusion and Emma comes across to me.

"We're not sure if we believe you or not or even sure you're human." She looks over her shoulder at the others. "But we're stuck here, and we're stuck with you, so for the time being, we've decided that you should be the one to go first in the mating."

And just like that, my world falls apart completely.

JYR

"He's bleeding again."

"Here, use this."

I feel a soft, cool cloth pressing against me. Instantly, I'm on my feet, snarling, lashing out with my claws and beating the air with my wings.

"Don't touch me!" I'm eventually able to form the words. "Keep away or I'll destroy you."

I pry my eyes open to see the three mercs cowering as far away from me as possible, one of which is sporting a fresh surgical cut to his chest. He hadn't been able to get away from my claws fast enough. I'm clutching the cloth to my cocks and every part of me hurts like crazy. I tip my head back and groan out loud in defiance and despair that I'm still alive, sliding down the wall until I hit the floor and groan again at the pain.

"Sorry." I mumble towards the youngsters. "I didn't mean to hurt you. I thought you were Proto."

"It's okay. We know what it's like." The bolder one from earlier says.

The last thing I want to do is talk and yet, it would be a welcome distraction from the gak in my head.

"Why aren't you in the camps? Why are you here?" I roll my head so I can see all three.

They are young, reminding me of myself, once. Before Proto got hold of me and turned me into something more than Gryn. They are entwined with each other, obviously for comfort. This whole situation is frightening enough without them ending up trapped in a cell with me as their latest monster.

"We were in a camp, then Nyl tried to escape, and we were all brought here." One of them offers, after having looked at the others.

"Which one of you is Nyl?" The bolder one holds up a hand. "What are your names?" I sigh.

"I'm Bryn," the speaker identifies himself. "This is Ayn." The third merc eyes me with huge dark eyes. "Ayn doesn't say much." Bryn adds.

"I know a Gryn very like him." My heart is heavy as I wonder if my seniors are even alive.

"Do you think we could get out of here, Prime?" Nyl asks, tentatively.

"Do I think we could get out of this heavily fortified Proto base, filled to the brim with joykills, laser weapons, capturebots, with nothing more than our claws and wings?"

Nyl leans forward, anticipation written all over his young face.

"No." I close my eyes and lean my head back.

I can almost feel his disappointment.

"What did Proto want with you?" Bryn ventures after a long silence. I know they've seen my injuries, but that's one subject these young mercs don't need to know about.

"It doesn't matter."

"Proto did stuff to us too. But we don't heal like you. Ayn was sick for a long time after Proto took him last."

I let out a long, low growl. I don't want this. I don't want to help these mercs; I vrexed everything up last time I tried to do good and the last thing I want is more lives on my conscience. But the pain deep in their eyes speaks to my tortured soul. Viv would want me to help them. She believed she was damaged, and she was wrong. She was the purest thing that Ustokos has seen in a very long time, and I have to honor her memory.

"Any chance you've got any clothing to spare." I gesture to my cloth covered crotch. "I'm sure Proto would happily have me naked, but I don't want to oblige on this occasion."

Ayn leans forward, holding out a pair of trousers in the weird material that Proto always uses.

"One of the medbots brought these in with you."

"Guess Proto doesn't want me naked after all." I grin at them, pulling on the trousers. I'm rewarded by a weak smile from Bryn. "Now, when did you all last eat?"

The young mercs are painfully thin. All three have the build to be powerful males when they grow up and should be starting to put on their bulk, but Proto has clearly been limiting their rations. It takes a bit of noise on my behalf, but eventually a guardbot arrives and I tell him I need food. It ticks over at my request. Computing what I need, and, after a short while, a slot opens up in the wall at the back of our small cell. The scent of ration blocks fills the air and the three mercs fall on the proffered food, cheeks bulging as they stuff it in as fast as they can. Nyl offers me a ration block, but I shake my head. They need it more than I do.

"Let me have some of that water." Ayn passes me a cup, and I sniff at the liquid.

It doesn't appear to be drugged, and I gratefully swallow

it down. My throat is raw, and my guess is I descended into pathetic screams during my last torture. As the mercs eat, I take time to think, to work out a plan of escape. A plan that's going to have to involve freeing my seniors, these three and the remaining human women. That would be quite the haul if I can pull it off.

My eyes trace over the small cell. There's only one obvious exit, but as we have had food delivered via a slot, the walls are not as impregnable as they appear. It's a given that Proto is going to come back for me, because I know it's never finished, it's algo always calculating what it can extract, improve, or destroy. I believe that the next time I'm wanted is going to be my best chance of escape.

Nyl, Bryn, and Ayn sit across from me, stomachs full and eyes half lidded with the pleasure. They still huddle together, but their posture is reasonably relaxed.

"You three can all fly, can't you. Proto let you exercise whilst you were in the camps?" I ask.

"We can all fly. Nyl was one of our fastest flyers." Bryn says proudly as Ayn nods.

"Good—" I stop speaking because all of a sudden, I can't breathe.

The thoughtbond has sparked into life.

It's Viv, my mate and my *eregri*, and she is alive. Which means only one thing.

Proto lied to me, and she is in great danger.

VIV

The other women haven't spoken to me since they had their confab earlier. Lucy sits on the floor, knees drawn to her chest and her head tucked into her arms. Sophie paces on the opposite side of our cell to the door. Emma bites her nails. Bianca looks the calmest of the lot, semi-reclining on one of the ledges. She hasn't taken her intelligent eyes off me.

I try to make myself look small, insignificant. I want to tell the women that all is not lost on this planet, but if they don't believe me about Jyr, what hope do I have?

The door to the cell snaps open and three of the menacing bots swoop in.

"Take that one for breeding." One of them says and the other two swoop towards Lucy, who lets out a short yelp of fear.

"No!" I'm on my feet and advancing towards the bots. "Take me first."

There's an audible intake of breath from Emma. I don't think they thought I would offer myself up. Although from the look on Sophie's face, unbelievably, she's still not convinced.

"*Not permitted.*" The first bot replies. They heave Lucy to her feet, squealing and twisting as she fights with the bots.

I run at them, pulling at their metal pincers, trying to drag them off her. "I mean it! Take me first." I bellow.

The bots ignore me, and Lucy is slowly lifted off the ground as she continues to fight, until she sees she is in the air, and her body goes horribly limp. They move towards the door, and I take a running jump at the first bot, slamming into it with all my might. It twists around in a way that almost seems like it's angry.

"*Very well, take the compliant female.*" Lucy is unceremoniously dropped onto the floor, where she lies, unmoving, and I am grabbed instead. I don't fight and they don't need to lift me up.

The door to the cell shuts behind us and the bots hustle me forwards down the long corridor. I've no desire to be thrown to any Gryn for 'mating', but I expect it will probably be one of the seniors and I know there's no way they would touch me. While it means I can explain about the other women, I worry about what will happen when we refuse to 'mate'. I'm pushed and prodded a sharp left and then right. I try to stop worrying and memorize the route. At one point, I pass by something that appears to be a window to the outside of the base. We're high up, and I'm looking into what I can only describe as an enormous aviary. One or two Gryn fly around inside, listlessly.

Finally, another door slams open and I'm shoved inside. There is no sign of any warriors. Just two bright white bots, hovering serenely next to a smooth metal chair that has heavy restraints at the head, arms and legs. Ominously it also has restraints at the shoulders, indicating it's normally used for the Gryn. I notice with some amusement it's far too big for me.

The bots glide over, and lights appear on their cylindrical surface, resolving into smiling faces.

"*We are to examine you before you breed. For your safety.*" One of them says, its voice smooth, slightly feminine, and supposedly calming.

"*Please sit.*" The other bot adds.

With the meanbots behind me, I have little option and climb into the big chair. The restraints snap uselessly at me. I am far too small for it. A blue light bathes me as the bots hover nearby.

"*This female already carries Gryn young.*" A voice rings from out of nowhere. "*She is mated. Return her and bring one of the others.*"

I'm not able to move, my legs feel like lead. All of me feels like lead. I'm pulled off the chair by one of the bots, but I stumble, my brain not functioning.

"I'm pregnant?"

I'm pregnant with Jyr's child. Something that I thought I'd never want has suddenly become the one thing I do want. I splay my hand over my stomach.

"Wait!" I'm being dragged into the corridor. "What does that mean?"

"*You will birth a Gryn hybrid in approximately five Earth months.*" The AI replies. "*The start of a new generation of Gryn soldiers for export.*"

My mind goes into meltdown. FIVE MONTHS? This cannot be happening. I have to get back to the women and we have to find a way out of here. There's no way I'm giving up Jyr's child to this monstrous sentient AI. It has plans; it has emotions, even if it's trying to hide them, and it bodes ill for any organic life that ends up in its clutches.

I'm dragged back out into the corridor and compelled forward, despite my stumbling.

My eregri?

I look around wildly. I could have sworn I heard Jyr, so close, as if he was next to me. But that's not possible. Proto said he had been terminated, and I haven't felt him in my head since before I was kidnapped by Kaloz.

But he's in my head now and it's not a figment of my imagination. His warmth and love is a cloud of pink and orange that envelopes my heart.

Jyr.

I'm coming for you, my eregri.

My utter joy at feeling him again descends into the pit of my stomach. He has to blame me for us all being here. He has to think it's all my fault. I wouldn't blame him if he didn't want me, or the child I carry.

JYR

There's something extra in Viv's thoughtbond that I can't quite make out. I know she's scared but determined, like she always is. There's something else though, something that she's cradling inside her, both wanting to reveal and wanting to keep from me.

Whatever it is, I don't care. My love is alive and my heart sings with that of the mate bond. I offer a silent and heart-felt prayer to Nisis before I turn to the three mercs.

"You still want to get out of here, don't you?" They all nod hesitantly.

I close my eyes and try to visualize each of the mercs. I've never tried to put words in other's heads, not like Ryak does, but, because I know Proto will be watching and listening, I have no choice but to impart to each merc the part of the plan that they will have to execute. I dig deep within myself, taking my strength from my mate, to open up the communication between us all. When I open my eyes again, they are all staring at me, eyes wide at what they have just experienced. I find I'm panting with the exertion and spots appear before my eyes. The floor looks rather inviting as I sink down to rest.

I won't be doing that again in a hurry. Viv is definitely better at it than me.

They are on their feet as soon as I hit the floor, shouting, beating their wings, and making as much noise as they can, pointing at me. It's not long before I hear the cell door opening, and the three mercs quieten.

I haven't spent all my life fighting Proto not to have learned a thing or two about it. I keep my breathing as shallow as possible as I listen for the hum of the guardbot and feel the heat from its propulsion unit on my chest. With practiced ease, I'm clawing my way through the innards of the bot with all my might. Any damage caused to me heals up almost instantly, and the bot ends up a sparking ruin.

The mercs cheer loudly as the light dies out in its red eye.

"Enough," I say, gently but firmly. "We've got a long way to go from here. Keep behind me and do exactly what I say."

They immediately silence and serious expressions appear on their young faces as we creep out into the corridor. I don't believe I've been in this Proto base before, but they built most of them to the same specifications. If we are on the cell block level, then the rest of my seniors should be nearby, along with Viv and the other humans.

I plunge my claws into the locking mechanism on the exterior of the next cell and the door slides open to reveal Ryak, unharmed as expected. He sits cross-legged on a ledge and lifts his head as if he's been waiting for me.

"Just like old times." I grin at him and an alarm sounds.

"Just this time they've already experimented on us." Ryak unfolds in a fluid movement and is at the door in no time. "Who are your new friends?"

"They're just along for the ride, eh, mercs?" The three of them are grinning from ear to ear as Ryak joins us.

"Can you take these with you to get the seniors and Fyn? I need to find the humans and my mate." Ryak dips his head at me.

"Come with me and see how a real Gryn warrior deals with Proto." He says to the mercs.

They look between us. "Go with Ryak. He'll show you a thing or two." I encourage them.

I leave the group behind me as I stalk the corridors, keeping my eyes out for the bots and wishing I had something I could use as a weapon other than my claws, even if it's only to keep my distance from the joykills that will soon swarm this area. Another reason I have to get to Viv as soon as I can.

"*Gryn. Halt.*" The sound of a guardbot alerts me to a dead end, where it appears to be stuck. Unless that's where Viv is being kept.

"As you wish." I hold up my hands but advance towards it, increasing my speed by pumping my wings. The corridor too narrow for me to open them fully. I tackle the bot with outstretched claws, feeling a searing pain as it rakes a laser dagger down my side, but its flimsy carcass is no match for the claws that Proto enhanced to be stronger than any metal. Within seconds it's a shredded pile of wires and I feel satisfied with the violence I meted out.

I stab my hand into the door lock and it slides open to reveal my delicious mate. She waits for me, blue eyes flashing as she takes in my battle seared form.

"*Eregri.*"

I'm dimly aware of other bodies in her cell, but I only have eyes for her. She is real and alive. She is mine, and she is everything.

VIV

J yr stands in the doorway, a pile of robot parts behind
him. He's streaked in blood, and I can see a wound
on his side healing. He looks more devil than angel,
his dark eyes pools of blackness and his wings held
out so that he all but fills the doorway.

"*Eregri*" His first word to me is to tell me all I need to
know. He is mine and I am his. He calls it fated, and I call it
salvation.

I'm not even aware of myself running for him until I'm in
his arms, snuggled tight against his chest and breathing him
in. My hands rove over his body, into his feathers, until I'm
stopped by his kiss. His mouth is demanding and the rest of
him is warm. I meld into him, wanting to be part of him
forever.

"I'm sorry, I'm so sorry." I whisper when he finally lets
me up for air. "I shouldn't have let Kaloz take me. I shouldn't
have been wandering around the lair on my own." I
rush out.

"You have nothing to apologize for, my *eregri*." He
murmurs, running a clawed hand through my hair. "None of

this was your fault. It was my job to protect you, and I failed. I promise to always be there for you and to never let it happen again."

My heart leaps into the light. He isn't mad at me. Jyr is alive, and he isn't mad at me. The thoughtbond radiates with his love, and I push it back to him.

"I love you, my dark angel." I murmur into his chest. "I never want to lose you again."

"You won't. You have my promise as Prime of the Gryn." I look up to see the smile hitching the corners of his mouth and exposing his sharp canines. "And as your mate."

"That's better." I press my lips against his again until a fake coughing sound behind us reminds me that we have an audience.

"This is Jyr." I turn to them, holding onto his hand. "He's the alien I was telling you about." I feel Jyr puff up slightly. "My rather annoying mate." I give him a naughty grin. "Jyr, meet Lucy, Sophie, Emma and Bianca, the human women who were abducted at the same time as me."

Jyr lifts his wings and gives them a shake, the feathers rattling like swords.

"My ladies." He bows to them. Formal as anything. All the women stare at him, spellbound.

"A real life alien." Emma says hoarsely.

"So big." Sophie adds. I'm quite pleased that Jyr has rendered her near speechless for a change.

"We don't have much time, my *eregri*. Proto will be sending in the joykills, and we have to get out of here."

"Is everyone okay?" I'm suddenly gripped with the fear that one senior might have been injured or worse.

"I've seen Ryak and that bastid can survive anything. The others are just as robust."

"Fyn?" The young senior had started looking up to Jyr in

a way that was impressive. I'd hate for him to have been hurt.

"I believe Fyn might be one of us." Jyr says, cryptically. "I'll tell you later. In the meantime, lets go." He tugs at my hand, but I stay still, and he looks at me with a slight frown.

"You can come with us, or you can take your chances with Proto." I say to the women. "It's up to you. But I hope you understand now that I wasn't lying, and I'm only in league with these aliens."

The air is heavy with their hesitation until Bianca stands up and stretches out.

"I don't know about you guys, but I'm prepared to take my chances with the buff aliens, rather than the robots." She strolls over to me, eyeing Jyr appreciatively.

I have to bite the inside of my mouth to hold back my jealousy. She's incredibly pretty with her ice blond locks and cupid bow mouth. Just the sort of woman who turns a man's head. I risk a glance at Jyr. He isn't even looking at her; he is concentrated on the corridor behind us.

"If Bianca's going, I'm going." Emma announces as she takes Lucy's hand. "Come on, Lucy."

The tiny redhead's eyes look like they are about to burst out of her head. She can't take her eyes off Jyr either, but her gaze is anything but lustful. If I was to hazard a guess, it's somewhere between fear and disbelief. I suppose I didn't have the chance to be surprised at the existence of aliens, whereas these women have had the chance to get used to alien robots, so to find out there is something else alien out there is probably a bit of a mind fuck.

"I guess I've nothing better to do." Sophie says. "Look, Viv, I'm sorry for what we said earlier... It's just—" She waves her hands at our surroundings. "All this. You know."

"I know. But I promise it's much better when you don't

have to deal with the computers-that-say-kill." I give her a supportive smile.

"If only we could control-alt-delete." Sophie says as she rallies. "Best thing for any computer is to turn it off and on again." She huffs.

"Well, what are we waiting for?" Bianca strides towards the door and is stopped by a large wing.

"Follow me, Viv's humans. Keep quiet and move when I tell you." Jyr says rapidly. Warmth pools in my stomach when he refers to them as 'Viv's humans'.

He tucks me behind him as we move out into the corridor. Jyr rips a long sliver of metal from the destroyed bot, his claws making quick work in fashioning it into a crude blade. My hand is captured in his again as we creep forward. Every sense I have is on high alert, listening for the terrible sound of the joykill bots. As we approach a junction in the corridors, Jyr pulls up short, and I nearly run into the back of him.

He turns to us and holds his palm out flat, which I presume is the Gryn version of a shush. I find myself holding my breath. Jyr releases my hand and moves towards the corner. Raising his blade, he issues forth an almighty roar, leaping into the air.

Only for Kyt's grinning face to appear, causing my noble warrior to come to an ungainly halt.

"It's amazing what you run into these days." Kyt says as he steps out into the corridor, followed by Myk, Fyn, Ryak and three other skinny young Gryn. Jyr wing bumps his comrades.

"I see we have rescued the human females," Kyt turns his disarming smile on the women, "which is nice. But great Prime, what the vrex are we going to do to get out of here?"

"Vrex you, Kyt. You know Proto's bases as well as I do. We need to find an exhaust port." Jyr growls.

"We need to find something to carry the females." Ryak adds. He rests up against the wall, arms folded and gazing into the distance. "Or none of us are going anywhere."

"I'm happy to donate my clothing for the cause." Kyt says, his dark eyes full of mirth.

He appears to have lost the long coat that he favors around the lair and is only wearing a pair of thin tight black trousers like Jyr that leave very little to the imagination. His hands go to his waistband. I know well that Gryn are not interested in underwear, and I'm absolutely sure that the women are not ready to see what these alien warriors packs between their legs.

"Er, Kyt," Ryak fortunately interrupts his strip tease, "I don't think that will be necessary." He slams his claws into a nearby wall and a hidden door slides open, revealing a mass of wiring.

All the women have been very quiet since they met Jyr, but I spot Bianca giving Ryak a once over.

He reaches into the alcove and pulls out lengths of wire as the rest of the Gryn join him, scrutinizing the women and snipping off lengths and platting them together with impressive ease, given his clawed fingers.

"Is there anything we can do to help?" Emma offers. Myk holds up a perfectly platted sling and sizes her up. Her mouth makes a silent 'o' as she steps away from him. His gaze rests on her for a moment. Then he puts the sling over his head and shoulder, like the others have done.

"All we need to do now is get past the joykills and out of this base." Jyr says.

"So, we just have to dodge the killer robots and get outside?" I ask. He nods. "What about the aviary?"

"What's an aviary?"

"It's a place you keep birds—" I stop my explanation when I see Jyr's sweet frown. "It doesn't matter. What matters is that there's some sort of cage covering this base. I saw it out of a window earlier, when Proto took me. There were a few Gryn flying inside it."

"Vrex!" Fyn swears. "I was in this type of camp before. After you all escaped, Proto started building bases inside the camps where it experimented on us. To avoid further losses."

"And how do we get out?" Jyr asks, his eyes narrowing at Fyn.

"We don't." He says, his wings rustling with annoyance. "Except—"

"What?" Jyr demands.

"I heard that there were underground passages that led to outside the perimeter, but we were always tranqued when we were inside the base, so no chance of finding them." Fyn says and I see a shudder run over him.

Jyr drums his claws against the wall. We're running out of time, and he knows it.

"Kyt," he turns to his quartermaster. "You know the layout of these bases better than any of us. Are there any underground passages?"

Kyt places a single claw against his lips, looking almost as young as the skinny mercs that are observing us with a kind of hushed awe.

"I guess I probably know where they might be. As not all the bases have them, it will be a guess though."

"Well, I'll take a guess over being blasted to oblivion by joykills." Ryak says. "Let's go."

JYR

There's a deep booming from somewhere inside the base. It's ominous because the sirens have ceased their whining, and we move through the long, twisting corridors with a growing sense of unease. Kyt calls a halt, and I leave Viv with the other humans to creep forward.

"Where the vrex are we?" I hiss at him.

He points forward and I see that the corridors have ended. We are at the central stem. It's where the main power core is, an enormous glowing cylinder covered in circuits that towers above us and descends deep into the bowels of the base. The entire atrium is well lit, and which means I can also see several guardbots and joykills circling.

"Please tell me we don't have to use the central stem?" I groan, running my hand over my face. I would be hard enough with a raiding party of Gryn warriors, but with the humans and the young mercs, I can't see how we stand a chance.

"We have to use the central stem." Kyt says, his gaze still intent on the circling bots. "Sorry, I know you didn't want me to say that." He adds with his customary mirth. "It's the only way to access the lower levels."

"Vrex, vrex, vrex!" I mutter under my breath, looking back down the line of Gryn and humans.

Viv looks back at me, her face calm and her thoughts collected. She trusts me entirely to get her out of this situation, and that's what I'm going to vrexing do.

"Okay, we need a diversion."

Before I can stop him, Myk strides past me out into the central stem, grabbing my makeshift sword on his way past as he tosses his sling to Kyt. He lifts into the air with a roar and all the bots immediately turn towards him.

"Vrex it!" My plan, such as it was, is already going sideways. "Get a female and get going, follow Kyt." I yell out and each human is unceremoniously grabbed by a Gryn, save for the large two-toned hair one. Two of the mercs grab her and lift her, squirming, into the air as Kyt, a blur of feathers and human, speeds down the central shaft.

I turn to collect my Viv, and she walks towards me, smiling happily as I hold out my hand to her. With a sudden rush of wind and metal, she's cut off by a wall that springs instantly between us. She's trapped. I punch repeatedly at the wall, gouging at it with my claws, but it resists my every effort.

"Jyr!" Myk calls from high above me.

He's disposed of most of the bots, but as I look up, a further slot opens and joykills pour out.

"We have to go!" Myk says.

"Never! I have to save my mate. You go, get the others to safety, get back to the lair. If I get out of this, I'll meet you there."

Myk circles me briefly and then dives away, down the shaft and is gone.

I race over to the next corridor in the curved walls of the atrium. This one is not blocked, and I think I know the base well enough to double back around to find Viv.

Because there is no way I'm being parted from her, ever again.

VIV

Jyr disappears before my eyes, a wall appearing out of nowhere and blocking my view of him. I hear on the other side as he battles with the metal, trying to get to me. I bang my fists against it, uselessly.

Have we really come this far only to be parted again? I'm not prepared to believe that, not for a moment. Our thoughtbond is strong, and Jyr is determined he will find me again.

The corridor behind me is, mercifully, still empty of bots. I check to see if there isn't some hidden mechanism to release the wall that is blocking me from my mate, but to no avail. I hesitate for a second, wondering whether to stay put and wait for Jyr or to try to double back, to find another way to the enormous atrium I was just staring into.

I'd be a sitting target if I stayed here. Even if Jyr found me, we'd have to go back the way we came, and that's going to waste time we don't have. I have a burning sensation in my stomach that tells me Proto is playing with us. Could it even have been playing with me when it told me I was pregnant? I haven't had a period while I've been on

Ustokos, but that doesn't mean anything. I wasn't regular on Earth and with the stress of dealing with being abducted by aliens, a blip in my menstrual cycle is hardly a surprise.

I try not to think too hard about what having a child with Jyr will mean as I make my way carefully back down the corridor and look for any that branch off. Finally, I find one and hurry down it, hoping that Jyr has the same idea and is heading my way. As much as I have the hum of his being in my head, I have to be in reasonable proximity to him to do any of the weird thought transference.

I can hear noises behind me, and I increase my pace until the corridor ends and I'm in a large oval space that joins with other corridors. I steal forward, intending to hurry across the open area and scurry down another passage that might lead back to the central atrium.

"Looks like it's my lucky day." I spin at the sound of the familiar voice. "I get to show Proto what a good soldier I am by recapturing Jyr and his mate."

"Kaloz!"

He leans against the wall, holding a silver gun like thing in his hand and it's pointed at me. He pushes away from the wall and stalks towards me. I step back until a hard surface hits me. Kaloz keeps coming until he's closed the gap and towers over me, hot foul breath in my face and the scent of his feathers is all dirt and decay.

"Such a pretty little mate." He hefts the gun in one hand, holding it between us menacingly. With his other hand, he lifts up a lock of my hair and brings it to his nose, inhaling deeply. "So sweet, so edible." He grins to reveal his yellowing sharp teeth. "After all the trouble you've put me through, I think I deserve a taste of Jyr's prize."

He leans in to lick me, and I lift my knee sharply towards

the bulge in his groin, but he dodges away, leveling the gun at my head.

"You think you're fierce," he snarls. "You're nothing. Just a fertile womb to Proto. I think I'll ask it to give you to me as a reward for delivering up Jyr. That way I can ensure you don't get the chance to fight back."

It's as if he has looked into my darkest fears, even though I know he hasn't got the basic thoughtbond that the senior Gryn share.

"Fuck you, Kaloz." I grin at him. "Fuck you so fucking hard that you split in half and the pieces are eaten by a maraha then shat out. Fuck you, because Jyr will find me, and you'll have nothing, not even Proto. My only sadness is that Jyr will kill you too fast. If it were up to me, I'd kill you so slowly you would beg for death. But then that's the difference between my mate and me. He cares and I don't."

Kaloz snarls at my insults but I need to buy time. Making him angry probably isn't the best idea, but I want to stay in one place for as long as possible. For Jyr to find me.

"She's right about everything, but not caring." Jyr's deep voice rings out across the open space. "She has shown you, me and all the lair more care and concern than I ever did. She made it a better place, and she made us a family."

Kaloz keeps his back to Jyr and I see him fingering the gun.

"Watch out!" I yell as Kaloz spins and fires a beam of light towards Jyr. His huge wings beat, but he's not quite fast enough. The laser hits its mark, and he crumples to the ground.

"No!" I race forward, but Kaloz catches me and, despite my kicking and squirming, I can't get free and I can't get to Jyr. Kaloz clamps a hand over my mouth, as if that will stop me from calling out to my mate.

But the thoughtbond is empty. It echos. I go limp.

Without Jyr there's nothing worth fighting for.

"That's better," Kaloz says, smugly. "Your mate is dead, and you will do as I say as I'm certain you don't need all your limbs to bear a child."

"Fucking bastard." I snarl, trying to bite down on his arm. He smashes me in the side of my head with the laser gun, and I see stars as he heaves me over his shoulder.

JYR

Vrexing bastid, the laser blast Kaloz hit me with vrexing hurt. It set all of my insides on fire. Joykill laser whips had nothing on what he just used on me.

If I had any doubts the vrexer was in league with Proto, his ability to use its weapons was the final piece of evidence. It was entirely possible the whole story about his lair being overtaken by joykills was a fabrication. And if Proto has learned to lie, that changes everything.

I remain on the floor, paralyzed, as my body attempts to heal itself against whatever disrupter Kaloz used. I hear him threaten Viv, and I will myself to heal faster. Our thought-bond is temporarily severed, as everything I have is being used to fix my physical form. I hear a loud crack, followed by Viv's sob and my blood boils, all the anger I have been holding onto firing through me. No one hurts my mate. I made her a promise.

The feeling returns to my legs, and I force myself to my feet. My vision is blurred, but I catch sight of Kaloz wings as he disappears down the corridor that leads back to the central stem. I hold on to the wall as everything spins. My wings are next to useless, dragging behind me as I stagger like the drunkest merc at a celebration. I can't even hold them up normally. Looking down at my torso, my abdomen is a bloody mess. But the entry wound has healed. Only a few scorch marks remain.

I drag myself after Kaloz and Viv, frustrated at my body and at the lack of the thoughtbond. I can't reassure her I'm coming. That I would always come for her.

The more I move, the looser I feel, but I'm still struggling to stay upright as I round a corner and hit something hard but yielding.

"Vrex, Jyr! What happened?" Ryak grabs my shoulders and hauls me upright, checking me over.

"Kaloz happened. He shot me with a vrexing laser, and he's taken Viv." I clap my hand on his arm. "What the vrex are you doing here? You should get the vrex out of this base with the females." I try to sound mad, but my heart isn't in it.

"We're family, Jyr and we don't leave anyone behind. Not you and not Viv." My vision clears completely to see Kyt and Fyn stood behind Ryak. Behind them are the young mercs, smiling nervously. "Let's go get your mate."

I'm not sure whether to be relieved or angry, but in my chest, something is free. I can trust again, and Viv taught me that. Ryak pulls my arm around his shoulder.

"I think he's taking her to the central stem." I lean on my brother Gryn and allow him to help me as my strength returns.

I'm able to hold myself upright by the time we reach the atrium, and we're in time to see Kaloz drop Viv to the floor in front of a joykill. Fyn launches himself into the air. Both the joykill and Kaloz react instantly, firing their weapons, which Fyn dodges easily. Kaloz spots the rest of us heading towards him and pulls Viv to her feet. She sways, blood running down one side of her delicate face and her eyes unfocussed.

"Any closer and I'll drop her." Kaloz spins her out until she is teetering on the edge of the central stem over the void below.

"Jyr." She says groggily. She scrabbles at Kaloz's arm.

"You can't win this time, Jyr. Give it up before you get everyone killed." Kaloz waves the weapon at us.

"Only one Gryn is dying today." I say, my teeth gritted. "And it's not any of us."

Kaloz opens his hand and lets go of Viv. She screams as she topples sideways, arms flailing as she tries and fails to keep her balance.

"Viv!" I'm already diving for her, paying no attention to the joykill cackling above us as I stoop hard, pumping my wings to increase my speed after Viv, who tumbles unchecked towards the bottom of the shaft. With one final flick, I shoot underneath her, and she drops into my arms, her scream hoarse in her throat.

"Hold on to me." I murmur in her ear, inhaling the sweet scent of her hair as I spin around the stem and fire myself upwards, back towards my warriors, only to see them descending in a similar stoop to my own. Kyt spins and fires a laser weapon back up the stem before resuming his descent.

A body falls past us, it's Kaloz, blasted by his own weapon, I hear him hit the ground with a nasty squelch. I feel a pang of annoyance that I didn't get to deliver the killer blow to the vrexer, but it doesn't matter, as long as he is gone.

"Go! Go! Go!" Ryak screams at me, and I follow without hesitation.

We reach the bottom, and they turn in formation into a wide tunnel.

"Wait!" Viv cries out. "Jyr, stop, we have to stop."

"We can't," I look up, joykills are coming after us.

"Please!" She pleads.

Maybe she's been hurt by Kaloz. Against my better judgement, I row back with all my might to land us at the bottom of the central stem, and she tears herself free of my grip.

"Control-alt-delete." She says with a grin.

"What?" I'm looking up at the massing joykills.

"This is the main power source for the base, right?" She says excitedly.

"The central stem is, yes." I spin around to see where the others have gone.

"Proto has to have an off switch, doesn't it? It's a computer after all."

I turn back to her, my mouth falling open. Why the vrex didn't I think of that?

With a roar, I'm running across the open space towards the fuel core. Plunging my claws into the metal and tearing through it like rare maraha until I find what I'm looking for. The one cable that feeds everything. Steeling myself for the resulting electricity bolt, I yank on it, snapping the fragile wire and the light from the core stutters and goes out, followed, in sequence, by the lights all around us.

Within seconds I'm back at Viv's side as the air starts to rain joykills, smashing onto the floor next to us.

"Control-alt-delete." She says matter-of-factly, smiling up at me. "Maybe Proto forgot, after all its time being the dominant entity on Ustokos, all computers have an off switch."

It hadn't even occurred to me to turn Proto's power source off. My mate's more recent contact with tech that doesn't intentionally want to kill her puts us at an advantage for once. Although I suspect that Proto will quickly adapt.

I grab her and get airborne, heading in the direction the others took as fast as I can.

At the end of the tunnel, my warriors wait for us, along with the females. The powering down hasn't quite reached them, and the area is bathed in an eerie blue light.

"Kyt reckons we just need to go through that hatch, and we'll be outside the perimeter." Fyn says.

A loud explosion rocks the base and shakes the floor.

"Then I suggest we do what he says and get the vrex out of here!" I climb up the wall, using what little hand and foot holds are available to reach the door in the ceiling, just as the lights go out and some of the females make squeaking sounds. I give the hatch a shove and it pops open, air rushing in along with the light of Ustokos twin suns. I heave myself out and reach down to grab hold of Viv, who I haul up after me.

We are outside the base and outside the caging. Above us, I see a huge hole ripped in the caging fabric and multiple Gryn are bursting out. Further deep rumblings shake the ground as everyone makes it out of the hatch.

I pull Viv into my chest and capture her lips with mine. Her face lit by the fires that start to consume the base. She is so beautiful, my heart nearly stops. Is she really mine? The feel of her tongue entwined in my mouth confirms she is no apparition. She is entirely in my present.

"No time for that, Prime." Kyt claps a hand on my shoulder. "We don't want to be here when this place goes up."

It's been a long time since we caused Proto to lose such a valuable base, and I should be ecstatic, except all I ever wanted is in my arms and that's all I need.

My mate, my *eregri,* my Viv.

VIV

"I am not doing that. Ever again!" Emma extracts herself from Myk's sling and takes several hurried steps away from him, smoothing down her hair.

The trip back from Proto's base was not exactly easy. It rapidly became clear that we were some distance from the lair and the flight would be a long one. For me, that was more than fine. I got to spend all of it snuggled up against Jyr's warm body, feeling his muscles bunch and move easily as he flew steadily onwards. And I got time to spend thinking about his child, the one that might be growing in my womb, and how I could be sure that it was true before I told him.

From Emma's comment, not everyone enjoyed the trip back as much as me.

"I don't know, Emma. It wasn't all bad." Bianca unwraps herself languidly from Fyn, who, to my amusement, gets as far away from her as he can without appearing to do so. When she looks around for him, he's already out of her clutches.

The three young mercs look completely beat. They were

malnourished and the long trip back has clearly taken it out of them. At least one looks as if he's about to fall asleep where he stands.

"Fyn," I call him over. "Can you get them settled in the barracks? Make sure they have extra furs and don't miss the next meal?" Fyn looks to Jyr briefly, who nods.

"Of course, Lady Prime." He gives me a brief and unexpected smile. He shepherds the mercs off the landing platform and into the liar.

"I love it when they call you Lady Prime." Jyr murmurs into my ear, pressing a gentle kiss to my earlobe that sends a frisson of desire rippling through me. "It shows that you're mine, all mine." His dark eyes are filled with a longing, and I gently cup his cheek in my hand.

"I am yours, my love. Now and forever." I let my feelings for him resonate and the thoughtbond fills with every possible color. "I love you, Jyr."

"And I love you, my sweet Viv."

We are complete.

———

"WHAT DO you wish to do with the humans?" Jyr asks me.

"They're going to need quarters, away from the rest of the lair. They're also going to need a trip to a trading post because what they're wearing isn't going to last long." I scan their thin jumpsuits with a critical eye.

"Hey! What if we don't want to stay here, *lady prime*." Sophie says, somewhat sarcastically.

She stands slightly in front of the others, arms folded and looking defiantly at me. I feel myself bristle and cringe at her tone until I see the tears hovering in her eyes. She's as terrified as I was when I was first brought here.

I untwine myself from Jyr and walk over to them, placing a hand on Sophie's folded arm.

"These are the good guys, I promise. If you don't want to stay, then you don't have to." I swallow hard. "But I'd like you to stay, so would Jyr."

I look over my shoulder at him. He holds himself tall, his wings shining with life in a brief bolt of sunlight. His seniors flank him, Kyt managing to look disheveled, but bad angel handsome, Myk leaning on the sword that Jyr fashioned from the joykill bot, he's streaked with dirt and is every inch a feathered grease monkey, Ryak seems to have come through the whole ordeal with not even a feather out of place. Fyn reappears and joins their group. He sets his wings and folds his arms, his jaw clenched with the internal conflict I always detect from him.

"You would all be most welcome to stay with us for as long as you want. The Gryn offer you food, shelter and protection." Jyr says, his deep voice almost velvety smooth as he wants to appear welcoming.

"Can you get us back to Earth?" Lucy asks. Her eyes have been like saucers ever since we landed and she is incredibly pale, even for a redhead.

"That, I regret, is the one thing we cannot offer you. You've seen what the tech on this planet can do. Organic life lost the war with Proto many turns ago. If it brought you here, it has no intention of returning you."

Jyr walks over to us. He takes Lucy's hand, holding it in his huge one and I try my hardest not to allow my jealousy at him touching another woman eat me up.

"I am truly sorry that you have lost your planet." He says. "We all understand how hard that must be. Please do not judge us and stay for a while. If you still wish to leave, we can make whatever arrangements are necessary." He releases Lucy's hand and wraps his arm around my waist, pulling me into him.

"It's okay." Emma says, glancing at the others. "When you put it like that, we'll stay, and thank you for everything you have done for us." The women nod hesitantly.

"In that case - who fancies an alien version of a hot tub!" I cry, clapping my hands together and making Lucy jump.

"That sounds like the best thing that anyone has offered since we arrived here." Bianca says, a brief smile flitting over her solemn features.

As I lead the way through the lair, slowly, not like Jyr hurried me through on my first ever visit, I can hear them all chatter a little. Having reached Jyr's chambers, I usher them in and through to the poolroom. Jyr and the rest of his gang have followed us, silently like the predators they are, but once the women are inside, I turn and place a hand on Jyr's chest.

"That's quite far enough. The humans need privacy to bathe, not like you Gryn." Jyr opens his mouth to protest, and I hook a hand around his neck, pulling him down for a kiss. "You'll get what you want later, hun." I mouth in his ear. "Just as long as you get your sightseers out of here for an hour."

He gives me a quizzical look, the slight frown on his face makes me want to jump his bones in a way I've never felt before.

They won't be staying in our chambers, will they?

His concern murmurs down the thoughtbond.

"Ryak will find the humans some proper quarters, won't you, Ryak?" I pop my head around from behind Jyr's massive form to surprise the big, secretive Gryn. His blink is the only outwards sign I've been successful.

"Yes." He hesitates, his brow creasing. "I can do that." He says as I can see the cogs in his brain turning.

"Then it's settled. Now fuck off, all of you!" I add with a smile. My gang of enormous warriors troop, somewhat reluctantly, out of the door, all feathers and muscle.

Jyr oscillates on the threshold.

"Did we do the right thing?" He asks me.

"We saved three Gryn and four humans today. Not to mention the other Gryn who were in that base. I think we did good." I wrap my arms around his waist and press my cheek against his muscular chest. "Those mercs you found, they're just babies. Now they have a life and a family again." I smile up at his concerned face. "You did that."

"So did you, my *eregri*. I am truly blessed with you. Not because you are my boundless flight, but because you have an endless heart."

A flood of calmness runs through me. By being a hero, I saved everyone but myself. By working with my mate and his warriors, together we saved all. The warmth of being part of the Gryn is a feeling I never want to lose.

"I hope your heart has a tiny bit more room." The words tumble out of my mouth before I can stop them.

"What do you mean?" Jyr pulls back from me to look me in the eye.

"I think I'm pregnant." I place my hand over my stomach. "We're going to have a child, Jyr. You're going to be a father."

JYR

It's as if I'm buoyant in the warmest thermal, spiraling up into a clear blue sky, the likes of which Ustokos hasn't seen for many turns. My mate is going to have my child. She will grow ripe and round with my young. It is more than I dared to hope for.

I stride through the lair and mercs scatter in my wake. I reach out and grab one of them before he scurries off.

"Where is Fyn? I need to see Fyn, now!" I growl at him.

"He's in the food hall." The terrified merc stutters.

"Have you eaten today?" I fire at him. He can't do anything but shake his head.

"Good, then you will accompany me." I throw an arm around his shoulders, and he shoots a glance at his barrack mates hovering around the doorway. "All of you." I give them the benefit of my best smile, which, given how at least one of them blanches, might not have been the best idea.

Still, it's with a phalanx of mercs at my wings that I enter the food hall. To find Fyn sitting at a table on his own, shoveling maraha into his mouth with an air of exhaustion.

"Vrex off and eat, you bunch of vrexers!" I laugh at the

young ones scurrying away to obey my command. Fyn looks up at me, his gaze guarded as always.

"Did you get the young mercs settled in?" I ask as I slide onto the bench opposite him.

"Ryak's putting them in my barracks. I took them to Orvos. He wants to keep them in the surgery for a few days. One of them doesn't seem to be able to speak." Fyn replies, picking at the remaining meat on his platter. "They've suffered more than most of us."

"But not more than you or me." Fyn's head jerks up, his eyes full of fire until he remembers his place.

"I'm nothing special." He mutters.

I reach across the table in a movement so quick he shouldn't have time to see it coming. He catches my wrist and I cease moving, holding his gaze.

"What the vrex, Jyr?" He pushes my hand back at me forcefully, a hurt look on his face. "I saved your vrexing life back there-"

"Look." I point at his chest, and he jumps away from me before looking down.

He stopped me before I could do any worse, but there's still a long thin cut from my claw on his pectoral muscle. As he looks, the cut seals itself and within seconds, all that is left is the smear of blood on his skin.

"Proto did more than just torture you, Fyn. It did the same to me, to Kyt, Ryak and Myk. We're different."

"I'm not different. I'm Gryn and that's all I need to be." Fyn's features harden.

Which is exactly what I wanted you to say.

He blinks at me. Once, twice. "What?"

"You heard me." I grin. "Sit down. Finish your meal." I wave at his platter.

Reluctantly, he climbs back over the bench and settles

himself, folding his wings back tightly in case I try anything else with him.

"The thing is—" I rub at the back of my neck, "Viv believes she is with child."

Fyn stops eating and stares at me.

"So, we really can mate with humans? That's good, right?" He says. I forget he's still a youngster himself.

"It's a lot to take in. The responsibility of bringing Gryn young into this world, when we don't know if there are any Gryn females left. I suppose we have to give every opportunity a try." My shoulders hunch as I drop my head into my hands. "I don't want it to be a mistake. I want to be a good father, to bring my youngling up in a proper family." All my doubts creep to the fore as I speak them out loud. "I want it to be right."

"You'll make a great father." Fyn says with genuine feeling. "And as for a family, the lair loves the Lady Prime as much as it loves you. Your youngling will be loved just as much."

His face softens for a moment and it's enough to chase any concerns I might have away. I have everything I need, except one.

"Fyn, if I'm going to be with my mate during her pregnancy, I'm going to need a new Command. Proto isn't going to take kindly to us destroying that base, and we're more in demand from the other species for protection than ever. We need more of everything, including recruits, and they'll need training."

"How about Ryak?" Fyn shovels some more meat into his mouth, licking at his claws. "He'd make a good Command."

"Ryak would never accept, he enjoys being in the shadows too much."

"Kyt then. The mercs like him. He'd be good." Fyn suggests, as I repress a laugh.

"Kyt is good at two things, tech and taking mercs for a ride. He couldn't be Command and he wouldn't want to."

"Who then?" Fyn shrugs.

"For vrex sake, Fyn! I'm asking you!" My laughter rings through the food hall, causing the mercs to stop what they are doing and look over at us. "I want you to be the new Command, Fyn." I roar.

A drumming sound starts, quiet at first and growing swiftly louder, until the mercs burst out into a chant of his name as Fyn stares in disbelief.

"So? Do you want it? Do you want to be Command of the Gryn?"

"You vrexing bet I do!"

VIV

"The humans are settling in well?" Jyr asks as we slowly descend in lazy beats down to Orvos' surgery.

"They're settling in, but it's going to take them some time. I had to adapt to being on Ustokos straight away, they've been locked in Proto's base for all this time. It's like they've been abducted all over again." I explain. "But, they've told me they want to get involved in lair life, so I thought you and the seniors could discuss things when you're next in szent." Jyr makes an incredibly soft landing and gingerly lowers me to the ground.

Ever since my pregnancy began to show, he's been treating me as if I might break. After I had a bit of morning sickness this morning and he fussed, I decided a trip to Orvos might be in order.

If anyone can tell the Prime of the Gryn not to fuss, it's going to be Orvos. He doesn't take any shit.

"I want them to be happy, so you're happy." Jyr nuzzles at my hair like he always does and it sends a naughty shiver down my spine. He inhales and releases a groan. "You tempt

me again, my mate. I'm not sure it's good for our youngling."
He splays a massive, clawed hand over my slightly
protruding belly.

"Utter nonsense." Orvos voice calls out from behind us.
"You should mate regularly and often. That is best for a
Gryn youngling." He grins at me, "And it's parents. Come
with me, my dear. How can I assist?"

He leads me into the surgery, with Jyr sulking behind us,
and he settles me on a ledge.

"There is nothing wrong with me other than a touch of
morning sickness, but this one," I point to Jyr, "thought it
was worth bothering you."

"Male Gryn are always hopelessly overprotective of their
pregnant mates. I suspect it's something you will need to get
used to." Orvos gives Jyr an indulgent smile and he huffs in
annoyance.

Orvos gives me a quick examination and announces, to
my relief and more so to Jyr's, that both mother and baby
are doing fine.

"Proto said that I'll give birth in around five Earth
months. I think that's about half a turn, maybe a bit less. Is
that true?" I ask Orvos. Part of me doesn't want to believe
such a short pregnancy, but given how big my belly is
already, it could be true.

Not that I have anything at all to compare it to.

"Gryn females would gestate for half a turn. How long is
it for humans?"

"About three quarters of a turn."

"That's far too long." Orvos clucks his tongue. "Babies
need to be birthed. Gryn genes are strong. I would expect
you to go the full half a turn, but that's all."

"You're not filling me with confidence, healer." I
admonish him.

"Nor me." Jyr growls. "If you are to assist with the birth, you should brush up on your knowledge." He scoops me up in his arms and sweeps out of the surgery in a rustle of feathers. I hear Orvos sighing deeply behind us.

We make it out of the door before Jyr dissolves into laughter.

"Is it a good idea to wind up the lair's only healer?" I ask him, trying to keep a serious face.

"What? Oh—" Jyr sobers as he considers his options.

"I'm joking, you big idiot," I smack him on his chest and he adopts a hurt expression. "But you heard Orvos, this female needs mating, and mating hard."

Jyr opens his great wings and we're in the air, rowing swiftly up to the top of the lair, heading for our chambers.

I shed my clothing as soon as the doors are closed, dropping each individual piece like a breadcrumb trail as I walk towards the pool room. Jyr's eyes fill with lust as he takes in my changing body, and he makes me feel like the only female in the universe. With regular bathing in the Ustokos mountain waters, my scarring has improved, although I know it will never disappear forever. What's more, I don't want it to.

It no longer defines me. It's become part of my story, and only a tiny part. The rest of my story is ahead of me, and it's written in the huge wings and dark eyes of my handsome mate. Jyr, Prime of the Gryn and my boundless flight.

EPILOGUE

VIV

Our sweet, perfect baby girl is nursing quietly when I hear Jyr entering the outer chamber. Within seconds he sweeps into the bedchamber, locking the door behind him and clambering onto the bed with a sigh. I hold my finger to my lips, and he gives me a wolfish grin, burrowing behind me.

"Have you given any more thought to names for this little one?" I ask as I recline in Jyr's arms, making sure I don't disturb the feeding baby.

I tune into his tension, attempting to iron out the kinks in his mind, to make him feel less responsible for everyone. I know that's not possible. I'm the same way about the young mercs who seek me out for help and comfort, as well as the other humans. But thinking of baby names for our newest member of the lair might take his mind off things.

The birth of our gorgeous daughter did not go that easily, given that neither of us knew what to expect. I wanted everything to be calm and collected, even deciding to give birth in one of the shallow healing pools, which Orvos considered a good idea.

Reality was something else entirely. Jyr wouldn't let Orvos near me for the first part of my labor, he was like a Gryn possessed. It was only when the doctor threatened to tranq him that he came to his senses and let him assist. Having suffered through most of my labor with only a half-terrified, half-crazed Gryn for company, moving to the pool seemed unnecessary and a few hours later, she was born.

And it was worth every single second to see the look on Jyr's face as he held his daughter for the first time.

"How are things going for the celebration? Did you ask Fyn?" I can't contain myself. Who'd have thought match-making was a thing for me?

Jyr groans, rolling his head back. "He's agreed to ask her, but that male, he's clueless!"

"He's young, that's all." I laugh at Jyr's frustration. "He's been watching her for ages, he just needed someone he respects to give him a push in the right direction."

"The lair needs more younglings. Do you think she'll agree to come to the celebration with him?" I feel his concern through the thoughtbond.

"I hope she will, as long as he's sensitive about it. She's quite shy. And not every Gryn is as smooth as you." I elbow him in the ribs.

I make my mind calm. Jyr can't solve all the lair's problems and sometimes he has to let nature take its course.

"I was wondering about Syara." Jyr suggests, snuggling me against him. "It was my mother's name."

"I think that's a beautiful name, just like our baby." I try to hold back my ever present tears and fail. "Syara it is."

Jyr captures one drop as it rolls down my cheek, licks his finger and kisses my wet skin.

"Can I hold her?" He asks tentatively.

"You know you don't have to ask." I smile up at him. "She'll be finished in a minute or two. Hungry little monster that she is."

The infant finishes nursing, and I lift her onto my shoulder, gently patting her between her wing nubs until she releases the most unlady-like belch.

"She's all yours." I hand the tiny baby to her father, who takes her, dark eyes enraptured with wonder at the new life he has created.

He rocks her gently as she gurgles up at him, her dark eyes missing nothing and her mouth open in a semblance of a smile for her daddy.

"My Syara, you are as beautiful as your mother." He croons at the baby. "Who will soon fill this lair with even more younglings."

"Hold your horses! What do you mean, fill?" I say in a loud whisper to avoid frightening the baby.

Jyr gives me a toothy smile, all semblance of tiredness gone.

"Orvos has agreed to look after her tonight, and I get you all to myself." His grin becomes wicked, even as my core heats.

My mate really is a very bad angel indeed.

Book 2: Read Lucy and Fyn's story in *Fear: A Sci-Fi Alien Romance*

You can get an alert for all my new releases before anyone else by signing up for my newsletter. You'll also get sneak peaks from my latest work, cover reveals as well as a FREE steamy sci-fi romance novella 'Angel and the Alien Brute' as a thank you for signing up!

So if you want all of the above, sign up HERE or at www.hattiejacks.com/subscribe

You can also follow me on Amazon or Bookbub too!

ALSO BY HATTIE JACKS

JUST WHO IS THIS HATTIE JACKS ANYWAY?

I've been a passionate sci-fi fan since I was a little girl, brought up on a diet of Douglas Adams, Issac Asimov, Star Trek, Star Wars, Doctor Who, Red Dwarf and The Adventure Game.

What? You don't know about The Adventure Game? It's probably a British thing and dates me horribly! Google it. Even better search for it on YouTube. In my defence, there were only three channels back then.

I'm also a sucker for great characters and situations as well as grand romance, because who doesn't like a grand romantic gesture?

So, when I'm not writing steamy stories about smouldering alien males and women with something to prove, you'll find me battling my garden (less English country garden, more The Good Life) or zooming around the countryside on my motorbike.

Check out my website at www.hattiejacks.com!

Made in the USA
Coppell, TX
01 February 2025

45238685R10173